THE LAST OPERATOR

SAMCOGLEY.COM

Also by Sam Cogley

The Adam Knight series

SHADOW OPERATIVE

SKYFIRE

ROGUE STATE

NEPTUNE-SIX

The Penumbra Division series

THE LAST OPERATOR

For more information visit samcogley.com

A *PENUMBRA DIVISION* THRILLER

THE LAST OPERATOR

SAM COGLEY

Copyright © 2025 by Sam Cogley

All rights reserved.

No part of this book may be reproduced in any form or by any electronic or mechanical means, including information storage and retrieval systems, without written permission from the author, except for the use of brief quotations in a book review.

All the characters in this book are fictitious, and any resemblance to actual persons living or dead is purely coincidental.

FOREWORD

This novel is set in the days leading up to, during, and in the aftermath of September 11, 2001.

The Last Operator is the work of fiction, though it unfolds against one of the most pivotal and painful moments in recent history. While the characters, organizations, and storylines in this book are the product of my imagination, they are played out on the backdrop of real events. In some cases, I've taken liberties replacing real people with fictional characters, and blending the imagined with the actual.

Writing and researching this book took me back to the memories of the day. Back then, I stared at my TV screen trying to understand what had happened. Putting this book together was a difficult subject to revisit, and I'd like to think I approached it with respect. I hope you agree.

With that said, I hope you enjoy reading **The Last Oper-**

ator—a book that will not only entertain, but pay tribute in its own way to a moment in time which changed our lives forever.

Thank you. Sam Cogley.

FEBRUARY 1, 1993

PROLOGUE

LANGLEY, VIRGINIA

Some woke to their alarms. Not John Bishop. He got out of bed to the beat of never-ending wars.

He zipped up his jacket, the chill of the morning biting more than expected. He had left home at four a.m., the car waiting to take him to his office. He had hoped the morning would have got warmer with the sun's rays breaking through the clouds. As with everything in his line of work, there were no guarantees.

With his paperwork behind him and prepared for the upcoming meeting, he crossed the grounds from the Original Headquarters Building to the New Headquarters Building. The simplistic distinction between the two was typical of the CIA. The older facility had been erected in the sixties and served as a base for the agency until 1988. Instead of bulldozing the aging structure, they combined the buildings into a sprawling super-complex.

Most of those who had called the former building home

were moved to the glass palace, so named by some, or the annex, as it was known to others. To Bishop, it was just another set of walls. It mattered little to him. Bureau 61 had never been invited to the gleaming new HQ, instead remaining in the outdated and claustrophobic spaces of the old CIA confines.

If he were honest, he preferred it that way. He never enjoyed having the CIA brass breathing down his neck. That was the whole reason Bureau 61 was conceived in the first place—to be a shadow within a shadow. Everyone knew the CIA. What they did, and how they did it. Not Bureau 61. They operated where the wider CIA could not.

Bishop reached into his pocket and took out a creased packet of cigarettes, having already gone through half of them since arriving. He was a chain smoker to be sure, but the number he had burned through on this particular morning spoke louder than words.

A black Chevrolet Caprice entered the vast facility, rolling through the security checkpoint and moving toward Bishop at the entrance. The forgettable design was the standard ride for those at the agency to get around in. Bishop lit his cigarette and took a drag as the car came to a stop. The rear door opened, and a familiar face stepped out.

Dressed in a black jacket, matching the paintwork of the vehicle, Aaron Quade yanked up his collar. His widened eyes and puffed cheeks revealed to Bishop that his right-hand man was not ready for the welcome of the brisk February morning. He shut his door and gave a wave to his driver, the armored Caprice promptly disappearing around the corner.

"Sorry I'm late, boss," Quade said. "We got stuck on the Beltway."

Bishop waved off the apology. "It's not the worst morning to be tardy."

Quade frowned, likely catching the meaning of the cryptic statement. Bishop motioned onward, and they entered the lobby of the new building, the heating inside the complex immediately warming Bishop's bones.

The pair shed their jackets and strode to the security section, flashing their ID passes to the guards. They tossed their wallets and keys into a tray for a separate screening and walked through the metal detectors. Bishop left his cigarette pressed between his lips, while Quade remained a step behind, their examination over within seconds.

They collected their belongings and made their way to the elevators where a vacant car awaited. Bishop punched in their desired floor. Beyond, a latecomer ran to join them. Quade instinctively moved aside. Bishop had other ideas. Instead of placing his shoe in to stop the doors shutting, he pressed the close button, ensuring their ride remained private, much to the scorn of the other man.

Quade smirked. "I suppose you don't have any prior intel on what we're about to walk into this morning."

"If you're asking if anything official has appeared on my desk, then no, it hasn't." Bishop exhaled, and a steady stream of smoke filled the confined space.

Quade, though not a smoker himself, did not so much as wrinkle his nose.

It was one of the things he liked about the younger man. He never complained. Despite a fifteen-year age gap, the Floridian in his thirties agreed on many aspects of their business. Sure, they would disagree, and the resulting argument would be a passionate one. But they were adults. Quade was at Bureau 61 to do a job, and he did it, even if it meant setting himself up for emphysema in his later years from all the passive smoke.

Then again, at Bureau 61, lung damage was the least of anyone's worries.

The elevator chimed, and they stopped on one of the upper levels. The corridor beyond was busy, the wide-open hallways of glass walls welcoming them to the rapid movement of analysts sharing urgent conversations on the polished floors of the new building. Everything was pristine, a stark contrast to the grimy halls where Bishop and his team operated on the opposite side of the grounds.

They exited the car and walked to the reception area at the very end of the corridor. Donna was on duty at the desk and looked up at the duo as they entered. She shook her head at them and glared at Bishop.

"You're late," she said.

"Blame Quade," he told her.

"I got stuck in traffic," Quade protested.

"A likely story." Donna stood and gestured to the door next to her desk with one hand, offering Bishop an ashtray with the other.

Bishop extinguished the cigarette with a nod. "Thanks."

Her frown softened into a weak smile, and she allowed them in. There beyond stood a large polished table, which could easily seat a dozen people, perhaps more, depending on the meeting. On the opposite side, floor-to-ceiling windows offered a view of the grounds and the older CIA building.

"Ah, John. Please join us."

The words came from Jeffrey Phibbs, who sat at the head of the table. Bishop had only been acquainted with him a week earlier after Phibbs was assigned as the new director of the CIA. In such a brief period, Phibbs had a way of making it seem like they were friends. He even called him by his first name. Bishop saw through the façade. To the director, he was a relic. A dinosaur from a time the agency was trying to forget.

"John, I'd like to introduce you to Mr. Henry Manning. The new Secretary of Defense." Phibbs stood, as did the other man next to him. "This is John Bishop, the director of Bureau 61. And Aaron Quade, his deputy director."

They all shook hands.

"A pleasure to meet you both," Manning said. "Please, sit down."

Everyone took their seat. Phibbs remained at the head of the table, Manning beside him, and Bishop and Quade opposite. The secretary and the director opened some file folders next to their glasses of water.

"It's so very good to finally meet you, Mr. Bishop," Manning began. "Your reputation proceeds you."

"I'm sure that it does," he responded in a prickly tone.

"Yes, well, I've heard a lot about you in my time with the Congressional Oversight and House Intelligence Committees. Your work has been nothing short of exemplary." The secretary waved a hand over his documents. "Your work as an operative in the field, as a member of the operations team here at Langley, and finally as director of the branch, is second to none."

"I've kept myself busy."

"What you've been able to achieve under such conditions is truly miraculous. There are some in this building who would argue that if it weren't for Bureau 61 we might still be fighting the Cold War."

"You can take that to the bank."

Manning cleared his throat. "Indeed."

Bishop had no intention of making him feel comfortable. "May I ask a question?"

"Of course."

"If this is a routine meet and greet, fair play to you. However, if this is something more, I'd like you to cut the crap and just get on with it."

Silence filtered through the conference room, the secretary stunned at the audacious words and the tone with which they were spoken. Though it should not have surprised Quade, even he appeared shocked alongside Director Phibbs.

"Very well, Mr. Bishop. We can dispense with the formalities, if you'd like." Manning closed his folder. "I'm here to inform you that the CIA is being restructured."

Bishop glanced over at Quade, sharing a knowing look.

"As part of that restructure, Bureau 61 is to be disbanded. Relevant staff members will be rolled over into other divisions, while the rest will be offered redundancies."

Bishop delved into his pocket and slapped his packet of cigarettes on the table. "Your administration has been in office all of five minutes and you're already rearranging the furniture. Do you people have any idea what you're doing?"

"I can assure you, Mr. Bishop, that this is not a partisan decision. The Congressional Oversight Committee has been reviewing the numbers—"

Bishop scoffed.

"John." Phibbs leaned forward. "Over the past six years, Bureau 61's budget has been shrinking by the year. This has been on the cards for some time. You know that. Now with the Soviet Union out of the picture, those who are in charge of our bank balance have decided that a branch like yours is no longer required in the post-Cold War world."

Bishop opened the cigarette packet. "Let's discuss what

this is really about. This is the CIA steering away from HUMINT. You think SIGINT will do the work for you."

More silence filled the room, Bishop recalling the same conversations he'd had with previous CIA directors on countless occasions. The agency had grown increasingly reliant on SIGINT, or signal intelligence gathered by electronic means instead of HUMINT, or human intelligence which depended on real people.

Phibbs shifted in his seat, placing his hands on the folder in front of him. "SIGINT is the future, John."

Bishop took out a cigarette and lit it up. "That's a mistake."

Manning slid his chair slightly backward. "Do you mind, Mr. Bishop?"

"What? We can't smoke in federal buildings anymore? I suppose you'll take that away soon, too?" Bishop puffed a swirl of haze in the secretary's direction and refocused his attention on Phibbs. "No matter how good the technology is, you cannot bank on it as the sole method to procure intelligence. You need to have boots on the ground. Miss one tiny shred of information, and God help us, we could have another Pearl Harbor on our hands."

Phibbs coughed. "HUMINT will still have a vital role to play."

"Just not for Bureau 61?" Bishop grabbed Manning's glass of water and tapped some ash inside it, much to everyone's astonishment. "You know, in sixty-one when the Bureau was founded, the whole idea was for us to be the ones to do the dirty work. The Bay of Pigs was such a debacle they needed to find someone to fight in the shadows against communism. The administration of the day wanted a team of people who could get things done, and do it so that they could never be embarrassed again. I believe it was called plausible deniability."

"Mr. Bishop, the Cold War's over."

Bishop turned to Manning, unable to restrain the mocking smile appearing on his features. "If you think there aren't more battles to be fought out there, Secretary, you're more of a fool than I thought you were."

"John, the decision has been made." The CIA director rushed his words, no doubt wanting to end the unsavory conversation. "In three months, Bureau 61 will be officially disbanded. You've got that time to settle your operatives' current assignments and bring them home."

Bishop stood and flicked his half-smoked cigarette in Manning's glass. Quade rose with him, a hand on his arm, dragging him to the exit.

"Who's going to do all your dirty work now, Phibbs!" Bishop spat, trudging over the threshold with a final parting shot.

The question lingered as the door shut behind them.

SEPTEMBER 8, 2001

1

VENICE, ITALY

The shot rippled through the air, the bullet slamming into the stone wall with a deafening thud.

Harvey Wulf ducked and narrowly avoided another attack, the next round smashing a window. The marketgoers around him scattered, diving for cover from the storm coming their way on the busy street. Wulf barreled past a fruit stall and then by the fishmonger, the morning catch still glistening in the sunlight. He found a safe corner and hid behind it, sneaking a peek at his stalker.

He was tall, with blond hair and defined cheekbones. Scandinavian perhaps? The man shoved his way through the chaotic crowd, stepping over toppled stands as if they were barely an obstacle. Wulf took a breath. He had to keep moving.

He pressed on under the nearby bridge, cutting to the other side of the market. Those who were there had heard the earlier gunshots and fled to safety. It worked to Wulf's advantage, providing him a clear passage.

Unfortunately, his pursuer was quick.

More bullets sprayed his way, striking the pavement at the heels of his feet. Wulf stumbled, though regained his footing, and went left toward the canal. He was not as fit as he once was, his lungs seemingly ready to collapse under the strain. He realized if he wanted to see out the day, he would have to dig deeper.

Behind him, the footfalls of his pursuer echoed against the wall of the surrounding walkway, with no hint of him slowing down. Wulf could not call the Scandinavian's fitness into question. He was younger than Wulf and built like someone who lived in a gym.

He searched for some cover ahead, but there was no refuge he could use to catch a breath or offer an escape. All that greeted him was exposed ground. In the canal near him, a gondola drifted by, the lone gondolier steering it with his oar, free of any passengers to serenade through the romantic city.

He had a stupid thought. Would it work? There was only one way to find out.

Wulf hitched his leg up to the side of the walkway and pushed off with all the energy he could muster, landing in the middle of the gondola. He managed to stay upright, regaining his balance immediately.

The gondolier, also remaining on his feet, stared at him with his jaw agape. "Hey, what the hell are you doing!" he berated Wulf in rapid Italian.

The attacker closed in on the edge of the canal. With little time to spare, Wulf snatched the oar from the gondolier in the striped shirt and thrust him into the canal. The startled man yelled out, his arms flailing as he splashed in the water, creating ripples under the boat.

The gondola continued drifting at a nice pace, despite losing its only crew member. Wulf used his new vantage point to surprise his pursuer and pulled out his sidearm from his waistband and fired on his position.

His stalker avoided the shot and hid behind a pillar.

The boat edged under a low bridge. Wulf put his gun back in his waistband and took his chance, setting his feet apart and bracing himself under the stone arch. He lunged, his hands finding a metal support railing along the other side of the bridge. He heaved up the few extra pounds he had recently packed on and hoisted himself over the top.

His pursuer fixed his gaze on him in the distance.

Wulf made a dash for it in the opposite direction, having gained some yardage on him. He bounded onto an adjoining street lined with iconic Venetian buildings, where more people congregated. The locals went about their business while tourists snapped photos of the picturesque scene.

Church bells rang in the distance, the sounds mingling with gondoliers singing and the horns of nearby trains blaring from beyond the city.

Wulf hurried across the road, slipping through a small gap in the traffic, checking behind to see what kind of lead he still had. As he suspected, his pursuer had gained and was pushing through the crowd. Wulf quickened his pace as best he could and entered a dark alleyway. Sitting at the far end, a group of workers were on a break, eating sandwiches. Their voices blended as one, the conversation punctuated by exaggerated hand gestures. Between him and them was a ladder affixed to the roofline.

Wulf bolted for it and stopped at the bottom to glance

sideways at his chaser, closing ever farther. He scaled the first set of rungs. Before the workers could protest the use of the equipment, he reached the top and kicked the ladder to the ground on their heads.

He peered out from his new position. Using the mental map of Venice he had constructed in his mind during his brief stay, he ran across the rooftops, jumping from one to next, his feet slipping every so often over a loose tile.

A bullet cracked, splintering the timber frame of a window to his left. He jumped to another roof and turned right, glimpsing his pursuer now with him on the rooftops of the city. The Scandinavian fired again, and again, the rounds pelting into the walls of the second story and the tiles at Wulf's feet.

Wulf locked on to his target fifty yards away and removed his weapon from his pants, firing a wayward spray behind him. The other man appeared undaunted, continuing his assault, forcing Wulf to zigzag away from the gunfire. At the end of the roofline, he darted right and out of the Scandinavian's line of sight, zeroing in on a second-floor window. He slid through the half-open entry and closed it in his wake.

There, waiting for him inside, was his temporary home and the operation he had built during his time in Venice. The quad screen setup and the two computer towers in the cramped space was the engine room at which he worked. He booted up the computer's operating system and ran his hands over the keyboard, bringing up the relevant applications to prepare for data delivery. With the internet connection live, he brought a microphone to his lips.

"Hello, old friend," he began. "I'm sorry I have to make this quick, but I have to warn you. An attack on the United

States is imminent. I repeat, imminent. I'm sending all the intel I've gathered. You need to—"

A bullet whistled through the window, shattering the glass. Wulf dived and rolled across the floor to avoid more rounds raining down on him. The brunt of the assault took out his computer, the monitors fragmenting and the inner circuitry spewing from the towers in a hail of sparks. Wulf, unscathed, hurled himself up and ran for the exit.

He could only hope his message had got through.

2

ANCHORAGE, ALASKA

Bishop sat in his foldout chair, his eyes fixed on the endless expanse before him. His breath resembled that of a ghostly cloud, the temperature no more than thirty-five degrees Fahrenheit. It was cold for the time of year, but with the first light of dawn over the horizon, he knew the chill would be short-lived. If he was fortunate, it might reach fifty in the early afternoon, a perfect fall day in 'The Last Frontier.'

He reached past the fishing pole, locked into place in the metal rod holder to his right, and grabbed his backpack, unzipping it to find a thermos inside. He unscrewed the lid and pulled out a ceramic mug from the bag, filling it to the brim with a rich black coffee. The warmth permeated through his hands, radiating him with a much-needed rush of heat. He took in the moment, savoring the aroma, before finally taking his first sip.

Ecstasy washed over him in an instant. As he enjoyed the drink, he peered past the winding river at the landscape that framed his home. At the edge of the property, he had a front-row seat to the sunrise touching the eastern side of Mt. Susitna. Or the Sleeping Lady, as it was known to the locals, due to the shape of the mountain resembling a reclining woman.

The view was magnificent, a sight he had cherished in his days since moving from DC to Anchorage. It had become more than his home. It was his sanctuary. He glanced to his left at the empty patch of ground, a plum-sized lump forming at the bottom of his throat. With another sip, he pushed the bulge deep within and closed his eyes.

Then a sound.

His fishing pole...

Bishop snapped his eyes open to find the pole jerking inside the rod holder, the line dancing across the water's surface. He put down his mug and gripped the handle with both hands, heaving himself from his chair and preparing for the battle.

The fish was a fighter, its strength matched by the forceful current. He let it have its way with the bait, giving it the illusion of victory, before slowly reeling it in. The fish did not relent, not even for a second. There were many varieties he could catch in the river, but none that had such determination. It was a silver salmon.

He walked down the edge of the bank and continued to wind the spool, drawing the hunter and the hunted ever so closer. The next few seconds were paramount if he wanted to get a fresh meal. The water rippled, Bishop's line tightening. Then the salmon lifted, its fins and tail slicing above the surface.

Bishop brought it as close to the bank as he could, straining with all the effort he could muster. With a final flick of the spool, he tossed the rod in his direction, the salmon landing on the gravel bordering the river. He took the large fish in his hands, its tail still thrashing in his palms. With the hook removed, he carried it to the bucket next to his chair and gently placed it inside.

He checked his watch and decided it was time to go. Packing all his supplies, he finished the coffee and slung his backpack over his shoulders. With the bucket in one hand and fishing pole in the other, he began the familiar trek back to his house. The journey was easier after sunrise, but even in the dark he had no issue traveling, the contours of his property burned to memory.

The damp riverbank gravel gave way to larger stones and then to the soft earth of the open ground. The river snaked to the south, while to the north, the wilderness stretched out in an expanse of black spruce. The scent of the pine resin from the trees drifted with the cool breeze.

As was tradition every morning, he stopped about halfway along the path at a solitary paper birch. Its pale bark glowed under the sun, its golden leaves also catching the early light. Some had already fallen, beginning to blanket the ground beneath.

Bishop stepped closer to the weathered headstone protruding from the dirt, where some of the foliage fluttered over its sharp edges. Etched in the stone was a name and date: PATRICIA BISHOP 1947-1997.

He frowned, the discomfort in his throat rising once more.

"Well, I did it." He held out the bucket with the fish inside. "Got your favorite. Didn't think I had the fight left in me, but I managed to snag him."

He approached the headstone and put his fishing pole

down, brushing away the leaves. The memory of the day he had lost her returned to him in a stormy haze. "Seems there's still a bit of scrap in this old brawler yet."

With that, he yanked his rod up from the ground and turned, continuing toward his house. The two-story abode appeared on the other side of the crest, the familiar silhouette standing against the brightening sky.

When he and Pat had first moved in, it was nothing but an empty husk in need of demolishing. Bishop had seen something within its decaying bones, and instead of knocking it down, they had restored it to its former glory. He had renovated large portions to make it livable again, and even added an extra bathroom, a study space, and a wraparound porch.

He climbed the steps and nudged open the door, entering the kitchen. Darkness greeted him, the curtains still drawn. A small blinking light, however, cut through the shadows next to his oven, along with a piercing alert klaxon.

Bishop froze for a moment, then dropped his gear at his feet, flipping on the lights and flooding the cooking area under the warm globes. Never one to waste time, he went over to the alarm and switched it off, the light and sound instantly ceasing.

He could not remember when it had last gone off.

Had it ever?

He scaled the stairs to the upper level of his house, his mind racing at what awaited. At the end of the hall, past his bedroom, was the room he had built with his own two hands.

It had started as little more than an empty space until he had knocked down a wall, expanding the area so he could fit in everything he needed. If someone were to step inside, they would have likened it the bridge of the *USS Enterprise*. Only much more rustic.

Three sturdy timber desks lined each side, supporting an array of computer systems. It was a hodgepodge of technology. Monitors and towers varied in make and model, mostly artifacts from the eighties and early nineties. A radio setup dominated one corner, with speakers hanging from the ceiling along with different styles of microphones which he had salvaged from his time at Bureau 61.

A blackboard framed one side of the door, scribbled with notes, while the other had a corkboard pinned with documents, putting together puzzle pieces of some outlandish jumble of intelligence.

His study was all that remained of Bureau 61, his days of commanding the best undercover operatives in the world now nothing more than a museum exhibit. A shrine to a sad man whose life had faded, thinking that perhaps there might still be some good left for him to do in his solitude.

Above the computer to the right, a similar red alert light to the one downstairs glistened in steady but insistent intervals. He went to the chair and sat, booting up the computer, the near-ancient operating system steadily coming to life. A window finally popped up and read: INCOMING MESSAGE.

Bishop pursed his lips. It was not a glitch after all. He tapped his fingers on the keyboard and pulled up the document. It was an audio file. He rolled his chair to the radio on the other side of his office and activated the speakers, linking them with his computer.

He returned and played the message.

A voice materialized, some background noise evident in the mix. "*Hello, old friend. Sorry I have to make this quick, but I have to warn you. An attack on the United States is imminent. I repeat, imminent. I'm sending all the intel I've gathered. You need to—"*

A crack echoed in the transmission as the message ceased. It was a sound Bishop knew all too well.

A gunshot.

He checked to see if there was anything else piggybacked on the audio.

Nothing.

He straightened in his chair, the muscles in his back tightening. If another person had sent such a communique, he would almost dismiss it as a hoax.

But not Harvey Wulf.

If Wulf believed America was about to be attacked, then he meant it.

3

LANGLEY, VIRGINIA

Jeffrey Phibbs walked into his office with his tuna salad, closing the door to the busy conversations in the corridor behind him. Sunlight spilled from the windows, the warmth of the early September day cast across his desk. While he welcomed the heat, the intense glare would make eating his lunch a challenge. He crossed the room and adjusted the blinds just enough to shield himself from the intrusive light.

He went to his seat and pushed aside a growing pile of folders which had accumulated during the morning. No matter how quickly he sifted through them, they never seemed to stop multiplying. He nudged the mouse to his computer to the opposite side and opened his bag, removing the plastic-covered meal he had bought from the luncheon station downstairs. Lifting the lid, he picked up the fork and enjoyed the first bite.

It was fine, though not what he would have preferred. If Phibbs had his way, he would have indulged in a hot dog drenched with ketchup, mustard, and every other topping that he could get his hands on. Unfortunately, he was not the lean forty-five-year-old he was when he became the CIA director.

His thoughts drifted to his wife who would have been happy at his lunch option. In truth, he suspected Nicole would have been happier if he simply gave the job away. Eight years was a long time to be in such a position. Strangely, though, she never voiced her opinion on the matter. Maybe she knew that if she did, he would actually go through with it. Then what would that mean for her? Him, home all day, moping around, complaining he had nothing to do?

He smirked at the notion and had more of his salad, skewering a hefty lettuce leaf and a chunk of tuna. As he chewed, his phone rang. Speak of the devil, he thought, reaching for his pocket and taking out his cell. He flipped it open, checking the caller ID.

It was not Nicole.

In fact, it was not a number familiar to him at all.

He took the call and brought the device to his ear. "Hello."

"Good morning, Phibbs."

The tone was deep and gravelly.

Phibbs nestled his fork in the middle of his lunch. "Who is this?"

"I'm surprised you don't remember."

Phibbs's posture stiffened, a sudden realization overcoming him. "Bishop?"

"That's right."

"As in John Bishop?"

"Very good, Director."

The former head of Bureau 61 was a hard man to forget. When the decision was reached to shut down the elusive branch of the CIA at the start of his tenure as director, Bishop had made every day until the end a living hell.

"How did you get this number, John? This is my personal—"

"Think about who you're talking to."

"If you want me to be impressed, you've done so—"

"I couldn't give a crap if you're impressed or not, Phibbs. I just need you to listen."

Phibbs swiveled around in his chair, to the brightly lit confines of the CIA grounds beyond his window. "Well, as they say, you've got my undivided attention."

"Good. About twenty minutes ago, I received a message from a very reliable source. He claims that there's going to be an attack on the United States."

Phibbs closed his eyes. He could have just hung up the phone, but he supposed his salad could wait. "Who's this source of yours?"

A moment of silence filled the line. *"Harvey Wulf."*

Phibbs paused, remembering the name. "Can you trust him?"

"I wouldn't have had him doing jobs for me if I didn't."

"That was some time ago, John. Who's to say that in all these years he hasn't—"

"I know Wulf. I assure you, he's reliable."

Phibbs stood and stepped closer to the window. "Very well. Did he give you any more information?"

"He said to me that he sent intel along with the message, but the audio was cut off. With the way it came to such an abrupt end, I can only assume it was lost before being relayed."

"John, this isn't much to go off."

"*I understand that.*" Bishop's tone softened. "*If I could offer more, I would. You have to appreciate I wouldn't have contacted you if I didn't think there was substance to this.*"

Phibbs let the moment linger, recalling the pair's time together in '93. Sometimes, they came to an understanding with one another. It was rare, but it happened. "You know I need more to go on. We have reports daily of potential attacks on American soil. It's either false intel, or something we can lock down before it escalates."

"*Just do me a favor, Phibbs, and double-check everything coming your way. If it's big—*"

"I got it." Phibbs nodded subconsciously. "Thank you, John."

The line went dead, and he snapped the cell shut, tucking it back in his pocket. He returned to his desk and picked up the landline phone, dialing a number through to the agency's IT division. It rang only once before being answered.

"This is Director Phibbs. I want you to check something for me. I had an unauthorized call on my cell from someone outside the agency—"

"*Sir, that's not possible.*"

"Well, it happened, so it is. Check it out for me."

"*Right away. I'll get to—*"

Phibbs slammed the phone down and returned his attention to his meal. He picked up his fork ready to eat more of the early lunch, his thoughts drifting to the conversation with the grizzled sack of bones that was John Bishop. He could not shake the memory of the last time he had seen the man walking from his office, carrying a cardboard box of his belongings. Despite his staunch, no-nonsense demeanor and a career filled with victories, he had left the CIA a defeated man.

Phibbs reached for the receiver again and dialed through to the reception desk. "Felicity, I want you to organize a meeting for twelve p.m. I'd like to go over all the intel for the past twenty-four hours from our major global stations—"

"Sir, we've had that meeting two hours ago—"

"I know we did," he shot back. "I want to do it again. Get all station heads together. Twelve p.m., Felicity."

He set the phone down and rubbed his chin.

Despite the way John Bishop went about his work, his abrasiveness, and the knack that he had at making enemies, above all else, he placed his country first.

He was a patriot.

And if he was onto something, Phibbs had to heed his warning.

4

ANCHORAGE, ALASKA

The scent of salmon weaved a pungent trail through Bishop's home, the smell mingling with the side of poached eggs he had cooked. From the kitchen to his study, the aroma lingered all the way up the stairs.

The office space had become alive in other ways, too, the hum of the computers and the buzz of the radio filling the room. Bishop moved faster as well, at a speed he had not attempted for some years, rolling on his chair from screen to screen.

He had hoped with each replay of the message he may have gleaned a hidden detail to unlock the mystery. Each time, the transmission remained the same, the interruption of the gunshot jolting him. Someone was after Wulf. Was he still alive? The urgency of the call to Bishop spoke volumes, only magnifying the seriousness of what he had claimed.

An attack on America? Imminent?

He recalled his past with Wulf back at Bureau 61.

Unlike most individuals scouted to work for the mysterious division of the CIA, he was no typical operative. He was not ex-military, or a former government employee, and certainly not a foreign national with similar combat or diplomatic expertise whose loyalty could be guaranteed.

Instead, Wulf was a computer expert. A prodigy with a reputation. He had bounced around from company to company, either getting himself fired because he pissed off the wrong people or simply got bored because the jobs no longer stimulated him.

Bishop offered him something more. In the mid '80s, when Bureau 61 was building its 'IT' division, he presented Wulf with a more enticing opportunity. A chance to work in the shadows, spying on the hidden corners of the emerging World Wide Web which was taking shape, along with enemy networks, particularly those of the Soviet Union.

Wulf could be eccentric. He was a hacker, so it came with the territory. But he always got the job done and did so in a way that left no trace in his wake. Bishop lost contact with him in 1993, though told him where he could be found. He assumed the CIA would have snaffled him up in another program. Perhaps they had, and he no longer enjoyed the working conditions, hence why he had contacted Bishop instead of Phibbs.

The computer behind Bishop pinged with a notification. He set down his half-eaten breakfast and swiveled in his chair, rolling along the hardwood floor to the flashing red monitor. The program he employed to trace the numbers of unknown callers had come up empty. Wulf's call, masked in a similar manner, had thwarted the tool. It hardly surprised Bishop. Harvey himself had designed it and would know how to counter it. Just another item of software Bishop had taken from Bureau 61 before he had left, which was now obsolete.

That was the crux of the problem. Most of the gear he had was prehistoric by modern standards. The programs, the algorithms, everything he relied on was out of date. Then there was his other issue. Harvey Wulf was better. If he did not want to be found, he would make sure he was a ghost.

Bishop slid through the menu of results, scanning all the relevant findings, confirming what he already suspected. Not only had Wulf shielded his number from any attempt to trace it, he had also scrambled his GPS location at the time of the transmission.

He might as well have been invisible.

"Dammit, Wulf, what's all this about?" Bishop muttered, crossing the room and finishing up what remained of his breakfast.

He returned downstairs to the kitchen and put the plate and utensils into the sink, intending to clean them later. He paced the dining area, pausing by the jacket on the rack he had worn outside that morning. Reaching inside the pocket, he took out a packet of cigarettes. There were only two remaining. He sighed and sparked one with his lighter, traipsing up to his command center once more.

Bishop had swung at every pitch, striking out each time. There was one option left. A long shot. He sank himself into a chair and pulled up the audio again. To the untrained eye, it was a simple recording. But what if Wulf had hidden something by piggybacking his data within? It would have to have been compressed and would likely hold only a few fragments.

He brought the file to the center of the monitor and launched another piece of Wulf-invented software. The hacker had designed it to peel back every byte like an onion, layer by layer. A progress bar appeared in the corner of the screen, accompanied by an execute button. Bishop clicked on it and let the program do its work. The computer whirred a little harder, the old CPU straining to unravel the message.

Seconds turned into minutes, the progress bar slowly inching from top to bottom. As it did, Bishop continued enjoying his cigarette, the smoke wafting throughout his office. He tipped the ash into an ever-growing ashtray next to the mouse. Finally, the bar filled and a notification window appeared.

Bishop grunted at the results, stubbing the cigarette in frustration. Nothing. Not a single byte of data. It only confirmed what he knew. Wulf was in trouble. So much so he had no time to relay the intel to Bishop by other means. If he was dead, the information had likely died with him.

His hand instinctively moved for the mouse, and he played the audio message through the speakers, turning up the volume as high as it would go.

"*Hello, old friend. Sorry I have to make this quick, but I have to warn you. An attack on the United States is imminent. I repeat, imminent. I'm sending all the intel I've gathered. You need to—*"

The transmission ended as it had every other time. He reran it repeatedly, listening beyond Wulf's words. In the background, sounds took shape, rising above the sentences and static. Bells. Talking. Singing. A horn. The grumble of engines. The splash of water.

Bishop hoisted himself up on the bench and drew the speakers lower to his desk, so that he could press his ears to them.

He shook his head. His equipment would only take him so far.

He stood and walked to the window, taking his last cigarette and igniting it. He opened the catch to let out the smoke drifting throughout the room and gazed out at Pat's gravesite. His heart thumped, and his pulse quickened.

What if Wulf was not dead?

Bishop's mind sifted with the thought that Wulf might reach out again. If he didn't, it would mean him going to Wulf instead. He lingered on the notion of leaving his self-imposed exile. The idea felt almost alien.

With a flick of the ash from the windowsill, he went back to the desk and picked up the phone. It was not an advanced piece of tech he had scavenged from his Bureau 61 days. It was just a plain old telephone with a rotary dial he had found when he had bought the house. He extended his index finger to turn the numbers, the rhythmic clicking echoing inside his office.

"*Alaska Airlines, how may I help you?*" asked the cheery female voice on the other end of the line.

"I want to book the first available flight out of Anchorage," Bishop said.

"*And your destination, sir?*"

"Seattle."

5

Noise coalesced around Bishop as he neared the gate to his flight. PA announcements blared throughout the terminal overhead, interspersed with the whir of motorized luggage carts, while the steady thud of surrounding foot traffic played in melody to the shrill cries of tired children.

The morning had come and gone, his drive through the city in the brilliant afternoon doing little to lift his mood. It had been the farthest he had ventured in years. He normally limited his trips to short drives to the store for food, cigarettes, or the occasional visit to his doctor. The traffic in Anchorage was nothing compared to the carnage in other parts of the globe he had visited, but after so much time in seclusion, he felt as if someone had thrust him into downtown Mumbai.

A line had already formed at the gate, his booking one of the last to be added to the manifest. The queue moved in an orderly fashion, the only disruption from a young boy in tears around six years old, causing trouble for his mother and airline staff. Eventually, the kind women at the counter calmed him with a coloring book and a packet of crayons. Even then, the child only settled under sufferance.

The poor kid.

With every step Bishop took toward the counter, his breath became shorter, and his chest tightened. A lifetime of cigarettes had left their mark, and likely would continue to do so if he survived the years ahead. This feeling, however, was slightly different. It was not the decades of inhaled smoke suffocating his lungs.

He knew exactly what it was.

"Sir?"

Bishop snapped from the darkness in his thoughts to discover the queue had shifted, even though he remained rooted in place. He glanced behind at the frustrated passengers and then in front at the airline attendants who were ushering him forward. He quickened his step and handed one of them his boarding pass. She smiled, checked the information, and swiped the magnetic strip, returning the ticket to his fingertips.

"You're in row ten, seat C. Enjoy your flight, sir."

Bishop nodded his thanks and headed down the air bridge, closer to the hatch. The cabin crew welcomed him on board and took his pass again to confirm where he was sitting. As he stepped over the threshold into the cramped fuselage, his pulse spiked, a surge of adrenaline rushing through his body. For a moment, he thought his legs would give way under him.

Bishop pushed through the discomfort, refusing to make a scene of himself.

The line inched forward, those ahead of him stowing their bags in the overheard lockers. Bishop located his seat and placed his own bag in the space above his head. The pack was light with the essentials inside. A newspaper, some pills, a bottle of water, and a laptop. The rest of his belongings had been checked in, the luggage likely already crammed in the storage section of the aircraft.

He sat and closed his eyes, mentally preparing himself. Perspiration beaded on the top of his nearly bald head, the hot lights in the ceiling not helping matters. Every so often a drop would trail down his forehead and the side of his face. Remaining as calm as possible, he reached into his breast pocket and took out a folded handkerchief, dabbing the sweat as if he had just eaten a hot chili dinner.

Footsteps rang out, accompanied by the sound of whimpering. Bishop reopened his eyes to find the difficult child from earlier taking his seat with his mother on the opposite side of the aisle.

"I don't want to, Mommy!"

The boy squirmed as she adjusted his belt.

"Do we have to go?" he asked.

The mother buckled him in. "Don't you want to see Grandma and Grandpa?"

He dropped his head, and his shoulders sagged. Taking the plane was the price one paid living at the edge of the world. Not that he could help that.

The PA crackled, instructing the flight attendants to cross-check the doors and prepare for departure. Bishop's back stiffened, the surrounding muscles tensing. The boy mirrored his unease. Comfort briefly permeated through him that he was not experiencing distress alone. Though he would have preferred the child was not carrying the burden.

The 737 jolted, then rolled from the gate, the turn of the wheels rocking everybody aboard. Bishop lunged for his newly bought cigarettes in the other breast pocket, catching himself before pulling one out, realizing smoking had been banned by the FAA many years earlier.

Oh, for the good old days.

The plane taxied onward, and the cabin crew went through the routine safety spiel. Though some words had changed over the decades, the well-rehearsed script was the same that Bishop had listened to more times than he could count.

The aircraft reached the end of the runway, and the pilot once again hailed the staff over the PA system. He ordered them to their seats to strap in like every other passenger. A male and female attendant hurried by Bishop into the back of the plane, while he closed his eyes once more.

Images cascaded through his thoughts all at once. The gloomy afternoon. The howling of the wind. The dark clouds in the distance. The sound of sirens.

"Mommy, please! I don't want to do this!"

Bishop opened his eyes again to the kid clutching on to his mother, his fingers like claws digging into her shirt. Bishop looked down, finding the coloring book and crayons at his feet. He gathered them up and handed them to the boy. "Here, you dropped these."

He turned, removing his attention from his mother. The kid took them instantly, thanking him in his own way. With a roar, the plane's engines pushed the aircraft down the runway, propelling everyone into their seats. The child's eyes widened at the pressing feeling.

"Don't worry," Bishop said to him. "Everything's going to be okay."

The words hung between them, meant as much for the boy as for Bishop himself.

6

SEATTLE, WASHINGTON

The Seattle-Tacoma International Airport overflowed with the energy of weary travelers, the crowds coming and going in all directions. Even at such a late hour, Bishop found himself shocked at the commotion.

He raised his carry-on bag as a shield against the current, getting caught in the tide taking him to the opposite end of the terminal. Somehow he freed himself from the pull and located a path to the baggage claim section.

By the time he stepped outside, the pickup bay had become a conveyer belt of people in vehicles arriving and collecting their loved ones before speeding off, only to be replaced by another. The taxi rank and shuttle bus lines were much the same, the slight patter of rain turning an organized queue into a free-for-all. For Bishop, the drizzle barely registered, having packed a thick jacket. A habit formed in Alaska and one difficult to break.

The jostle of the crowd admittedly unsettled him more

than he cared to admit. It seemed everyone was in a rush. To be fair, he was, too. Though, his fight was against an unseen clock.

As he neared the front of the line, the cab with the passengers ahead of him pulled away, while another arrived, ready to take him aboard. Before he could even make a move for the trunk, a trio, two men and a woman, shoved their way in front of him, the rain getting that much heavier. It was as if he were invisible. Or they just didn't care. He went to protest, but before he could speak the words, their bags were stowed and the cab already down the road.

Once, he would have grabbed each of the men by the scruff of the neck and floored them. At that moment, the realization hit him all at once. He was not the person he used to be. His sojourn away from civilization had aged him more than he had thought. The world had sped up into a merry-go-round, leaving the likes of him behind.

Another taxi rolled up and popped its trunk. Bishop remained still until a gentle hand touched his shoulder. He turned to find the mother and son from the plane, the child much more relaxed since the landing.

"Do you need help with your bags?" she asked, likely noticing him in his momentary haze.

"Uh, no." He shook the fog clear. "Thank you, though."

The rain pelted down harder, and he tossed his luggage in the trunk, sparing one last glance with his fellow travelers. Without another word, he got into the car so they could get the next taxi in line.

"Where are you heading?" the driver asked.

Bishop took a piece of paper from his pocket, scribbled with the address, and handed it to him. "Bellevue."

"Fancy."

Soon, they were on their way, the driver navigating from the airport and beyond onto Seattle's highway system. The local, about sixty, similar in age to Bishop, weaved in and out of the traffic with ease. Throughout the smooth ride, the man must have sensed Bishop's desire for solitude, remaining quiet for the twenty-minute trek.

The scenery changed drastically off the exit, the cabbie being correct in his earlier statement. The area exuded wealth. Lush trees lined the streets, framing sizeable homes, some contemporary, others older with a Mediterranean design. The neighborhood, owned by the rich and famous of Seattle, were mostly tech and computer tycoons.

Bishop had come to the right place.

The driver made a left turn, before stopping at a modern abode, which had glass windows lining the front half of the house. "This is your stop."

Bishop peered through the rain-streaked window at the home, its opulence almost catching him off guard. He handed over his fare to the man and tipped him generously. An intensified shower of rain welcomed him outside, and he collected his bags as quickly as he could, rushing to the reprieve of the rooftop over the door to the small mansion.

Despite the late hour, lights from inside bled through the drawn curtains. He proceeded to the doorbell and pressed it, the faint sound of the chime carrying in the night. A moment later, footfalls approached on the other side of the door, and a woman opened it.

She was slightly older, her hair a little shorter, but still stunning nonetheless. "Oh my God..." she uttered.

"Good evening, Danielle," Bishop said.

"John?" She turned and called out inside, "Honey!"

More footsteps echoed from deeper within the home, the

thuds growing closer until a man appeared by Danielle's side. He had barely changed, his hair cut sharper with a gray streak through it, the only difference.

"Hello, Quade."

"I don't believe it." Aaron Quade stood there just as shocked as his wife, attempting to process the arrival.

"Can I come in?" Bishop asked.

"Of course. Let's get you out of the rain."

Bishop hauled his bags indoors, his shoes leaving wet prints all the way to the dining area. The former deputy director of Bureau 61 flipped on some lights and bathed them in a subtle pale glow.

Quade exchanged some quiet words with his wife, and she soon left them on their lonesome, disappearing down the hall.

Bishop put down his luggage and removed his jacket, draping it over the back of a chair. Quade rubbed his hands together and entered.

"You're the last person I expected to see appear out of the night, John." He took the seat opposite and sat. "That doesn't mean it's not good to see you. Did you fly down from Alaska today?"

Bishop nodded. "Just got in."

"I wish you'd told me ahead of time, we could've had a bed ready for you and—"

"I'm not on vacation, Quade."

"Oh?"

"I'm here because I need your help."

"Anything for you. You know that."

Bishop steepled his fingers on the table. "ExoCipher. Your company has some tools I require."

Quade smiled. "So, you found out about my new job?"

"I've kept an eye on you ever since the end of Bureau 61. You stuck around with the CIA until '96, then co-founded ExoCipher with some lucrative investors. You knew which way the wind was blowing. With how much the agency was relying on SIGINT, you realized they'd need to outsource their activities. You provided them with the goods, employing staff all over the States and the world. I even read a recent write-up about the company in Forbes. You've done very well for yourself."

Quade appeared to struggle with accepting the unexpected praise. "Thank you, boss. That means a lot."

"With that said, I'm not here to blow smoke up your ass. I need your assistance." Bishop leaned forward. "I received a message from Wulf."

Quade raised an eyebrow. "Harvey Wulf?"

"He claims the US is about to be attacked."

"What? When?"

"I don't know. That's what I have to figure out." Bishop explained everything to his old friend. He knew Quade held Wulf in a similar regard as he and would believe any intel the hacker had found.

Quade exhaled. "Holy hell..."

"I've brought the audio file with me. As it stands, Wulf's the only one who can give us the information on this potential attack. We have to find him."

"And what if he's dead?"

"One thing at a time."

Quade sat quietly, contemplating further. With a hand on each side of the table, he rose from his seat, determination painting his face. "Very well. Let's go to the office."

7

The ExoCipher Building loomed before Bishop, its towering glass facade rising from the rainy darkness. Even at night, its sleek design seemed to capture the imagination, the glimmer of the moon and the lights within catching all the right angles.

Quade led them up the steps, past the two guards who roamed near the entrance. The director of the company gave them a casual wave, the pair doing their best to stay dry while doing their job. Quade approached the static revolving door, which during the day would have been rotating with the regular ebb and flow of staff and visitors. Next to it was a less elaborate entry.

He swiped his card through a scanner, and the door opened with a soft click. "After you, boss."

Bishop accepted the invitation and went into the lobby. Two more guards patrolled the shadows, the movement mirroring the hush outside. The reception desk was quiet, too, no personnel manning it after hours. Throughout the day the place was likely a hive of activity. Bishop, having dug deep into the company's brief history, knew it was worth millions with thousands of employees spread across the globe. Not bad for a start-up that in 1996 had been nothing more than Quade and a few investors willing to take a punt. He had come a long way. Bishop could not help but be proud of him. Not that he would ever say so.

They went over to a bank of elevators, where Quade once again swiped his security credentials. A chime sounded, and the doors in front of them slid open. Both entered, only to be enveloped by the metallic silence sealing them inside. Quade punched in their destination, and without a word, they surged upward through the building.

The drive over had been filled with a much more active conversation, Bishop retreading on everything he knew so far about their former colleague's message. Quade, as he had always done, listened intently. Despite the years and success, little had changed. He was the same level-headed presence Bishop had trusted to take up the deputy directorship of Bureau 61 back in 1988. If there was one difference Bishop could point to, it was that Quade was more reserved. He had his own secrets now, and Bishop had to accept that.

The elevator chimed once again, and they stepped out at their destination. The overriding theme of glass continued, the transparent walls offering Bishop a view of the entire space. Offices lined the perimeter, with cubicles filling two massive bullpen-style areas. Unlike downstairs, the level hummed with much more movement.

People worked at various desks. It was not a full team, more akin to a skeleton staff. The personnel appeared to be liaising with their peers overseas, their tireless work following the rising sun across the world.

"Boss?"

Bishop found himself standing on the spot, taking everything in, the operation putting even the newest CIA building to shame. He nodded and continued his trek with Quade, weaving through the graveyard shift and on to a door leading to a back room.

What awaited him inside was nothing short of spectacular. The computer lab setup was a modern marvel of technology. Cutting-edge computers and monitors lined the walls, while built-in speakers protruded from the ceilings. In some ways it was a sterile environment, every inch a shade of white and light gray, contrasting his more agricultural arrangement back in Anchorage.

"Welcome to ExoCipher's audio lab," Quade said. "This is where we break down and analyze every piece of auditory intel that comes our way. If I were allowed to say, I'd tell you we've saved the CIA's bacon more times than I can count in here."

"So, just like the good old days, then?"

Quade chuckled. "Take a seat here. Do you have the file with you?"

Bishop unzipped his jacket and revealed a burned compact disc. He slipped it from the plastic case and handed it to Quade, who smirked at him.

"A CD for an audio file?" Quade picked up a black thumb-sized component from one of the tables. "Haven't heard of USB drives yet?"

Bishop glowered. "I guess I'm not as up to spec as I once was."

"At least you didn't bring in a floppy disk."

As Quade inserted the CD into the tray, Bishop's mind flashed to his Alaskan home setup. All his computers still had floppy drives installed in them. He even found himself using them from time to time as well. "Just because something's old doesn't mean it's useless."

Quade pulled up a seat next to him at the workstation and jolted the mouse to bring the monitor to life. The ExoCipher logo, which had been bouncing from one side of the screen to the other in a never-ending loop, vanished.

"Okay, let's see what we've got here." Quade cracked his fingers and clicked through a series of menus. From a separate folder, he dragged the audio file into the graphical user interface of a piece of software. With another click, he played the message.

"*Hello, old friend. Sorry I have to make this quick, but I have to warn you. An attack on the United States is imminent. I repeat, imminent. I'm sending all the intel I've gathered. You need to—*"

As always, the audio ended with the crack of a bullet firing near Wulf's microphone. Quade sat for a moment contemplating what he had just heard before replaying it a second and a third time, his face darkening with each subsequent hearing.

"I'm glad you bought this to me, boss."

"Do you hear it?" Bishop asked.

"The background noise?"

"Can we use this fancy gear to pinpoint the location of his transmission?"

"Possibly." Quade went to work, running the file through a set of algorithms, his hands working quicker than Bishop could register. "It might take some time, though."

Bishop leaned back in his chair, while the screen between them flickered, the program disseminating every element of the message through its advanced acoustic recognition. Waveforms bounced across the monitor, isolating the sounds and collating them into separate fragments.

Quade put his hands together. "I assume you talked to Jeffrey Phibbs about Wulf's warning?"

"He was the first person I called."

"And?"

"He said he'd look into it."

"Do you believe him?"

Bishop paused at the question, remembering the last time he had seen the CIA director. It was the day he had packed his belongings in his old Bureau 61 office. Even after all the disagreements they'd had in the short time they had known each other, the man at least had the honor of seeing him off. "Phibbs might be many things, but he's no fool. He'll have scoured every intel report for the previous three months searching for something out of the ordinary. I doubt he'll find anything, though."

"Why do you say that?"

"Because you haven't."

Quade raised an eyebrow.

"Every shred of SIGINT that runs through ExoCipher ends up at the agency with one of their analysts. If there were any intel about a potential attack, you would have seen it first. You've said nothing since I showed up at your door, so I can only assume little of significance has crossed your desk."

"Hmm." Quade nodded. "What does that say about us if Wulf found something we didn't?"

"That you probably should've hired him."

"Believe me, I tried." Quade let out a short laugh, his joviality quickly waning. He stared at Bishop, deep concern creasing the corners of his eyes. "In all the rush, I've never got to ask how you are. I know most of our communication over the years has been by email. The last time we spoke you told me that Pat—"

The computer chimed, a notification window materializing on the monitor, sparing Bishop from answering any awkward questions.

"What do we have here?" Quade acknowledged the notification and rang up the results. "This is good. Really good. Have a look at this."

Bishop narrowed his eyes at the data. "You're saying you've determined exactly what those background sounds are?"

"Every sound we've been able to program into this software has been."

"How? Those church bells. They could be church bells from any city in the world."

"They could be. When we cross-check the other audio in the transmission, it allows us to narrow the search field. The algorithm has discovered the vocal signatures are conversations and singing. It's picked up the language, too. Italian." Quade pointed at the screen. "There's also a train horn. It even detected a faint flow of water. Put it all together and the program tells us that the church bells were in fact rung from the bell tower of St. Marks Basilica."

"St. Mark's Basilica?" Bishop tilted his head. "The water? The singing? They're gondoliers, aren't they?"

Quade nodded. "Rowing down the Grand Canal."

Bishop straightened in his chair. "Venice."

Quade smiled and returned his attention to the monitor, bringing up another window, producing a map of the city. Colorful dots were overlayed on the image along with a circle in the northwestern corner. "From the decibel levels of the fragments in the audio file, it's managed to trace the transmission to an area with the diameter of two hundred yards, not that far away from the Santa Lucia Train Station."

Bishop grabbed the mouse and zoomed in on the position. "There's some apartments within that zone."

"It would appear so."

Bishop fell into his chair once again.

"Where to from here?" Quade asked.

"From here?" Bishop puffed out his cheeks, exhaling slowly at the discovery. "It looks like I'm getting on another plane."

SEPTEMBER 9, 2001

8

QUANTICO, VIRGINIA

Jack Tyler loathed returning to the FBI Academy. He had paid his dues, slogging through the training to become a special agent twelve years earlier. Despite the experience he had gained across the Northeast field offices and the coveted position in the Behavioral Analysis Unit he had scored at the Bureau HQ in DC, coming back always made him feel like he was a rookie all over again.

It probably had something to do with the subject matter. Chemistry was not his strong suit. As he sat in the auditorium with other agents from all over the country, he did his best to appear engaged with the lecture. Of course, he was listening to Professor Pasternak. He was not foolish enough to have traveled from the office to zone out.

"Are you going to take any notes?"

He glanced at Special Agent Monica Brunelli next to him. Or just Monica, as he had called her since they had begun working together at the J. Edgar Hoover Building eighteen months earlier. She was a bookworm. You had to be to get into their line of work. She, however, took it to another level.

Tyler tapped his temple. "It's all going in here."

She rolled her eyes, obviously aware of how legendary his photographic memory was back at HQ. Tyler knew she was jealous. But there was something more. It was a front. She liked him. If he was being honest with himself, he liked her, too. Neither had made a move. He figured she was waiting for him. The idea of getting involved with someone at work was not one he considered appropriate, no matter how he felt about her.

Was that a mistake? She would only wait for so long.

He shrugged off the thought and turned his attention back to the stage where Pasternak was placing a thin sheet of metal on the lab table. A large screen behind him projected the image of his demonstration, helping the agents get a better look.

"As you can see here, this is aluminum. It has the ability to be shaped and modified under certain circumstances. With the right chemicals, it becomes quite flexible." The professor picked up a bottle and showed it to the crowd. "Ammonia. A cleaner we all use around our home. The alkaline solution is powerful when in concentrated form."

He poured a small amount on the sheet, and the faintest of bubbles rippled on the surface. "Now watch when I add hydrogen peroxide."

With the tip of another bottle over the initial layer, it foamed some more, along with a faint hiss.

"Hydrogen peroxide is more aggressive. As it reacts with the ammonia, it breaks down the aluminum faster. Notice the discoloration? That's corrosion." He grabbed a third bottle, pulling off the cap with his gloved hands. "Here's where it gets interesting. Bleach. On aluminum, it can go a long way, especially when combining it with our previous two chemicals."

Pasternak dripped a liberal amount onto the already fizzing metal. Seconds passed, and the reaction intensified. The professor tilted the sheet on its side, pushing at the weakened area with his finger. The metal warped ever so slightly. "This is what we have to contend with out in the field. All these items are within easy access of criminals..."

The professor's words faded into the background as Tyler thought ahead. Soon he would be on vacation. He and Brunelli would head back to the office in DC, catch up on some work, then he would sign off for the last time for three weeks. He struggled to suppress the smile.

The lecture came to an end, and the FBI's best and brightest filed from the auditorium. Brunelli zipped up the folder of notes she had gathered, no doubt something she would pore over on their trip back to the Hoover Building.

At the exit to the hall, they squirmed through the crowd, Tyler exchanging waves with former colleagues, and even recognizing some familiar faces from his days in the very place when he was taking his first classes. The pair stepped outside and made their way to the parking lot where their signed-out car had baked under the warm morning sun. Tyler used the key fob to unlock the doors and hopped in behind the wheel. While Brunelli settled into the passenger seat, Tyler reached into the rear, opening his briefcase to confirm his plane tickets were still inside.

Brunelli shook her head. "I see what you're doing, you know?"

"What?" he asked in faux defense.

"I get it. You're going to be gone for a while."

"I was just checking to see if the boarding passes were there."

"Sure you were."

Tyler got the car started and weaved them into the slow crawl of vehicles edging out of the parking lot, which had bottlenecked at the exit.

"When do you arrive in Monterrey, anyway?" she asked.

"Four days. I'm heading to New York first to see my sister. Then down to Miami to visit my parents. After that, I'll be on a jet to Mexico."

"Way to not gloat, Jack."

"Hey, you've got more vacation time banked up than I do. Nothing's stopping you from getting away, too."

"No, but who would I go with?"

The question lingered for a moment, naturally an attempt to bait him. Tyler gestured a car in from the left. "I take my vacations alone. You could always do the same."

"That's not really how I like to do it."

"Fair enough, I suppose." Tyler frowned. "Why don't you look into one of those tours? You could do Europe. Paris. Rome. London."

"With a group of drunk spring breakers getting wasted every day? No thank you."

He chuckled, and they finally found a gap through the checkpoint, hitting the open road. An uncomfortable silence took hold. One Brunelli felt too by the way she reached for her paperwork, unzipping the folder and flipping through the notes. Tyler kept his eyes ahead, pretending not to notice that their journey had suddenly taken a very awkward turn.

SEPTEMBER 10, 2001

9

VENICE, ITALY

Bishop emerged from the Fiat cab at Piazzale Roma, stepping into the embrace of the early afternoon. He pulled out his sunglasses and placed them on to contain the glare of the sun bursting through the overcast cloud cover.

He strode to the driver's window and pressed a handful of Italian lira into the man's palm. Though the euro had officially taken effect, the physical banknotes were still yet to be produced. For now, the old currency would have to suffice.

The cabbie gave him a wave of thanks and drove off, leaving Bishop in the bustling square, allowing him to take a breath. At least the drive from the Marco Polo Airport had steadied his nerves after the flight. It had been his biggest concern traveling to Italy. Anchorage to Seattle was one thing. An intercontinental journey sealed inside the fuselage of a 747 was another matter entirely.

He delved into his pocket and unfurled the map Quade had printed for him before he had left the United States. On it was a bird's-eye view of Venice. Bishop was currently located on the eastern side of the old metropolis, where the last bridge from the mainland allowed cars to travel. The Santa Lucia Train Station stood to the northwest, and beyond that, toward the west, was the apartment complex from which Harvey Wulf had presumably sent his transmission.

He set off across the Constitution Bridge, aware he would be on foot the rest of the way, the city's strict no-car policy making sure of it. Though he was not there to sightsee, it was impossible not to get caught up in the grandeur of his surroundings. He had been to Italy many times, but in all his years of traveling the world, he had never visited Venice. Despite the constant chatter of the tourists crowding the streets and gliding along the canals in the various water taxis, there was a strange serenity about it.

For that moment, it was as if he had been transported to another age. Another time. He was no longer a relic from the defunct Bureau 61, he had become an Inquisitor of the State from the sixteenth century on assignment by order of the Council of Ten.

Bishop shook his head at the infantile fantasy and concentrated on his journey. He passed by the Santa Lucia Station, glancing at a train on the platform. The sea of tourists prevented him from determining whether it had arrived or was preparing for departure. Regardless, it was busy, to say the least.

He kept to the water's edge, following his map, passing a series of ferry wharfs. The lines of people waiting for a ride were long, the tourist season obviously not letting up. Bishop wondered what life was like for those who called the city their home. Did they ever get a reprieve from the constant flow of visitors, or had it simply become part of their lives that they would forever have to tackle? He chortled dryly, realizing in more ways than one he was a world away from his quiet escape in Anchorage.

As he continued his walk, he rounded a corner, veering from the water and entering one of the many narrow streets which formed the veins of the city. Paved stone greeted him underfoot, while on either side, storefronts and restaurants lined his path, their outdoor settings filled with patrons enjoying meals, while others queued for a table to become free.

From what little he had seen of Venice so far, despite its beauty, there seemed to be an endless cycle of waiting. Lines to get into other lines. Bishop's shoulders instinctively tensed, a flicker of claustrophobia creeping over him at the suffocating press of bodies.

He found some relief in a space around the San Germania, where a courtyard stretched out before the 1700s church. The throngs of people dissipated beyond, and he homed in on his target down one of the slimmer laneways. There, where the maps had indicated, was the apartment building. It was old, the red roof blending in with the rest of Venice's architecture. He attempted to breach the lobby, but it was locked.

He did not have to wait for long. A young couple breezed out, oblivious to his stalking presence. Bishop seized the opportunity and slid his hand in the door before it could close, slinking his way inside. The lobby was cramped, the walls cracked and worn. He went over to the mailboxes mounted on the wall, scanning the slots, each marked with a number and surname.

Bishop ran his finger down them. Most were Italian,

others appearing to be foreign nationals. He concentrated on the latter, reading them out one by one.

One stood out.

Knox.

Whenever Wulf went on assignment for Bureau 61, especially into hostile territory, he would adopt the pseudonym of a former US president. And Knox was the middle name of President James Polk.

"Apartment 2F..."

Bishop ascended the stairs, passing by an old woman coming the other way, the steps groaning beneath both their feet. Like the rest of the city, every part of the structure was ancient, its bones carrying the weight of centuries. There was a high probability it would crumble long before Venice sank into the sea.

He reached the second story and ambled down the hall, stopping at the 2F emblazoned on the door with faux-gold-plated numerals. He rapped on the painted timber, glancing sideways in both directions, the corridor clear of onlookers.

No answer.

Another knock. The same response.

With a subtle slide of his hand into his pocket, he retrieved a set of lock picks. Bishop had not used the tool in years. Not since his days as an operative before taking up a desk job at Langley. He hoped he still knew how to use them.

He worked them into the barrel, edging the tumblers in the process. It was slow going. Once, he would have opened five doors in the same amount of time. Finally, the lock gave way, and he twisted the handle.

A chaotic scene of epic proportions was his first glimpse inside. Someone had upended and scattered the sofa and chairs. They had also thrown two tables aside, and the lone window had been shattered, the jagged fragments of glass still littering the floor.

The aftermath of the gunshot he had heard in the message?

Bishop moved quickly through the small apartment, scanning every corner he could. The kitchen was bare, the bedroom untouched, and the bathroom empty. No trace of anyone. If Wulf had been there, he was long gone.

He returned to the carnage in the living area, his gaze falling downward. Behind the overturned tables were cables protruding from the power sockets. Bishop could almost see the picture before the destruction. This had been Wulf's computer setup, all his gear removed, leaving a twisted wreck in its wake.

Bishop sighed.

He went to tug a cord from the outlet when a familiar sound cracked over his head.

A gun.

The bullet tore through the air and thudded into the wall. In an instant, he threw himself to the floor as another burst flew through the broken window.

10

Gunfire hammered into the wall behind what had once been Harvey Wulf's computer setup. Bishop remained low, his hands over his head as the assault tore the wallpaper up in a blizzard of debris. Every so often, his assailant's aim would falter, and a round would strike the last remaining shards of glass in the window frame and slash at the weathered timber finish.

Bishop lifted his gaze at the sudden silence. His stalker was out of ammo. How long before he reloaded? Seconds, at most. He hauled himself up, his muscles groaning and his bones grinding under the stress. Even the last physical Pat had nagged him to take with their local doctor had not punished him as much.

He bolted for the door, slamming it open and bursting out into the hallway. Out of the corner of his left eye, he spied the man through the window who was intent on making him his next kill. Tall, blond, fair-skinned. Possibly Swedish. Scandinavian, for sure. His stare was cold, his focus locked on to Bishop while he slid another 9mm magazine into his sidearm. He moved assuredly across the rooftop of the adjacent structures, his posture that of a hunter, ready to take down its prey.

The questions swirled in Bishop's mind. Was this the same person who had come for Wulf? Had he already killed him? And if so, why was he still staking out his residence?

The answers to all his musings would have to wait. Survival was his primary priority. At sixty, out of shape, out of practice, and out of the game for decades, against a specimen in his prime. It would be tough going.

To his right side, a door creaked open. An elderly lady, between eighty and ninety, peered out. She seemed surprisingly spry, considering her frail figure. Her eyes flickered with irritation, likely having been woken from her afternoon nap in all the commotion.

Bishop pointed back in her home. "Get back inside!"

Whether she understood English, he could not say. She did, however, understand the danger, the killer behind them moving across the roof enough of a warning for her to take the hint.

The glass window exploded, and once again Bishop careened to the floor. The impact of the landing was worse than he had hoped, his breath driven from his lungs. He pushed through the discomfort, confirming he had not been hit.

His memories drifted to the Vietnam War. Of course, back then, he was not scrambling through the halls of a Venetian apartment building. Instead, he was dodging death in the dark jungles of the Iron Triangle. Still, to this day, after all the experiences he'd had during the rest of the conflict and then the missions served with Bureau 61 as an operative, nothing terrified him more than the Viet Cong.

The sleepless nights. The constant sensation that someone was watching you, even in the pitch-black of night. The moments when it felt you were getting the upper hand on the enemy, only to have the ground slip out from under you. And just like that, you were on the run, and surrounded, behind the lines.

He shoved aside the nightmares deep within, locking them to the darkest recesses of his mind. He dragged himself from the floor once again and rushed off down the corridor. Behind him, the blond slayer closed on the window and stepped through it, hitching his leg over the frame, swatting away at the persistent glass still in place.

Bishop went for the stairs, almost tripping down them from the surge of adrenaline coursing through him. He shot out his right hand at the rickety timber balustrade, hurrying down the steps, the lack of cartilage in his knee forcing bone to scrape on bone.

More rounds fired, slamming into the walls, grazing the railing and thudding against the door of a nearby apartment. Bishop reached the bottom and glanced upward. The man's footsteps inched toward the top of the staircase. Bishop could not outrun him, even with the slight lead he had over him.

With a tug of the balustrade, it wobbled ever so slightly. It gave him an idea. The question was, would he have the strength to pull it off?

Pressing his back against the adjacent wall, he waited, steadying himself. In the precious seconds he had up his sleeve, the shadow of the assassin neared that little bit more, the man appearing on the second level.

Their eyes locked, surprise flashing in the Scandinavian's chilling gaze. He took a step downward. Bishop hoisted his feet into the air, keeping the pressure of his back on the wall and planting the soles of his shoes against the bottom of the balustrade. He shoved with every ounce of strength, the railing groaning and breaking free from its supports in the stairs.

The balustrade snapped free from its base and crashed down. The assassin, caught off guard, hesitated. He attempted to dodge the railing, but it was too late, the heavy wood thumping into his hip. He tried to recover with a backward lunge. Instead, it made his situation worse, a foot getting tangled, forcing him flat on his face and in a knot of destruction.

Bishop did not waste a second, knowing his pursuer would soon regain his bearings. He ran through the lobby and out into the glaring sun. He hoofed it into the narrow laneway, only for the slam of the door to crash behind him. Fifty yards. That's all he had on the man. Running around the corner, he sprinted as best he could back to the courtyard at the front of the San Germania.

The crowds were still thick with tourists, oblivious to the danger heading their way. He wove through them, gasping for air, his smoke-scarred lungs protesting at the struggle. Perhaps giving up the cigarettes would have been a wise move, as Pat had suggested many times before he had lost her.

Gunshots rang out, followed by the panicked shrieks of the city's visitors. Bishop's heart skipped a beat, and he glanced over his shoulder. The Scandinavian had closed. He fired more rounds into the air and sat on something. The crowd thinned, and Bishop got a better view.

A black motorcycle.

The assassin revved the engine amongst the people scattering. Bishop moved on, pushing himself even harder, turning toward the waterfront. The buzz of the bike followed him with the screams of the people in the assassin's path cutting through the air.

Bishop raced past the queues of tourists lining up for canal tours, his legs starting to burn. He reached a corner and gathered a breath. But the Scandinavian only closed farther. He could only be thirty yards away now. Bishop dared look back at the Scandinavian skirting his way through the crowd, his motorbike snarling with every foot he gained.

Then another engine roared from his right. A flash of red flew through the people milling about, a scarlet painted motorcycle skidding to a halt in front of him. The rider, a woman, her hair dark, tied in a ponytail, and her skin an olive shade of brown, offered him a hand.

"Get on!"

Bishop took only a split-second to consider, throwing his leg over the back of the bike and grabbing her waist in a tight hold. His savior tugged them to the right and shot them down a side street away from danger.

At least for the moment.

11

The woman was no shrinking violet. With a flick of the throttle, the bike surged away, slicing through the stunned bystanders, missing any obstruction in her way with a precision Bishop could only have hoped to emulate.

"Who are you!" His voice was drowned out by the air pressing down on them from their rapid speed through the streets.

"Moretti!" she said. "A friend!"

Bishop frowned. He would have preferred a reply that shed more light on her intentions. She may have been just as dangerous as the Scandinavian on their tail, swerving through the crowds in a hurried pursuit. He had learned long ago not to trust a pretty face. But what could he do? Not being one to look a gift horse in the mouth, he clutched her waist more firmly. He was not about to jump from the ride. Not at this velocity.

"I didn't think you were allowed to have cars or bikes in Venice!" he yelled.

She whipped the motorbike left and then a right with a

smirk. "If the bad guys don't play by the rules, why the hell should I?"

At the next corner she took another right, the sound of the engine echoing against the storefronts. They cut through the Parco Savorgnan, the lush greenery of the park a welcome respite to the labyrinth of buildings stacked one on top of the other.

They bounded across the Ponte delle Guglie bridge, Bishop catching a quick glimpse of the gargoyles carved in the balustrades, keeping watch on their surroundings.

"Where are you taking me?" he asked.

"Somewhere safe!"

"You're going to have to lose our friend first. He's closing on us!"

"I'm working on that!"

They continued on, the paved path tapering further, the shocked expressions of those darting out of the way growing more pronounced the longer the chase persisted. As they crossed a short bridge over a narrow stretch of the canal, Bishop spotted a pair of police officers standing at the corner watching the foot traffic. Each stood by a bicycle.

Moretti sped past them. Moments later, their blond-haired hunter followed in hot pursuit. The cops got on their pedal bikes and chased after him, but the likelihood of them catching either of them was effectively nil. They would likely radio for reinforcements, though.

Sure enough, the distant wail of sirens echoed from the wider canal, the water boats of the Polizia di Stato now alerted to the activities of the two motorcycles. Moretti leaned into the turns, guiding them across another bridge and pushing them eastward through the ancient city. Yet, through all the daring maneuvers, the Scandinavian continued to gain.

Moretti eased off the throttle and twisted the handlebars to the left. The assassin mirrored the move, both passing by the Ponte Chiodo bridge, then heading toward the sea at the north.

Gunshots rang out.

Bishop glanced behind, the Scandinavian now within range and firing, the rounds pelting into the road near their tires. Bishop did a double take at their position, the bike closing on the water.

"Uh, I think—"

"Just hold on!" Moretti yelled.

Bishop followed her instruction, and she pointed them at the canal. With a rev of the engine and a hop over a wooden plank, she launched them over the waterway. They soared through the air, the gap easily thirty feet. Then came the jarring thud, the duo landing intact on the other side, the wheels staying upright as they went.

"Are you okay?" she asked.

Bishop barely had time to catch his breath. "Fine! Fine! Keep going!"

Moretti pulled them away, snaking them through the maze of yachts and boats lined up in the wharf. In the rear, the Scandinavian jumped the same canal, clearing it and landing even more effortlessly than they had.

Moretti took a left at the junction ahead and then a sharp right. In the distance, a group of police officers rode toward them on their bicycles, their hands raised in the air in a clear signal for them to come to an immediate halt. She did not take notice, jerking them left again out into a residential street lined with a few pedestrians. Moretti zipped by them and zigzagged through the following streets until they came across the Grand Canal.

More police appeared, this time on boats, the crafts steering to the nearby jetties. Moretti slowed, the path becoming increasingly congested near the casino. The crowds, unlike the others around the city, were much less inclined to make way for them.

They eventually broke free, inching through the horde of well-dressed men and women, near the docked police boats. As with every obstacle they had come across so far, she paid them no matter.

Bishop furrowed his brow. Where was the Scandinavian?

The roar of the other motorbike erupted from the north, and Bishop snapped his head in the direction of the sound, the assassin having gone around the long way to ambush them. He overshot them, however, giving Moretti the chance to escape. She took the advantage using the seconds on their side, zooming off beyond their pursuer's line of sight, near another of the canal's main bridges.

"We're going to get off here!" she said.

"We are?"

Moretti slowed by the edge of the water and came to an abrupt stop. She peeled herself from the seat and helped Bishop off in a single motion. She revved the throttle and let go, the bike shooting forward and tipping over the side into the canal with a deafening splash.

The woman yanked Bishop's hand, and they hurried down an alleyway, where they hid in an alcove. They held their breath, out of sight, waiting for the Scandinavian. His motorcycle grew louder, brushing past them, its brakes screeching as he skidded to a halt.

He hopped off his ride and slammed the kickstand into

place, resting his gun by his side. He stepped to the lip of the canal and peered over the edge with a hand on his hip, their abandoned vehicle at the center of his crosshairs.

The police sirens grew louder, and the assassin holstered his weapon. He returned to his bike and got back underway, spinning the tires underneath him. He sped off, the engine fading while he outran the approaching constabulary.

Moretti took Bishop by the arm. "Let's go."

She opened the door behind them, and Bishop trailed her inside. The bottom level of the building was vast, stripped bare like an old warehouse. It was once likely a set of apartments, now though little more than a shell. How long it had been abandoned for was a mystery.

They climbed the dilapidated stairs, Bishop half expecting the timeworn timber to collapse underfoot. The few windows not boarded up which remained in the structure cast feeble rays of sun through to help light their way. The shadows swallowed everything else up, the only sound the pitter-patter of leaking pipes somewhere in the depths of the darkness.

At the summit of the steps, Bishop followed Moretti to the far end of a hallway. She ushered him inside, and he ambled over the threshold. The sharp tang of strong tobacco tickled his nostrils on entry, the smell oddly familiar.

There, at a solitary table, sat another woman. She was older than Moretti, not that much younger than Bishop himself. Her hair was dark, with some streaks of gray, her face slightly wrinkled but still radiant. A cigarette dangled from her mouth, her lips curled with a grin.

"Hello, Bishop," she said. "Welcome to Italy. It's been a long time."

12

"Teresa Abella."

Bishop stepped closer to the desk, breathing in the secondhand smoke weaving through the air. The scent was pungent. A strong blend. Unfiltered. Russian, if his instincts were correct. "The last time I saw you, we were in a place much nicer than this one."

She nodded. "Milan."

"March 1981."

Abella dragged her cigarette and stubbed it in the ashtray on her desk. "It's nice to know I'm not forgettable. You, my friend, certainly are not. You cut a trim figure back then. I remember you having much more hair, too. What happened?"

"I got older."

She smiled. "I'm glad you outlived the game. I always suspected you were a survivor. Sit, John."

Bishop lugged the chair in front of the desk out, scraping it against the battered floorboards. He settled into it and glanced at the younger woman still standing by the door. "It appears I've got you and Ms. Moretti here to thank for keeping me alive to see another day."

"She's one of my best." Abella gestured to her with a wave. "Could you please give me and Mr. Bishop a moment?"

"Of course." She exited, pulling the door shut behind her.

Bishop refocused on Abella, peering through the dim light of the shadows cast by the solitary lamp in the corner of the room. "So, the operative now controls the operatives. The question is, are you in charge of the Military Intelligence and Security Service or its domestic counterpart?"

Abella reached for her packet of cigarettes. "I think you already know the answer to that."

"The foreign service it is then. If you were head of domestic operations, we'd be meeting in a much more official capacity. Not some ramshackle building. You obviously don't want to step on the toes of your colleagues in the Intelligence and Democratic Security Service. Of course, I don't have to guess. I know you took charge of the foreign service in 1997 and have built up quite the reputation since your career in the field."

"You seem to have me at a disadvantage." Abella's welcoming joviality disappeared. "Getting information on you was always difficult. I did some digging after our job against the Soviets in '81. While I knew you were connected to the CIA in some capacity, I couldn't find a shred of evidence that you ever existed."

"I guess I'm good at covering my tracks."

"Indeed." Abella opened the packet and took out a cigarette. "Would you like—"

"I thought you'd never ask."

She handed Bishop one and lit it for him before sparking

her own. The twin trails of smoke wafted through the office, creating a gray haze around them.

Bishop inhaled the rough texture of the Russian cigarette. It had been some time. "Your curiosity must have got the better of you when my name popped up on a flight to Italy."

"I won't lie," Abella said. "It got my attention. So much so I hightailed it from Rome to make sure you stayed out of trouble. I suppose I arrived too late."

"I apologize about that."

"You're not on vacation?"

"No, not exactly."

"I suppose you're no longer on the CIA's books anymore either. If you were, they would have sent someone younger and fitter."

Bishop grunted. "Nothing gets by you, does it, Teresa?"

Abella blew a plume of smoke in his face. "I'm simply putting everything together. What's going on here, John? What are you doing in Venice, and who was that man who was following you?"

"That's sensitive—"

"Need I remind you where you are? If it wasn't for me, you'd be dead right now. Tell me everything or I'll have you tossed out of the country."

Bishop could not help but admire her nerve. She was a tough cookie back in the '80s. Time had done nothing to dull her edge. "Very well. I'm here doing an investigation."

"You said you weren't with the CIA anymore."

"I'm not. This is more personal."

"I'm all ears, John."

He leaned across the desk and tapped some ash in the ashtray. "Yesterday, I received a message from a former... contact. He claimed that an attack on the United States was imminent. The audio was supposed to be accompanied by a data packet of all the intel he had. It never came through."

Abella stared at him. "And this led you to Venice?"

"The message ended abruptly. The last sound recorded was the crack of a gunshot. I tried to get back into contact with him, but he'd scrambled his number and masked his GPS coordinates. Eventually, I managed to pinpoint the origin of the transmission."

"That apartment building?"

Bishop nodded.

Abella twirled her cigarette in her fingers. "I'd be very interested in how you did that without his GPS coordinates."

"Another time, perhaps?"

"Hmm. Why did he contact you? If he knew of an attack, why not speak to the CIA?"

"Trust is earned." Bishop shrugged. "I have his. They don't."

"What did you find in the apartment?"

"It's been ransacked. I suspect whoever was after him got to his computer setup. They took the monitors and the towers. All that was left was some generic cables."

Abella raised an eyebrow. "Computer setup?"

Bishop hesitated for a moment, dragging on his cigarette and exhaling. "Let's just say he has a way with—"

"He's a hacker?"

"That's one of his skills, yes."

"So, this information he claimed to have had, he likely hacked it from somewhere?"

"I don't know. His message was brief. That's why I flew here to find him."

"And when you did, you were nearly killed."

Silence fell across the room, lost in the smoke.

"Well, John," she said. "I must admit, when I came to Venice, I didn't think our meeting would be this interesting. Maybe I should've. Did you recognize the assassin?"

Bishop shook his head. "No. If I had to speculate, I'd assume it was the same person who came after my contact."

"Why do you say that?"

Since the pursuit, Bishop had pieced together the fragments, arranging and rearranging them to understand what Wulf had been up to. "Let's presume my contact gained knowledge he wasn't supposed to. Let's also assume he did so in a way that got him noticed. Someone was sent after him due to the sensitive nature of that information, knowing that he would try to reach out to someone with it. He was intercepted and his computers taken. That much is clear. But what if they didn't get him? There's a chance he escaped, and that very assassin has been staking out his apartment just in case he comes back."

Abella finished her cigarette and flicked it in the ashtray. "And instead of your contact returning, you enter, getting yourself caught in the line of fire."

"It would seem so."

Abella steepled her fingers and brought them to her face. "That blond assassin of yours has disappeared from our radar, which means we've come to an impasse. If your contact is still in Venice, there's every chance he's gone to ground. There are plenty of places to hide here."

"It'd be like finding in a needle in a haystack." Bishop frowned. "That doesn't mean I'm about to give up, Teresa. My contact was adamant this attack was going to happen. I can't just leave without trying to find the proof."

Abella considered his words. Before she could speak, the

door knocked and opened. Moretti stormed in with a folder under her arm in a fluster.

"What is it?" Abella asked.

"The police," she said. "You wanted me to monitor their activities."

"Yes?"

"They've found something. A body in the canal."

13

NEW YORK, NEW YORK

Tyler stepped off the air bridge from his plane and entered the terminal. Though he was a tall man, the crowd seemed to carry him along as if he were a piece of driftwood flowing down a raging river.

Typical New York. He had visited twelve months earlier, and his arrival matched the same restless energy on display then as it did now.

And it was not just the airport.

It was the roads, the sidewalks, every inch of the pavement. Everyone was in a hurry, their heads down, moving without pause. No one stopped to talk. No one looked at each other. Tyler grimaced. He never liked big cities. Even DC had taken time to get accustomed to when he had landed his role at FBI Headquarters. Having grown up in Arkansas, he supposed, the slower lifestyle remained with him no matter where he went.

"Jack!"

Tyler followed the sound of the feminine voice through the surrounding din. An outstretched hand reached into the air beyond the waiting area seats. He strained to see better, but the crush of fellow passengers blocked his view.

"Jack!" she called again.

Tyler jostled himself onward, the tide ebbing, some going left, the others right. In the chaos, he spotted her. A redhead, the rusty shade matching his own. Her eyes, hazel, also like his, glimmered in the overhead lights. Then there were the freckles dusting her cheeks. He had luckily outgrown them. On her, they were endearing. On him, not so much.

His petite sister, a foot shorter than him, stood with her arms crossed in a defiant stance, radiating all the moxie he had expected. "Do you know how long it took me to get out here?"

"Did you take your way or the shortcut I showed you?" he asked.

"That shortcut is dumb."

"Yet here you are. Late, as usual."

She smiled. "Maybe next time I'll make you get a cab."

He wrapped his arms around her, and they shared a warm embrace. "I've always said you don't have to come all the way out here."

"I wouldn't strand you. I'm not that mean." She pulled away as some more passengers disembarking the plane accidentally shoved them. "It's good to see you."

"You, too, Kate. It's been too long."

"And whose fault's that?"

Tyler laughed. He knew it was only a jest on her part, but a pang of guilt hit him, nonetheless. He should have taken more time off work when he had the chance and organized more visits, considering they did not live that far away from one another.

"Come on, let's get out of here." Kate led him through the terminal, her lack of height doing little to dent her confidence. She nudged through everyone, making it to the baggage claim section where they stood patiently for the conveyer belt to spit out Tyler's bag.

"So, how long did you say you'd be in town for?" she asked.

"Just the one night."

Kate frowned. "I suppose that beach of yours in Monterrey can't wait, huh?"

"I—"

She pressed her hand against his arm. "I get it. You've probably been pretty busy at work."

"Like you wouldn't believe."

"How's Monica?"

Tyler froze, looking down at her. "What are you talking about?"

"You don't remember, do you?"

"Uh—"

A smile the size of the Brooklyn Bridge beamed across her freckled face. "That night you visited last year. We had all those drinks at that bar downtown. When we walked back to my place, you told me about this woman. You thought she was kind of—"

Tyler put up a hand to stop her going any further. Next to them the luggage tumbled onto the belt. Those lucky few whose bags came out first tugged them to freedom.

"I don't remember telling you this," he said. "Now I'm wondering what else I confessed to that night."

"Nothing as interesting as this. Do you two still work together?"

"We do."

"Well, spill the beans, big brother."

Tyler chuckled. "There's nothing to tell."

"Seriously?"

"Seriously."

"You're hopeless." Kate shook her head. "Are you ever going to make a—"

"Hey, my bag!" Tyler zigzagged through the waiting passengers in front of him to grab the black case and return to his sister's side. "Ready to go."

She stared at him with a look that made it clear he had not heard the last of the subject. Tyler ignored her as best he could and moved toward the exit. They went outside into the hustle and bustle of the traffic beyond the door, stepping over the crossing and making their way into the parking lot.

"So, I assume Mom and Dad have got your bed ready for you when you visit," Kate said.

"Yup, just like last time. In that tiny little back room."

"What's wrong with the guest room?"

"Dad's putting together a five-thousand-piece puzzle of the Battle of Yorktown, which is taking up the entire space."

Kate rolled her eyes. "He's been doing that puzzle for six months. Has he even done the edges yet?"

"No."

The pair shared a laugh as they reached her car. Kate opened the trunk, and Tyler nestled both his bags inside. He slammed it down and then joined her.

She started up the engine and reversed from their parking space. "Have you heard from Rick lately?"

Tyler shook his head. "I tried calling him last week. It went through to his voicemail."

"Yeah, same." Kate drove them from the lot and out of the airport exit. "I hope he comes around."

Tyler shrugged. "We're all gone. I went first. Then you. And now Mom and Dad are at the retirement home in Florida. I suppose he feels as if he's been left behind."

"I guess so."

"He'll be fine."

"Yeah."

"Anyway, what about you? You look great. Almost glowing, if you know what I mean." It was Tyler's turn to tease her. "Have you got something to tell me?"

"You're an idiot." She glowered at him while keeping an eye on the traffic. "But I do have some news."

"What is it?"

She smiled, easing into the left lane and pressing her foot on the gas. "I'll tell you at dinner. You're not going to believe it."

14

VENICE, ITALY

Olsson raised the bag of apples he had selected to the shopkeeper. The old Italian man behind the counter gestured to the scales. Olsson placed them on, the needle shifting to weigh his purchase.

The shopkeeper did the calculation and spoke in his native tongue. Olsson, far from proficient in the language apart from a handful of simple phrases, nodded, checking the required payment flashing at him on the register. He took out his wallet and flipped through it, selecting a few banknotes to hand over. The bills vanished into the till almost instantaneously, the shopkeeper retrieving his change just as fast.

Olsson took the coins and tossed them in his pocket with his wallet. "Grazie."

He walked from the shop onto the busy Venice streets outside the door, the tourist traffic as lively as it had been the day he had arrived to track down the hacker. The golden sun bathed the red roofs of the surrounding shops and houses, making it feel almost like paradise. While he enjoyed the scene, he had to remind himself he was not on vacation.

With a step forward, his hip flared, shooting a pain down to his knee. He grimaced, recalling the scuffle with the older American in the hacker's apartment building. Age and fitness may not have been on his opponent's side, but he was shrewd. Collapsing the stairwell balustrade had been a masterstroke, one Olsson wished he had anticipated. Ridding himself of the torment caused by it would take time.

Just as he was about to join the mass of people before him, a team of local police sped past much more urgently than he had seen so far on his assignment in Venice. In the distance, the shrill of the sirens still wailed from earlier, the pursuit through the streets obviously having spooked the constabulary into action.

They, of course, would not find him. After discovering the motorbike of his targets in one of the canals, Olsson had slipped into a narrow alleyway before the local cops could take him in, his bike now out of sight. With a black hat pulled low over his signature blond hair and a pair of dark sunglasses on, for all intents and purposes, he was now an apparition.

But that did not mean he could let his guard down. In the last few days, Venice had been rocked by two major pursuits. Such chaos would not go unnoticed without serious questions asked. With any luck, his mission would soon be over. No matter how proficient he was at his job, it was foolhardy to stick around somewhere too long. Eventually, someone would place a set of crosshairs on his back.

Olsson glanced both ways to check if the coast was clear. He took off, melding into the flow of nearby tourists, the clatter of their cameras and the various foreign languages doing little to soothe his pain. He fished an apple from his bag and sank his teeth into it, the juicy flavor offering at least some respite.

A buzz vibrated in his pocket. He finished chewing his food and found his phone, flipping it open. The caller ID was unknown. He did not need to see the name. He knew exactly who it was.

"Hello," he said.

"*Are you alone?*" the voice spoke in a mechanized tone, electronically distorted to mask their true identity.

"Stand by." Olsson weaved through a few more people and maneuvered down a side street to his hotel. Taking another bite of the apple, he traipsed through the lobby and walked the stairs to his room on the second floor. Balancing the fruit, his phone, and the key, he unlocked the door and entered, clicking it shut and latching the chain.

He pressed the cell to his ear and went over to the window, drawing open the curtain to shed some light and take in his canal view. "I'm alone."

"*Good. What's your situation?*"

"Just as you claimed would happen, someone else came looking into the hacker's business." Olsson checked his watch. "At approximately 1:05 p.m., he entered the apartment. I spotted him through the window and opened fire."

"*And his description?*"

"Early sixties. Caucasian. Nearly bald."

A silent understanding seemed to reach across the line.

"He fled, and I pursued on foot through the building and onto the streets," Olsson continued. "He was rescued near the wharfs."

"*By the police?*"

"No. I suspect either the foreign or domestic intelligence

agencies have operatives in the city. His allegiance lies with them."

"*You don't need to concern yourself with them. What matters is that our target's breathing, unlike the last one. He is alive, isn't he?*"

Olsson gritted his teeth, recalling the admonishment received from his superior for allowing the hacker's death. His orders had been explicit: to ensure the hacker remained unharmed for interrogation. "He's still very much alive. I did everything I could not to kill him. At the end of the pursuit, I found the motorbike I was chasing. It'd been dumped in the canal. There were no bodies. I guarantee that they got away."

"*And you made the chase believable?*"

Olsson winced, brushing his knee and thigh. "Very."

"*Good. That means the new player on the scene is going to continue his investigation. He will have found nothing at the hacker's apartment, leading him to pursue the possibility of backup data being left behind. You'll have to follow him closely from here on out. If he finds any form of the plans before the attacks begin and gets them to the CIA, it will endanger the entire operation. You must destroy any other file, no matter the cost.*"

"I understand."

The line went dead, and Olsson snapped his phone shut, sliding it back into his pocket. He rested a hand on his hip, peering out at the canal as he finished his apple. The crunch of each bite resonated within the stillness of the small hotel room. He drew the curtain closed and crossed into the bedroom, swinging ajar the wooden door of the closet.

He kneeled and pressed the required code into the panel of the safe, opening it with a quiet thud. Inside the compartment lay his Glock 17. And nestled beside it were stacks of spare ammo. He had already spent several since his arrival in the city but cared little as he always packed extra.

Next to the arsenal sat his DeSantis New York Undercover shoulder holster. He unraveled the leather rig and slipped his arms through the harness, adjusting it until it fit nice and snug. With all the speed he had acquired over the years of doing the job, he removed his sidearm from the safe and slid in a magazine, holstering the gun. He then took two spare magazines and put them in the pouches on the opposite side.

Olsson went into the living area and removed his jacket from the sofa, placing it on to conceal the bulk of his firearm underneath. He confirmed, with a quick glance in the mirror, that it was obscured.

But there was one more thing. His nuclear option.

Olsson returned to the closet and slipped out the last item. A briefcase. He hefted it to feel the weight of the contents. He had done many things in his time. This, however, was something new. While he was partial to the standard tools of the trade, he could not help but be curious of what lay within the case.

He closed the safe and pocketed another apple for later.

Even a triggerman needed to eat.

15

Bishop disembarked from the water boat behind the two Italian women, with a helping hand from Moretti. The foreign service agent exuded the same strength as her superior. Beneath the hardened shell, however, was a gentler side. Not vulnerable, but cerebral. It was clearly a quality that Abella valued in her people.

The trio moved along the edge of the waterway until they reached a building with a beautiful white marble facade. Arched windows lined the structure, along with elegant curves, evoking the artistry of shape and soul from the Renaissance period.

They approached the door where a sign hung above, the modern light box out of place in such a location. On it was the text 'OSPEDALE' lit up in red on a white backdrop. Abella entered first, her heels clacking against the floor of the hospital with a sped and rhythm Bishop remembered from their brief assignment together in the '80s. Her appearance had softened with age, but she was as sharp as ever, her presence still commanding, her demeanor that of a consummate professional.

Before embarking on his one-man mission to Italy, he had considered reaching out to her. He ultimately decided against it. Too many years had passed, with the potential of too much having changed. When someone transitioned from the field to a desk job, management often expected them to break their old habits. Diplomacy had to be conducted by the book instead of on the fly. Bishop knew the bureaucracy side of the game all too well.

He was glad that Teresa Abella had not been tempted by those paying her wage. The qualities he had admired in her remained.

The inside of the Venice Hospital mirrored the elegance of its exterior. Ornate stonework and polished timber blended to create a spectacular architectural masterpiece. Unlike the streets outside the door, the halls were relatively quiet. Abella continued to take the lead and approached the reception area. She murmured to the woman behind the counter, and they were sent to the right.

Bishop quickened his pace to catch the others, his muscles aching from the chase. It had been many years since he had used them in such a way. By the time he reached their side, they arrived at a door flanked by a duo of police officers clad in blue. Abella again spoke in muted tones. The older of the two men motioned to the door, allowing them in.

The morgue, in contrast to what Bishop had seen so far, left him underwhelmed. While the ventilation was cool from the AC in the ceiling, the room itself was cramped, the lighting harsh, and the chemicals lingering in the air making him feel lightheaded. At the center of it all stood an impeccably dressed man in black, flipping through the pages of a clipboard. He was young, barely thirty, with a thick mustache and long wavy hair. Abella approached and extended a hand.

He shook it. "Teresa Abella, I presume."

She nodded.

"I'm Inspector Conti. I received word to expect your arrival."

Bishop turned his gaze as Abella handled the conversation with Conti. He knew the delicate nature of such situations intimately. When they had learned of the body being discovered, she'd had to swallow her professional pride and reach out to the domestic intelligence service and advise them of her activities on their turf. She had obviously smoothed over any misunderstandings. If not, they would not have been standing in the morgue with their consent or that of the Polizia di Stato.

"These are my associates. Ms. Moretti and Mr. Bishop," Abella said, making the introductions.

"Welcome to Venice." The youthful inspector waved them forward and gave everyone a clear view of the body on the table before him.

The corpse was naked, save for a sheet draped across his crotch. Bishop stared at the face. His unkempt brown hair and stubbly facial features were familiar, even if the passing of time had altered them.

"Is this him, John?"

The words came from Abella, the question caring, yet one expectant of answers.

He nodded. "That's him. That's Harvey Wulf."

The Inspector popped a pen from his breast pocket and wrote the name on his paperwork. "Very interesting."

"Why's that?" Bishop asked.

"It doesn't match his driver's license." Conti led them to

another table in the corner of the morgue. "These are all the effects that were found on him."

Everything had been placed in clear plastic bags. Bishop picked them up one by one. A fresh pair of blue jeans. A black-and-white Letterman jacket. A ghastly green baseball cap. And a pair of red Air Jordans. They were new, going by the vibrant color, yet worn with plenty of scuffs and scrapes.

Inspector Conti collected another bag with a brown wallet within. He unsealed the top and retrieved it, opening the contents with a snap of the button. "We found only three items inside. Some cash. American and Italian currency. A North Carolina driver's license belonging to a Mr. James Knox. Not Harvey Wulf."

Bishop nodded. He had not revealed his contact's name to anyone, not even to Abella. There was little point in hiding it now when the man lay dead. "It's definitely Wulf."

"And this Knox?"

"A...pseudonym."

Conti glanced at Abella with a raised brow. "I suppose I should have expected there was more to your arrival than met the eye."

"What was the third item?" Bishop asked.

"Hmm? Oh." Conti revealed another laminated article from the wallet. "A library card."

Moretti stepped closer. "Which library?"

"Biblioteca Nazionale Marciana," Bishop read from the card.

Abella turned her attention from the personal effects and back on Wulf's corpse. "Where did you find the body, Inspector?"

"It was washed up in the canal near the magistrate's court."

"Cause of death?"

He led her to the table while Bishop continued staring at the card. "No bullet or knife wounds. As you can see here, there's severe blunt force trauma to the side and back of the head. We have witness accounts of a chase taking place on foot. One description matches our Harvey Wulf here."

"And the other?"

"We've not been able to find the individual, but it appears we're searching for a tall, blond Caucasian male. Late twenties to early thirties. The witnesses also claim they heard gunshots fired along with a pursuit on the rooftops. We believe Mr. Wulf fell from one such rooftop, coming down on the pavement before drowning in the canal."

Bishop glanced up from the library card, catching both Abella's and Moretti's gaze. They shared a silent understanding. The assassin who had targeted Wulf and Bishop was one and the same.

"It lines up with another incident that's been looked at from a few hours ago. Two motorbikes. A tall blond man on one. A male and a female on the other." He pulled out a small notepad and checked some scribbled details. "Mr. Bishop, and Ms. Moretti. You might be able to help me. The descriptions are uncannily similar to your own."

Abella placed a gentle hand on the inspector's shoulder. "I'll ensure your department has a full report on the foreign service's activities since our arrival."

He glared at her. "I'm sure that'll be most interesting reading."

"In the meantime, as a token of our thanks, we'd like to give you the address to Mr. Wulf's apartment." She gestured to Bishop who took the cue and handed the folded-up map he had brought with him to Conti.

The group continued exchanging details, naturally holding back Bishop's role, along with the sensitive information about Wulf, the message, and any of the potential intel he had. Satisfied with what they had to say, Conti allowed them to leave. Bishop returned the library card, and then he, Abella, and Moretti departed, stepping back out into the glare of the afternoon.

Bishop remained deep in thought behind them as they waited for a boat to take them on their way.

"You're thinking about something, John," Abella said.

"How can you tell?"

"You've been quiet."

"I just saw a man I considered a friend dead."

"It's more, though, isn't it?"

Bishop paused. No longer was he alone. He now had allies by his side. "I want to go to the Biblioteca Nazionale Marciana."

Moretti titled her head. "The library card?"

He nodded. "Perhaps, if we're lucky, it'll contain a message from the grave."

16

Olsson lowered the binoculars and peered across the canal at the three individuals emerging from the entrance of the hospital. One was the older American who had investigated the hacker's apartment. The others, both Italian. One more senior than the other. The younger one was the person who had rescued the American on her motorbike when he had begun his pursuit.

He brought the binoculars to his eyes again. The American man now had associates helping him. An unexpected development which could prove to be either a blessing or a curse. His target had obviously come to the medical facility to view the hacker's corpse. His reason was two-fold. One: identifying the deceased as a courtesy to relatives, perhaps also giving himself a sense of closure. And two: he was searching for clues.

If Olsson's employer was correct and the American was in Venice looking for data regarding the upcoming attacks, his motive was clear. He would not stop until he had the truth. And if, as Olsson suspected, the others were from an Italian intelligence agency, their combined intellect and resources increased the likelihood of them finding that truth.

His disadvantage? It was three against one. Olsson could not help but smile. He had faced far worse odds before.

The trio lingered on the wharf, chatting for a few more moments before boarding a boat. The older of the two Italian women spoke to the driver, and they set off, creeping away from the edge and chugging down the canal.

Olsson snapped his binoculars shut and tucked them into his breast pocket. Heaving himself up from his crouched stance in the obscurity of the rooftop, his knee burst with pain. He cursed and grabbed his briefcase, leaping through the window he had left ajar. He bounded down the staircase and out onto the street, the boat with his targets aboard remaining within sight.

Twenty yards farther down, he found a water taxi free of any passengers queueing for its services.

The driver waved Olsson away. "Mi dispiace. Non prendere passeggeri."

From what Olsson could gather, the ride was not in service. That was not the answer he was hoping for. He remained calm and took the diplomatic approach, revealing his wallet and the wad of cash within.

The driver shrugged, motioning him aboard. "Va bene."

Olsson yanked the mooring rope and tossed it into the back of the taxi. He jumped next to the other man and stuffed the banknotes into his hand, pointing ahead. "Seguimi."

He hoped his feeble Italian was accurate. It seemed it was. They pulled away and moved in behind the other boat. Close enough to keep them in his crosshairs, but far enough in the rear so they did not appear in pursuit.

The cool breeze of the canal ruffled Olsson's hair, the setting of the afternoon sun sending a chill through the city and casting long shadows across the buildings. He put down his briefcase and took out his binoculars, fixing his gaze on the boat ahead. The trio appeared relaxed in conversation, though the distance and his inability to lipread rendered their words a mystery.

Had they found something at the morgue inside the hospital? For all he knew, they had discovered nothing and were simply returning to their base of operations. He continued to watch in case they produced any hint of their intentions.

They glided under one bridge, then another, before turning left onto the wider canal. They went right at the next junction to an adjacent waterway where other boats flowed in the opposite direction. Most filled with tourists, others only a handful enjoying a more intimate journey.

Churches, hotels, and homes of all shapes and sizes framed his way, the scene telling the story of Venice's history and character. In the distance, the songs of melodic gondoliers echoed off the weathered stone structures, while along the water's edge travelers reveled with their cameras, taking shots of the timeless beauty surrounding them.

Olsson tugged his hat a little lower over his brow, counting the bridges they passed.

One. Two.

They turned left.

Three. Four.

They turned right.

Then left again.

He narrowed his eyes. The other vessel was leading him southward, clear of the heart of the city, moving them closer to the sea. A flutter of anticipation stirred in his chest at the possibilities. Where would it lead him?

They drifted onward, the sound of the propellers humming and the wake of the other boats creating a gentle ripple. They moved under another series of bridges in quick succession, finally arriving at the end of the canal. Beyond, in the dim afternoon sun, an island emerged. The San Giorgio Maggiore Church stood atop it, its white stone walls gleaming and its tower looming in the darkening sky.

The turnoff was a hub of activity, boats coming and going in a chaotic waltz. Some veered to the left, others to the right. His target went to starboard.

The driver glanced at Olsson, who motioned to follow. The boat eased into the sea, both men keeping a sharp eye on the other vessel. It steered closer to land and arrived at one of the wharfs. Olsson pointed fifty yards farther down. The driver understood and glided the taxi past a pair of gondolas. Olsson lifted his binoculars again and scouted his targets, disembarking their ride, heading from the wharf on foot in a northward direction.

Olsson's boat closed on land. He hoisted his case and jumped before they made contact, the jolt of the impact sending a pang of pain through his knee. He did his best to push the feeling aside and moved into a hurried walk.

The American and his Italian counterparts weaved through the crowd toward the restaurants that lined the walkway. He hoped they had not come all this way to order a bite to eat.

The mass ahead of Olsson thickened, the surge making it difficult to keep his pace. They were a tourist group, their guide holding a paddle in the air to corral them. Olsson groaned, trying to sidestep them, but the tide seemed endless.

He grew weary of being polite and barged through instead, the people bouncing off him like bullets ricocheting off armored glass. Startled shouts burst his way. He paid them no mind, pushing on until he broke though.

With his path dispersed, he eyed his three targets once more, putting some extra pep into his step. Just like the taxi driver, he maintained a gap to avoid suspicion. They moved by the restaurants, allaying his initial concerns and blended in with the crowds crisscrossing the square beyond.

Olsson mapped out the area, the geography unfurling in his mind. Within walking distance there were the Palazzo Ducale and the Sala della Cancelleria Segreta. Both Museums. There was also the Carmagnola Head and, of course, St. Mark's Basilica. Both famous attractions.

Every step took him closer to all the possibilities, but as those ahead of him moved onward, another option emerged. The Biblioteca Nazionale Marciana.

Olsson raised an eyebrow as they made a beeline for the library's entrance. He rolled his shoulders, confirming his gun was still snug beneath his jacket. A heft of his briefcase too confirmed his surprise package had not been lost. Whatever they were looking for, Olsson intended to be right there when they found it.

17

The Biblioteca Nazionale Marciana was a masterpiece. Its gleaming Renaissance facade caught the waning sun, casting a luminous glow over the marble-and-stone structure.

Bishop led the way, traipsing beneath an arch toward the entrance. Above, pilasters adorned the upper story, the mythological statues looming over them, their unblinking eyes as watchful as the scattered security cameras tracking the patrons' every move.

They passed by curious tourists, their conversations a blur of foreign languages, arms gesturing in all directions to take in the panoramic sweep of the surrounding landmarks. Bishop, remaining on point, nudged the heavy door, revealing the library's interior.

The scene struck him all at once. It might as well have come from the pages of a fairy tale. High vaulted ceilings soared above, adorned with majestically painted frescoes, the intricate imagery far beyond Bishop's understanding. Polished wood lined the walls, while chandeliers, centuries old, hung from the ceiling like distant stars.

The area expanded, the museum element giving way to a vast sanctuary of books. Towering shelves filled the section and many various alcoves, the volumes stored exuding the scent of ancient parchment, wood, and dust. Carved stone stretched upward to a second level containing more books, where arched openings faced the main floor.

Moretti pointed to the information desk beyond the computer banks. They walked by those taking in the sights of the library, while others perused its books or sat at the workstations, clacking at the keyboards, likely using the internet connection to stay in touch with home.

The queue was short and the wait brief. The librarian called them forward, and Bishop approached.

"Uh, parli Inglese?" he asked in the hope the woman spoke English.

She smiled. "Si. Yes."

"I need the history of my borrowed books. I'm a little worried I might have some pending returns."

"Okay, do you have your card with you?" she asked.

He shook his head. With the personal effects from Wulf's corpse as evidence, obtaining the card from Inspector Conti would have been impossible. "Unfortunately, I misplaced it."

"That's fine. If you give me your name, I can search for the information."

"It should be under James Knox."

The librarian tapped the letters into her computer. "James Knox. That was easy. You're the only one in our database."

"And my returns?"

"You've only ever borrowed one item, Mr. Knox. You returned it the same day."

"That's right. I forgot," Bishop said, continuing the

charade. "I was leaving town and brought it back because I wouldn't be able to return it in time. Which book was it again?"

"*The Life and Times of Leonardo Da Vinci.*"

"A good read. Where might I find it, so I can borrow it for longer this time?"

The librarian punched in more commands, and a printout whirred behind her. She swiveled on her chair and reached for the paper, turning to hand it to Bishop. "Top level to the left."

"Thank you very much."

"You're welcome."

Bishop guided the others up the stairs.

"You were right." Abella glanced over his shoulder at the document. Not only did it have the location of the book, but the details of James Knox's membership. "He signed up to the library, borrowed, and returned the book within an hour. All on the eighth of September. The only reason someone would do something like that is if they were leaving a—"

"A message." Bishop nodded. "It would seem we've come to the right place."

The vantage point above offered an even more breathtaking view of the building, the magnificence of the space not lost on any of them. Bishop ambled to the bookcase at the end of the hall, passing by the numerous arches along the way. With the document in one hand, he ran his index finger across the row with the other.

"Here we go." He slid the leather volume out, revealing an ancient portrait of the Renaissance man himself on the cover. "*The Life and Times of Leonardo Da Vinci.*"

"What are we searching for?" Moretti asked.

"I'm not sure yet." Bishop went to the table, put the book

down and flipped it open. "Perhaps he highlighted some text. Maybe some folds which spell out a code. Anything out of the ordinary."

Bishop trawled through it first, scanning each page. Abella followed. Moretti rounded out the group, her brow furrowing while she read. Bishop grew increasingly frustrated. Behind them, an old clock with Roman numerals ticked, only adding to his heightening agitation.

"I'm not seeing anything here," the youngest of his companions said. "Is there a chance you might be wrong?"

"I'm not wrong."

Abella placed a consoling hand on his shoulder. "There's nothing here, John."

"There has to be." Bishop returned to the table and yanked the book from Moretti's grasp.

He skimmed it again, his fingers tightening on the leather binding.

Not even a hint.

He sighed and tossed the tome down. Without another word, he made his way to one of the arches overlooking the lower level. Moretti resumed her search in the text, while Abella approached him once more.

"Perhaps we've got this all wrong," she said. "What if he never intended to leave the clue in the book? What if his thinking was more abstract? Do you remember anything in your past together that might have had something to do with Leonardo Da Vinci?"

Bishop chortled. "We never sat down to discuss the greats of the Renaissance period."

Silence lingered as Bishop's gaze remained fixed on the lower floor. The books seemed to stretch endlessly. Then an object caught his eye, his posture stiffening and his shoulders tightening.

"What is it, John?" Abella asked.

"Follow me."

Bishop hurried down the stairs with Abella and Moretti quick on his heels. They shadowed him to a stone wall where a glossy poster hung from some wires affixed to the ceiling. An illustrated picture of Leonardo Da Vinci took up a vast amount of the image, the portrait not that different from the one on the cover of the book. At the top, in bold text, it read: LEONARDO DA VINCI EXPERIENCE EUROPEAN TOUR. In smaller lettering at the bottom, the cities of the tour were listed: LONDON, PARIS, BERLIN, FLORENCE, ATHENS, AND ISTANBUL.

Bishop stared at the poster, while the women discussed the locations and dates which were printed, pondering if it might lead them to their next clue. Bishop was so captivated by the image of Da Vinci that he barely heard their voices. Almost without thinking, he reached out under the poster's corner. He dragged his hands across it until his fingers brushed against something attached to the back.

He froze and tightened his grip on the object. It was stuck down with some tape. He tugged it free and held it in the light. A USB drive. Not dissimilar to the modern storage device Quade had introduced him to at ExoCipher during his visit.

Bishop turned to the Italians, still debating with each other. His revelation quickly silenced them.

"A backup copy?" he muttered in hope, having secretly harbored the possibility.

In unison, all three of them shifted their gaze to the nearby computers.

Bishop hurried over to one that was vacant and sat, clicking the mouse to rid the monitor of its screensaver. He checked for a USB port and inserted it.

It did not fit.

"Am I doing something wrong?" he asked.

"Uh, you've got to put it in the other way," Moretti said. "Like upside down."

Bishop frowned, twisting it in his hand and sliding it in with ease. A file folder appeared on the screen, and he clicked on it.

A second layer of files unfolded before him, each hopefully brimming with the answers to his questions. Just as he was about to click the first, the lights inside the library flickered and the computers' screens went black, plunging the beautiful old building into an eerie hush.

It did not last long, a shocked cacophony of confused voices erupting from the library's patrons.

"What the hell!" Bishop wailed.

"A power outage?" Moretti pondered.

Bishop's stomach churned, a gnawing suspicion creeping within. He removed his cell phone from his pocket and flipped it open. The screen remained as dark as the monitor in front of him. "This is no regular power outage."

A shriek echoed at the door to the museum section. There, next to the screaming woman, a tall figure stumbled, dropping a briefcase near a sculpture.

Bishop locked his gaze on the man. Despite the hat and sunglasses, the unsteady gait which he had inflicted on him was unmistakable. "It's him!"

Abella caught on immediately, her finger pointing at the blond assassin. "Moretti, go!"

18

Olsson stumbled, his knee buckling as he tried to pivot in the other direction. Agony shot through his leg, and he collided into the nearby sculpture, his grip on his briefcase loosening and the small EMP device spilling out of it. The woman walking next to him spotted the mess of cables and wires scattered on the floor and screamed out at the top of her lungs.

He gathered himself and peered at the computer station where the American and the two Italian women followed the sound of her panicked wail through the dark library, its lights all extinguished from his detonation of the device. The American's eyes were fierce, recognition flashing at the sight of him under the guise of his hat and sunglasses.

The elder of the Italians pointed in his direction. "Moretti, go!"

He cursed under his breath and bolted into the museum section, then out the door into the open courtyard beyond. Leaving the EMP device behind was not ideal, but it had done its job. As his employer had instructed, he kept a close watch on the American. Sure enough, it paid off, the advice leading him to a backup of the stolen information confirming the upcoming attacks.

The hacker had been astute in making a copy. Now it had all been for nothing. The EMP device would have obliterated every electrical component in the building, including any hard drives, wiping them clean of every single kilobyte.

Olsson pressed on, gratified he had done what he was assigned to do. The hacker was dead, and so too everything he had stolen. He would have preferred, however, not to have sustained the injury. Each step he took gnawed at him, the knee protesting with every stride. He glanced over his shoulder, Moretti forcing her way through the heavy doors and taking chase.

Olsson barged through the masses, meandering about, slamming past them, the vast majority cursing in his wake.

"Everyone get down!"

Moretti's command was almost deafening. Though, the lack of awareness on the tourists' part was his saving grace. While some followed her instruction, most remained oblivious to the situation taking place around them.

He sprinted as hard as he could and cut to the left, getting lost in another throng of people. His breaths were ragged, his steps uneven. That damned American, he swore, recalling the source of his injured knee in the hacker's apartment.

He would not allow himself to be beaten by the man.

In the rear, the Italian operative spotted him. "Move! Move!"

Olsson scurried alongside someone dressed in a black jacket similar to his. He ripped off his own cap and tossed it on the stranger's head before racing beyond him, the man probably having no idea what had just happened. He snatched a horrible cream Panama style hat off another gentleman, throwing it on and weaving in front of a group of tall African tourists.

Rounding the corner of a building, he leaped into a tight alleyway. From his new vantage point, he spied Moretti slowing, stopping the man in his black cap. She yanked it from his head and threw it aside in frustration. Olsson smiled and hurried down the alley. Footfalls sounded behind him, the clap of pursuing boots echoing in the claustrophobic space. He risked a glance to the rear.

Moretti.

She was as speedy on foot as she was on a motorcycle.

At the end of the backstreet, he drew his sidearm from his shoulder holster and aimed it down the gauntlet. The Italian, realizing his intent, dove into an alcove while he fired, the clatter of the pistol's bullets reverberating off the walls.

With a moment's reprieve, Olsson continued to run. St. Mark's Basilica towered overheard, the flow of tourists around it an additional hiding place to take advantage of. Moretti edged out of the alleyway and got caught in the sea of bodies. Unfortunately, they stifled him, too, slowing him down further.

The geography opened up into another square, offering Olsson an escape. His mind raced. He needed to get to the canals. West was his only option.

He reached the far side of the square and made the turn, a glimpse of the waterway just visible in his line of sight. He surged forward, his feet threatening to slip on the unforgiving paving stones. Nearing the canal, he slowed, quickly glancing around to locate his stalker. She had closed again, her strides long, her face determined. She would not stop until she had him.

Along the edge of the canal, Olsson eyed the traffic in the water. A gondola rowed by, while on the other a speedboat neared in a northbound direction. He mapped out the maneuver in his mind. If he was not injured, it would be no problem. With the bad knee, it was a gamble.

So, too, was the unending chase.

He had to do it.

Breaking back into a full sprint, he approached the lip of the stone wall flanking the canal. Without another second's thought, he jumped, propelling himself toward the gondola. He crashed onto the vessel, landing between the serenading gondolier and the bewildered couple. Somehow, everyone stayed afloat.

On land, Moretti appeared. Olsson fired his weapon, forcing her to scatter once more. The scant win over her gave him the precious time he needed.

In the opposite direction, the speedboat sliced his way. Before the gondolier could rise to protest his intrepid arrival, Olsson leaped again, landing on the floor of the powered boat.

The driver glanced at him, ready to hurl abuse at his unwanted passenger, but the barrel of Olsson's gun pressed against his jaw silenced him before he could act. A swift gesture with the weapon was all that was needed to make his instruction clear. The driver sidestepped and jumped into the water. Olsson took the wheel and breathed a sigh of relief.

Before he could think about how to reach his destination, sirens blared in the distance. The unmistakable sound of the Polizia di Stato. A police boat surged into view at the junction ahead from the right. Olsson swerved left and fired at the approaching vessel. The bullets banging into the hull echoed in the confined gauntlet. The rounds found their mark, striking the driver. The police boat skewed off course and smashed into the bank of stone flanking the water behind him, a burst of flames exploding from the wreckage.

Olsson stayed en route in a northward direction, figuring he could make it back to his motorcycle and get out of dodge while the opportunity was still there.

More sirens sounded, but they were too far away. They would not reach him in time. A powerful hum rang out behind his craft. Another speedboat.

Moretti.

She had tracked him down again.

He gritted his teeth and aimed his sidearm. One tore into her boat's frame, the other her windshield, shattering the glass. He pummeled it until his gun clicked empty.

Still, she closed the gap.

Olsson fumbled for the spare ammo in his shoulder holster when Moretti unleashed an onslaught of her own, the bullets raining on his boat, the near misses searing past his ear and cracking his own windshield.

He crouched, slipping another magazine into his Glock, pivoting to take his shot. An ache seared in his knee, his stance wavering from the movement. Before he could recover, a bullet hit him in the left arm, his grip on the steering wheel faltering. The wound throbbed, and his ride veered wildly and slammed hard against the stone bank.

The impact threw him onto the floor of the boat, and the vessel struck another object out of his view. The craft flipped, throwing him into the water, which threatened to consume him, sending a cold shiver through his body.

He looked into the sky for solace. Instead, he was met with an ever-darkening sky. It was not caused by the sunset. Rather, his boat tumbling back down upon him.

19

NEW YORK, NEW YORK

Screeching to a halt, the taxi pulled up to the curb at the corner of the block. Tyler instinctively reached for his wallet, only for Kate to put a hand out to stop him.

"Don't worry, Jack. I've got this." She unbuttoned her purse and extracted some cash, handing it over to the driver. "Keep the change."

Tyler snuck a peek at the wad of money hidden inside her personal black leather handbag, the crisp notes almost overflowing from the larger of the two compartments. The driver nodded his thanks at the fare and the generous tip, allowing them to step out onto the street. Kate went first. Tyler pushed his curiosity aside and joined his sister in the cool grip of the evening air.

He swung the door shut, and the yellow cab sped off, disappearing around the corner.

"You're going to love this place," she said.

"I'll take your word on that."

They entered the building before them, and he trailed her across the quiet lobby, the tap of her heels echoing in the vast emptiness. She pressed the call button, and the elevator doors parted almost immediately, inviting them inside. Tyler fell in step after her, and she punched in one of the upper levels, his ears popping with the sharp ascent.

"So, that new apartment of yours. When did you move in?" he asked.

Kate checked her face in the mirror of her makeup kit, adjusting a strand of her red hair behind her ear. "About three weeks ago."

"That explains all the cardboard boxes."

"I've been busy. It feels like a disaster zone in there."

"You said it, not me."

She slapped him playfully. "You could always stick around and help me unpack."

"Pete could help, couldn't he?"

She froze, evading his gaze. "Pete?"

"Yeah, the Pete you were in that share apartment with."

"We weren't...you know? There were two other people living there. We were all just roommates."

"Sure." Tyler could not resist, enjoying his chance at mocking her and her potential relationships. "I'm certain he could've helped."

"He was busy."

"Everyone's busy in New York City, aren't they?" Tyler rolled his eyes. "How are they all, anyway? Did they find another person to help them with the rent?"

"Are you kidding? They had someone in line before I had my foot out of the door."

The elevator chimed, and the doors slid open. Unlike the lobby, the upper floor buzzed with atmosphere. Soft instrumental music, hushed conversations, the clink of glasses, and the sound of cutlery against ceramic plates greeted them on the way out.

"Come on, you've got to see this place." Kate dragged him along, her hand around his until they reached the entrance of the restaurant.

The maître d' stood awaiting them, impeccably dressed from head to toe, the absence of even a wrinkle on his suit jacket a clear sign Tyler was out of his depth.

"Welcome to La Vue du Ciel. Do you have a reservation with us this evening?" he asked, his accent distinctly French.

"A table for two under Kate Tyler."

The man perused the black folder in his hand and smiled. "Very good. A window view." He picked up a pair of nearby menus and tucked them under his arm. "Follow me, please."

He took off with a brisk stride and guided them through the restaurant. The place was half full with a blend of patrons. Some appeared to be businesspeople who had come straight from the office. Others were more elaborately dressed, the women especially putting the effort in, their dresses gleaming under the radiant chandeliers anchored to the ceiling.

"Are you sure we couldn't have just brought a hot dog from the corner?" Tyler asked.

Kate ignored him, while the maître d' turned as they reached their destination, a subtle, snobbish smirk of disdain tugging the edge of his lips.

"Here we are." He popped down the menus and pulled out a chair for Kate.

She sat while Tyler slid out his own seat and set himself down. The maître d' unraveled the linen napkins and laid one on Kate's lap. He attempted to do the same for Tyler, too, but paused.

"Sir?"

"Yes?"

He hinted with the napkin, and Tyler blushed.

"Of course." Tyler shifted, allowing the man to do his job, placing the linen over his knees.

The maître d' upended the glasses already in front of them and poured water in both. "Provided are your menus and the wine list. Spend a moment to find the right selection, and I'll have someone return to take your orders."

With that, he departed, leaving them by the window to enjoy the sun setting over Downtown Manhattan. While Tyler would have loved nothing more than to one day go back to the countryside in Arkansas, even he appreciated the view of the city from the high vantage point.

Kate enjoyed a sip of her water and opened the wine list. "Anything in particular that you'd like?"

"They don't have Budweiser on tap, do they?" Tyler asked, only half-jokingly.

She glared at him. "We're in one of the finest French restaurants in all of New York, and you want a beer?"

"Are you telling me the French don't drink beer?"

Kate suppressed a smile. "I'll pick, shall I?" She cast an eye over the different wines. "That looks good."

Just as it appeared she had decided, a server materialized next to them. "What have we chosen this evening?"

Kate held up the wine list. "We'll have a bottle of this."

He smiled. "An excellent choice."

Tyler took a gulp of water and spied her selection, noticing the dollar amount next to it. He nearly choked, his drink going down the wrong pipe.

"Are you okay, sir?" the server asked.

Tyler waved away the concern and coughed to regain his breath. "Fine. Thank you."

"I'll get your wine."

The man left them while Tyler dabbed at his mouth with his napkin before placing it down. When he looked up, he found Kate staring at him, her mood anything but jovial.

"What?" he asked.

"You've been thinking about it ever since we got to my apartment," Kate said.

"I don't know what—"

"Jack, just say it."

Tyler tossed his napkin on the table. "I'd rather not be critical."

"I can see it on your face."

"Sorry."

The apology seemed to do little to satisfy her. He bit his bottom lip, realizing it was time to rip off the Band-Aid. "It's no secret you've been having money problems since you got to New York. It's nothing to be ashamed about. This town's expensive. And as you've been climbing the ladder here…"

He trailed off, Kate's stare just as icy as before.

"Go on," she said.

"I've heard you've had to borrow cash from Mom and Dad from time to time. I also know you were treading water in that share apartment. And now here you are, paying for a new one downtown all by yourself. Not to mention you're shelling out for cab rides and expensive French dinners. I just—"

"I've paid our parents back in full."

Her words made Tyler take pause. "You have?"

"I work in finance, Jack. Don't think for a moment I don't

know how to manage my money. The taxi. The dinner. I'm paying for them because you're my guest and I want to show you a good time before you leave. As for the apartment." Kate grinned. "I needed a place closer to my new job."

Tyler raised his eyebrows. "New job?"

"That's right. I made it to the big time. A position with Dawson and Riddle. They gave me a sign-on bonus and a contract I couldn't refuse. That's how I can afford everything you've seen today."

Tyler's posture tensed, a sense of guilt festering inside him. "That's great. I didn't realize. I assume that was the news you were going to surprise me with?"

Kate nodded. "And now you've gone and spoiled it."

He blushed. "Sorry."

She smiled, her darker demeanor evaporating in an instant. "At least I know you'll always have my back."

"Always." He leaned closer to her across the table. "So, this office of yours. Where do you have to drag yourself to every day?"

She nodded toward the window at the twin buildings taking up the primary focus of their view, the lights casting a twinkling glow in the night. "The World Trade Center. North Tower."

20

VENICE, ITALY

"It's fried."

Bishop eyed the USB drive nestled in Teresa Abella's hand, the woman's voice laced with a solemn finality. He plucked the storage device from her grasp and held it under the light inside the Polizia di Stato HQ. The temporary office which the head of the foreign intelligence service had requested from the local constabulary was a far cry from the dingy space she had previously maintained in her mission to Venice.

"And you're sure about that?" he asked.

"I've had my best people down here to check it out," she said. "If there was any data on it—"

"Which there was."

"It's now gone with no chance of recovery. The police and the power company have cordoned off the Biblioteca Nazionale Marciana. They've discovered every electrical device within a fifty-meter radius is destroyed. The local grid, the lights, computers, hard drives. Everyone who was carrying a cell phone. All toast."

Bishop sighed. All the pieces had finally fallen into place. The Scandinavian had been waiting in Venice for the possibility of someone like him coming along. They had destroyed the original data on the attacks, having killed Wulf for them. But what if there had been a copy? They obviously had to be sure. So, they waited. Sure enough, Bishop came along and led them right to it.

He stepped to the other side of the desk, which Abella had claimed as her command post, fixing his gaze on the briefcase recovered on the scene. He unlatched it and flipped it open, revealing the contraption inside. It was rudimentary. An almost agricultural assemblage of circuits, components, and copper coils wrapped around a bank of batteries. "What have your people made of this?"

"As you suspected, it's a small-scale EMP device." Abella pulled a file from the drawer and spread it out on the desk. The page covered in numbers might as well have been Morse code for all Bishop cared, the mess well beyond his comprehension. "Crude but effective. There's no doubt. This was what caused the damage at the library."

"Where could he have got a weapon like this?"

"It might not look like it, but it's a fancy piece of equipment. There are a lot of defense contractors out there who have been making prototypes similar to this one."

"This isn't some corporate gadget."

"No. My guys suspect the assassin, or whoever he worked for, built it. It may have even come off the black market. We just don't know."

Bishop brushed his fingers over the device as if doing so might trace its origins. "I want the CIA to look at this. The

USB, too." He placed the storage drive back in Abella's palm. "They may not be able to recover the files, but it'll at least prove I wasn't chasing ghosts out here."

"I can take care of that for you." She frowned, the hint of optimism she had before they had set out for the Biblioteca Nazionale Marciana all but gone. "I'm sorry, John."

Bishop shrugged. "This isn't over yet."

"Do you think Harvey Wulf made another copy?"

"Not necessarily. But he knew someone was onto him. That's why he left the backup at the library in case the primary data didn't get to me."

"Then where can we go from here?"

Bishop drummed his fingers on her desk. Before he could speak, a knock sounded at the door.

"Come in," Abella said.

The door swung open, and Moretti entered with a laptop tucked under her arm. Gone was the ragged exhaustion painting her features from the pursuit, instead replaced with a woman recharged and full of energy.

"What have you got?" her superior asked.

"The photos of our blond assassin from the morgue have paid off dividends."

Bishop swiveled his chair sideways as the Italian agent opened the computer and set it down on the edge of the table, angling the screen so everyone could get a clear view.

"I've worked with the police, using what CCTV has been available to us."

She tapped the trackpad, and several grainy black-and-white images materialized. One revealed the assassin walking the streets with an apple, another capturing him mid-chase with a gun by his side; the rest were of him riding his motorcycle.

"I had our audio-visual people in Rome run it through the database and cross-checked it with other agencies. His name was Erik Olsson. A Swedish national." She clicked again, and an official dossier appeared. A file photo of the man stared back at them, while alongside it was a list of compiled details. "From what we've been able to piece together liaising with the domestic service, Olsson was a security consultant. He's been employed by several entities over the past decade. Some legitimate. Others not so much."

"And who was he with before being crushed by that boat?" Bishop asked.

"Himself. Olsson's been a private contractor for the last eighteen months. There aren't any details on his activities. Whoever he's been doing jobs for, it's likely off the books."

Bishop clenched his fists. "So, we finally get some good news, and it leads us nowhere."

"Not necessarily. Check this out." Moretti rang up more CCTV imagery, this time in video format. "These were captured from the Marco Polo Airport."

Bishop leaned closer. In the color vision, a man stepped off an air bridge and entered the airline terminal. He wore a green hat, a black-and-white Letterman jacket, and a pair of recognizable red Air Jordans. "That's Harvey Wulf."

"Right. He arrived on the morning flight to Venice three days ago." Moretti loaded up another video at a different gate.

Along with the crowd of departing passengers, a tall blond male disembarked with sunglasses covering his eyes.

"Erik Olsson."

"Correct."

"Where did they fly from?" Abella asked her junior.

"Istanbul."

"Both of them?" Bishop raised an eyebrow. "From Turkey?"

Moretti nodded, and the room fell into a heavy silence. Everyone contemplated the implications. Bishop stood and went over to the window, peering out at the sea of red buildings lit up from the exterior lighting in the Venetian evening.

"Olsson chased him from Istanbul." He turned, the women staring at him as he approached the desk. "We've been going off the assumption that Wulf acquired the information in Venice. He didn't. He got it in Istanbul. Wulf must have received it in Turkey and returned here."

"Why did he come back before sending it to you?" Abella asked. "If it was so important, surely he could have transmitted in Istanbul."

Bishop took a step closer to the desk. "Earlier, when we were looking into the lease on his apartment, it stated he'd been located there for six months."

"Yeah?"

"He's a hacker. What if the intel was encrypted, and he needed to come back to his home base in Venice to decode it? He may not have known what he had until he pulled it apart on his own computers."

Abella exchanged a glance with Moretti, both of them processing his theory. Bishop brushed the stubble on his cheek, a realization dawning on him.

"Damn, he was smart," he muttered.

"John?"

"Harvey Wulf." He returned his focus to Abella. "He's left another breadcrumb for me."

"Explain."

"That poster in the Biblioteca Nazionale Marciana. The

Da Vinci Tour. Do you remember the cities and the dates for the exhibit? Where's it currently being held?"

Abella appeared at a loss.

Moretti, however, raised her eyebrows in understanding. "Istanbul."

Bishop nodded. "Istanbul. The last leg of the tour."

"But what does it mean, Mr. Bishop?"

"Another backup, perhaps. Or maybe something else. I'm not sure. Regardless, I think Wulf suspected he was onto a secret so big that he had to leave evidence behind. There's only one way I can find out, and that's to go to Istanbul."

Abella stood. "It'll be sad to see you go, John."

"This was only ever going to be a brief visit." Bishop put his hands on her shoulders. "I appreciate everything you've done for me. You, too, Ms. Moretti."

The younger Italian woman blushed.

"Is there anything else I can do for you before you leave?" Abella asked.

"Some of those Russian cigarettes would be nice." Bishop gazed at the frozen CCTV footage on the laptop. "And one more thing if it's possible..."

SEPTEMBER 11, 2001

21

"Should I ask how you were able to pull this off?"

Bishop took the black plastic bag from Abella's hands and broke the seal at the top. He checked inside, sifting through the contents. Sure enough, every item was accounted for.

"I build relationships, John," she said with a grin. "That's what I do here. Before you ended your tenure at the CIA, you would've done the same."

Bishop fastened the bag and gripped it by the handle. His mind drifted to his days behind the desk as the director of Bureau 61. Abella was right. Beyond the politics of the position, the hard decisions made with other people's lives, the painstaking collection of intel, it was the rapport with others that had held the branch together. "It's nice to know it's not an art that's been lost in our game."

"If there's anything—"

Bishop raised his hand to stop her before she finished the sentence. She had asked at least three times already. There was no way he could ever repay her. If not for Abella and

Moretti, he would likely be dead. They had not just given him a chance, but everyone else one, too.

The PA system crackled inside the terminal of the Marco Polo Airport, a stream of announcements blaring in Italian. Bishop glanced at the passengers rising from their seats at the gate, shuffling into a line for boarding. Though he did not speak the language well, he understood the physical cue of others better than most.

"It looks like this is where we say goodbye," he said.

Before he could pivot on his heel, Abella took him softly by the arm and kissed him on the cheek. Bishop stopped, immobilized by the sensation. He could not remember the last time he had felt such warmth or affection.

Not for years...

"I'm going to tell you this now, John, because I may never have the chance again," she said, her voice low so others could not hear her. "You're in pain. I've seen what time does to people, and I can tell it hasn't been your best ally since we last met. I'm unsure of what actually happened. I just want you to understand that there are always second chances. It's up to us to take it when the opportunity arises. Please promise me when it comes, you'll be brave enough."

Bishop cleared his throat, certain his face had reddened under Abella's probing eyes. He managed a weak smile, his cheek muscles pulling in a way that was completely unfamiliar. Nothing more needed to be said. With a nod, he proceeded to step into the queue of travelers, taking Abella's weighty words with him.

He closed his eyes, and the past came rushing in. He saw himself and Pat trudging through the mud, fishing rods in their grasps, her infectious laughter carrying in the breeze. Then, the two of them on the porch of their Anchorage home. Finally, her grave. He stood by the headstone in the blanketed snow, a rose falling from his fingers, its crimson petals dancing. Fragments of a life lost to time.

Bishop opened his eyes, sweat beading on his forehead. The passengers ahead of him blurred, their forms twisting in a distorted chaos of color. He wiped his face with the back of his hand, his pulse rate spiking and his heart thumping. It was happening again.

He edged forward, pushing himself through the wave of disorientation. He could not miss his departure. The flight staff greeted him, and he handed over his boarding pass, repeating the same process he had in Anchorage and Seattle. They motioned him onward, and he crossed the air bridge into the plane.

A flight attendant smiled, pointing him toward his seat. As he ambled down the aisle, the passage bent and narrowed. How could he possibly fit down it?

A jolt from behind snapped him from the delusion, revolving his mind upside down and inside out. He turned to a man, who for a moment appeared as if he was going to chastise him for blocking the way, but his irritation subsided, no doubt noticing the stress in Bishop's features.

"Stai bene?" he asked.

Bishop dismissed the concern, focusing instead on putting one foot in front of the other. He reached his seat and placed his luggage in the overhead locker. Before sitting, he unzipped the carry-on and slid out his cell phone. Though the other was destroyed beyond repair by the EMP at the Biblioteca Nazionale Marciana, he always carried a spare, having left it and some other belongings in an airport locker when he had arrived in Venice. Old habits died hard.

He stepped into the row of three seats, setting himself

down by the window. Not a spot he would have preferred, but one he had to take with such short notice. More of the passengers boarded and stowed their bags, the flight attendants circling to help them with any of their needs. Bishop, meanwhile, steadied his breathing using some old techniques which had worked on his previous journeys in the past few days.

A pair of young ladies, barely twenty years old, approached the aisle and cast a quick sideways glance. They sat beside him, the one closest holding a Discman in her hands, the CD spinning within, probably cranking some tunes in her headphones that he had never heard before.

Bishop chortled, remembering Quade's mockery of him when he had arrived at ExoCipher with a burned compact disc. See? People still use them, he thought.

He reverted his attention to his phone, snapping it open and pressing through the main menu. His finger stopped at the contact list. There were no names attached to the particular caller ID, only a string of numbers. 1-1-1-1. He opened the SMS app and simply transmitted a blank message.

"Uh, I'm sorry, sir, you'll have to switch that off."

Bishop gazed up at the flight attendant gesturing to his cell. He ensured the message had sent and turned it off. With a satisfied smile, she moved on. Bishop closed the phone and stored it in his pocket.

With another breath, he prepared himself, glancing over at the two women again. They giggled, completely absorbed by whatever music of the day was currently popular. He could not help but think they had the right idea. Maybe he should have got a Discman for the trip.

Unfortunately, as good as the devices were, one of his old vinyls was unlikely to fit inside.

22

ISTANBUL, TURKEY

It was a far cry from his usual appearance.

Bishop studied his reflection in the hotel mirror, taking in the unfamiliar and frankly hideous ensemble. A green baseball cap, a black-and-white Letterman jacket, and red Air Jordans. The fit was snug and the sneakers comfortable. The style? That would take some getting used to.

He threw the plastic bag on the bed next to his luggage and zipped up his jacket. Abella had really come through for him. He took out a packet of Russian cigarettes from his carry-on and slipped them in his pocket. Not only had she supplied him with her favorite smokes, but she had also convinced Inspector Conti to hand over Harvey Wulf's personal effects, including the very clothes Bishop was now wearing.

Someone had luckily cleaned them, eliminating the canal's lingering damp stench. He exhaled, the guilt tightening in his chest. He'd had no time to grieve. It was not how things were supposed to be done. If there were another way, he would have taken it. The whole operation was a long shot as it was. He found solace in the fact that Wulf would have understood that more than anyone else.

He flicked up his collar and walked to the door, moving out into the corridor and down the elevator to the lobby. Carving a path through the sparse crowd of the hotel, he emerged outside at the taxi rank, the warmth of the late morning settling in over him.

A cab rolled up from the main road and stopped in front of him. The passenger window slid down, and the driver gave him a once-over, slipping his sunglasses down his nose. Though he barely reacted, the twitch of his eyebrows said enough. Bishop looked ridiculous, and they both knew it.

"Where to?" he asked.

Bishop removed the jacket. "The Ataturk Cultural Center."

He got in the car, and the driver pulled away. Bishop hardly settled before he could close the door and buckle his belt. The Istanbul native weaved them through the winding streets, the ageless soul of the sprawl enveloping him from all sides.

In a way, there were similarities to Venice. History had been similarly preserved, the bones of the Turkish city stretching back to its days as Byzantium and Constantinople, a jewel in the crown of the Holy Eastern Roman Empire. Crumbling fortifications from the ancient period remained standing as silent sentinels alongside buildings which were once grand cathedrals.

Then came the second layer of the metropolis. The sweeping domes and towering minarets of the Ottoman age. Mosques, palaces, and bazaars told the story of Islamic influence and its legacy of empire. And of course, the third layer. The modern face of Turkey, a fusion of east and west, fittingly where both worlds converged. Glass skyscrapers towered above, while luxury malls, high-end restaurants, and chic cafés pulsed with contemporary fervor.

The Ataturk Cultural Center was just such a place, purpose-built, unlike other museum spaces in the city which had been refurbished from former places of worship or ancient palaces. The cabbie arrived at the front of the building, and Bishop paid him in kind, stepping out and blending into lockstep with the rest of the crowd.

There, on the tall glass-and-metal facade, a sign hung, similar to the one at the Venetian library. The words were in Turkish, but there was no mistaking it. He had arrived at the current home to the Leonardo Da Vinci Experience. He shrugged on the Letterman jacket and joined the line, paying the entry fee and making his way through the entrance.

Another world unfurled within. The world of the Renaissance. He moved from exhibit to exhibit, starting with the man's collection of codices. Intricate sketches on reproductions of old parchments captured the thoughts of the visionary. They adorned the wall, blown up to a larger-than-life scale for all to see. Amongst them were the watchful eyes of the CCTV cameras affixed to the ceiling.

Bishop stepped closer and stared down the lens. He then ambled to the next section of the museum. It displayed Da Vinci's flying machines. Or rather, his ambitious attempts to design one. After that were examples of the wooden contraptions he had created, his exploration of physics and mechanics, and finally his military, hydraulic, and aquatic exploits, not designed to push the boundaries but secure favor with his wealthy patrons.

The experience then delved into Da Vinci's understanding of the human body and his fascination with anatomy, exemplified by the iconic *Vitruvian Man*. None of which could have been achieved without working on the actual flesh and bone of those who had passed. Quite scandalous for the time.

His artistic feats rounded it all out. The sculptures and his paintings. *The Last Supper, Lady with an Ermine, Virgin of the Rocks, Adoration of the Magi*. All the recreations were there. Including the *Mona Lisa*. As expected, she was getting the most attention, her enigmatic smile holding the gaze of those who flowed through the busy area.

Bishop glanced upward at the CCTV camera, just as he had throughout the entire exhibition. With a raise of his eyebrow, he acknowledged it as if it were a silent challenge. Having felt he had made his point, he shifted to an unoccupied bench in the corner of the vast space.

He could have done with a cigarette. But there was a time and place for everything. This was neither. He rested his hands on his lap and settled in. Five minutes turned into ten. Ten into twenty. Soon an hour ticked by.

Had he misread Wulf's clue? The doubt gnawed at him. If he had been wrong, the investigation was at a dead end. Bishop bowed his head, the weight of his failure pressing down on him.

Suddenly, the tap of footsteps approached. They came to a halt, and someone sat next to him. Bishop lifted his chin and glanced across at the young man who had arrived. A Turk, clean-shaven with short hair, his shoulders slight. He wore a green uniform with the logo of the Ataturk Cultural Center stitched on the arm. His dark eyes held an inquisitive stare.

The man's expression then shifted in an instant, a flicker of realization crossing his boyish features. Fear. Hesitation. He tensed, prepared to flee, pulling himself upward.

Bishop grabbed his wrist. "Not who you were expecting, huh?"

The Turk's lips quivered, his body immobilized. Even if Bishop let go, he doubted the man would run, too distressed to take the risk. Bishop decided to do the right thing and relinquished his grasp. As he suspected, the new arrival remained still, frozen in an awkward position.

"Please, you look like a moron. Park your ass down."

The Turk's mind seemed to crank. Bishop hoped the youngster's curiosity got the better of him.

It did.

He slowly sat, his gaze darting around him. "Who are you?" The man spoke in English with a strong accent native to his homeland.

"You first," Bishop said.

The uncertainty deepened, his chest heaving from the paranoia. "Ali Erdem."

"Ali Erdem." Bishop touched the logo on his museum uniform. "You've been watching me on the security cameras, haven't you?"

He did not respond.

"Who did you think I was when you sat down, Mr. Erdem?"

The Turk's reluctance continued.

"You're not in any trouble." Bishop sighed and unzipped his jacket. He took out a photo of Harvey Wulf from the morgue back in Venice, his body splayed on the cold steel table. "Did you mistake me for him?"

Erdem examined it, his eyes widening.

"I can see you recognize him." Bishop shuffled closer to him, lowering his voice. "You thought I was him when I came into the museum because of these clothes. He must've worn them so that he could distinguish himself to you. Because I know he wouldn't dress in these threads if he wanted to."

"I... Did you kill him?" Erdem asked.

"No." Bishop shook his head. "Just like I have no intention of killing you."

The room swelled with the noise of a tour group entering, all of them eager to get a glimpse at the *Mona Lisa* exhibit.

Bishop placed the photo back in his pocket and rose from the bench. "Come on, Mr. Erdem. Let's go for a walk."

23

NEW YORK, NEW YORK

"Oh, my head's killing me."

Tyler slumped against the glass of the passenger-side window. Outside, headlights and the high arching streetlamps of the dark morning smeared into a chaotic blur. Each flicker twisted, only exacerbating the dizziness spinning about in his head.

"Please, don't vomit in my car." Kate changed lanes in front of a slow-moving taxi. "It takes forever to get rid of the smell."

Tyler's stomach churned, and he pulled himself a little more upright. Familiar landmarks flew by, the green overhead signs drawing the route to the airport in his mind. "We're taking your way, aren't we?"

"Can you leave the driving to me, please?" Kate indicated and moved across the sparse traffic. "I don't need a drunk backseat driver in my car."

"Who said I was a drunk?"

She sniggered. "I was just teasing."

"Why didn't you stop me?"

"Stop you? What do you mean?"

"Well, I seem to remember we had dinner at that French Restaurant."

"And?"

"The meal was good. Don't get me wrong—"

"Liar. You hated it."

"No, I didn't, I—"

"You barely touched your frog legs and snails. That's why we went to the hot dog stand afterward."

Sour trickle rose in his throat at the memory of the foreign food. "Perhaps you shouldn't try to mess with my palate." He swallowed, pushing down the strain in his stomach. "Anyway, you made me lose my train of thought."

"Sorry." Kate peeled off the expressway via an offramp. "You were saying?"

"Uh, yeah, so we had that bottle of wine with dinner."

"Two bottles of wine."

"Two?"

She nodded.

"Right. Then the hot dog. After that, we headed to a bar."

"Two bars."

"Two?" Tyler closed his eyes in an attempt to remember. She was correct. "How much more did we have to drink?"

"There was no 'we' about it. You hit the beer taps and never looked back. I refrained from indulging. I've got work today."

Tyler blinked his eyes open to find JFK Airport in the distance. "What time did we return to your apartment?"

They came to a halt at a traffic light, waiting for it to give them the go-ahead. Once they got the green light, Kate took the turn. "About three a.m."

"Which means I got what, three hours of rack time?"

"If that."

"Jesus, Kate, you could've stopped me? You knew I had a flight. And you have work."

"What does it matter? You can sleep the hangover off on the plane. You'll be fresh as a daisy by the time Dad picks you up in Miami. And me? It's one day. I suspect I'll regret it at my desk this afternoon, but it's not like you come to town that often."

"Hmm."

"And you know what?" Kate drove them into the entrance of the airport parking lot. "I think you needed it."

Tyler chuckled. "Is that right?"

"Yeah, you had to blow the cobwebs out. How long has it been since you let your hair down?"

He pondered, his mind still a fog. "Probably last time I was here."

"You have to do something about that." Kate steered the car into a spot near the terminal. "I know you work hard, but you need to use some of your spare time to have a big night out every so often."

The pair stepped from the vehicle, and Tyler stumbled to the trunk to retrieve his luggage. He carried his carry-on with one hand and hauled his rolling case with the other.

Kate slammed the trunk down, and they walked over the crossing to the terminal. "Have you made any friends in DC?"

Tyler shielded his sight from the glare of the lights inside the airport. "I have friends."

"Do they include Monica?"

Tyler rolled his eyes as they lined up to drop off his bag. "Not this again."

The airline staff checked his luggage against his boarding pass, tagged it, and sent it down the conveyer belt. Tyler and Kate moved on to the security checkpoint with the remainder of the weary early morning passengers.

"I'm just saying that having a vacation is all well and good, but during the rest of the year, you have to figure out ways to unwind," his sister continued.

Tyler tossed his watch, wallet, cell phone, and carry-on into the tray and walked through the metal detector. Without so much as a beep, the staff allowed him through. Kate followed without issue.

He collected his belongings and pressed on. "And you think Monica could help with this?"

Kate winked at him. "What better way?"

"I can't believe I'm taking advice from my little sister about—"

"Sometimes you just need a push."

Tyler shook his head, and they approached a Starbucks. "Would you like one?"

She nodded. "The usual for me."

Tyler hailed the barista with a raise of his finger. "Cream with two sugars for her and a black coffee for me. Really, really, black."

The young barista smirked and set off to prepare their orders, the steam from the machines behind her already scorching from those who had frequented the store before them.

"Monica and I are just friends, anyway," he said. "I couldn't imagine anything worse if we got into a relationship and ruined it. Work would be a living hell."

"Don't you think it might be worth the risk?"

The barista returned with their coffees, and Tyler slapped the cash on the counter. He held the cup tight. With a deep sip, he allowed the heat to permeate through his muscles and bones.

"If it ends up failing, then one of us may feel the need to leave DC. That wouldn't be fair. We both worked our asses off to get where we are."

"I get that." Kate led him to the gate, having some of her own drink, the hot brew clearly sparking the same quiet satisfaction he had just felt. "All I'm saying is that we only live once. We're not getting any younger, and time is ticking."

"Yeah, well, come back to me when you find someone at your new job. And then tell me you feel the same way." Tyler checked his watch, the hour fast approaching seven a.m. "When are you due in the office, anyway?"

"Eight o'clock."

"Don't stick around on my account."

"I'll get there with plenty of time to spare." She smiled. "So, when are you coming back to New York? Please don't say next year."

He shrugged. "We should see each other on a free weekend. Maybe make a short trip to Philly and meet halfway."

"I'd like that."

The pair chatted until the boarding call rang out from the PA, their discussion filling the gaps from the day before. Tyler was going to miss her. It seemed as if it were only yesterday they and their brother, Rick, were at school together, raising hell for their teachers. Time really flew. And life had a way of pulling people apart in ways he could never have imagined.

The question was, would they follow through and meet

in Philadelphia, or would they fall into the same trap as everyone else, where the world moved too fast and promises to catch up went unfulfilled?

"Well, goodbye, big brother. Until next time?"

They hugged once more before Tyler threw his coffee cup in the trash can. "Until next time."

He joined the queue at the gate for his flight as his sister slipped away into the growing sea of passengers streaming into the terminal for the day's first flights. He boarded the plane and found his seat, stowing his bag and settling in for the trip. The coffee had filled the spot, but he still felt like hell.

He took a breath and closed his eyes.

Bring on Miami.

24

ISTANBUL, TURKEY

"You knew him, didn't you?"

Bishop led Erdem beyond the Da Vinci exhibition to a quiet wing of the cultural center. The foot traffic thinned, and the excited voices of other patrons faded in the distance. They walked up a staircase, emerging on a mezzanine level suspended above a vast hall. Below them was a monstrous skeleton of a Tyrannosaurus Rex. The few people meandering about gave it little notice, the once star attraction now ignored.

"I did." Erdem nodded. "Are you going to tell me who you are and how you were acquainted?"

"My name's Bishop. I was a friend. Wulf and I went back a long way. I hadn't seen him for eight years before yesterday in that morgue."

"Wulf?"

Bishop raised an eyebrow. "He must've used an alias. How well did you know him?"

"Not much at all. When we met, he called himself James Abram."

"James Abram?" Bishop recalled his days studying American history back in school, unable to forget the torture of memorizing all those different lists. "President Garfield."

Erdem furrowed his brow.

"Don't worry," Bishop told him. "It's a long story. How did you two meet?"

"Abram, I, uh, mean Wulf, approached me two weeks ago," Erdem said.

"And you'd never met him before that?"

"No. I was at a café around the corner from here, when he introduced himself. He wore the same clothes you're wearing now. Out of the blue, he sat down and opened his laptop opposite me."

"What did he want?"

"He'd hacked all my bank details and informed me that if I didn't do as he asked, he'd drain my accounts."

Bishop leaned an arm on the safety railing surrounding the mezzanine level. "Then what?"

"I wanted proof. He showed me everything on his computer. With a single click I would've been broke. I asked what I'd done to him. He said nothing."

"I don't understand."

Erdem peered around, his paranoia riding him hard. "He needed my help."

"In what way?"

The Turk cleared his throat, stepping closer to Bishop and lowering his voice. "I have more than one job. During the day, I work here. At night..."

Bishop mirrored him as he trailed off, his eyes darting from side to side. "At night?"

The man paused before continuing. "I'm, um, part of a group."

"A group?"

"Yeah. Uh, a collective..."

"Of what? Butchers, bakers, ice cream men?"

"Hackers." The words passed Erdem's lips louder than he likely expected. "I work for the Anca Syndicate as a low-level tech."

"This Anca Syndicate, what do you do?"

Erdem looked at him as if he were an idiot, or as old as the collection of bones on display. "We hack."

"I got that," Bishop snapped. "What and who do you hack?"

"We concentrate our efforts on the Middle East. Satellites, military installations, oil companies, the media. We get it all."

"Right. And Wulf knew this?"

"Yeah."

"So, you said he was blackmailing you. What exactly was he after?"

"Fort Knox."

Bishop raised an eyebrow.

"He wanted the lot." Erdem grabbed the railing with both hands, his knuckles whitening from his grasp. "The Anca Syndicate's servers are brimming with data. If I agreed to help him infiltrate the system so that he could download it, he told me I'd be able to keep my money."

"In other words, Wulf decided to hack the hackers."

"I suppose that's one way of looking at it."

Bishop relinquished his hold of the railing and brushed the creases from his jacket. "Did he tell you what he'd do with it once he had it?"

"Sell it to the highest bidder. I see some of the stuff that comes in. There's a treasure trove that many people would give anything to get their hands on."

Bishop took a step back and rubbed his chin. Money? It sounded like Wulf. While he had been invaluable to Bureau 61, he had not come for free. They had paid him well for his services. When the branch was disbanded, he obviously needed other ways to make a living. A man had to eat. "Okay. So, I assume you helped him. What did you do?"

"He wanted ease of access. Network info, login details, a rubber ducky."

"A what?"

Erdem rolled his eyes. "A USB payload so that he could get physical access."

"Right. Cut to the chase for me. Did it work?"

"He got it all."

Bishop took out the photo of Wulf's corpse again, clutching it tight with his fingers at the edges. "This is the result of a man by the name of Erik Olsson. This could only have happened if he was caught."

Erdem paused, no doubt replaying the events in his mind. "I—"

"Either you botched it, Mr. Erdem, or you snitched. He's dead because they were able to trace him."

"I didn't snitch. And I didn't botch it. If I had, I'd have been killed, too. Unless…"

"Unless what?"

Erdem brought his hands to his lips as if he were praying. "He worked remotely. Our guys are pretty good. If they suspected foul play, they may have tracked him via the open port, pulling his ISP. If that were the case, they could've assumed he was working on his own."

Bishop grabbed him by the scruff of the neck. "If I find out you were behind his death—"

"I wasn't!" Erdem held up his arms in surrender, the fear in his eyes genuine. "I wouldn't have risked that."

Bishop grunted and released him, putting the photo away in his jacket. He took hold of the railing again and stared out at the silent predator below. Of course, it was impossible to know if the Turk was telling the truth. Either way, Bishop still needed him.

"What's your role in all of this, anyway?" Erdem asked. "You might be a friend of Wulf's, but you're no hacker. You'd know what a rubber ducky was if you were."

Bishop glowered at the younger man. "Wulf found something big on that dump of data he stole."

"He did? You're saying he decrypted it? That quickly?"

Bishop narrowed his eyes. "What do you mean?"

"When the syndicate hack information from other sources, it's encrypted to ensure no one else can use it. Sure, it's possible to crack, but it takes some time, and someone very good at the craft."

"Yeah, well, he was that good." Bishop had wondered from the beginning why Wulf had taken so long to send him the message. Now he knew for certain. He had indeed returned to Venice to his specialized setup to decipher the intel. "You want to know how I'm involved?"

Erdem nodded.

"Wulf contacted me. He'd discovered attack plans in the data stolen from the syndicate. Unfortunately, the details weren't transmitted. Erik Olsson got to him before he was able to send them to me. All I received was an audio file claiming that it'd take place against the US and that it was imminent. It was apparently so important that he even left a backup copy."

"Do you have it?" the Turk asked.

"If I did, I wouldn't be here."

"And you've come here, thinking I might know about the attack."

Bishop nodded.

Erdem exhaled, looking at the ceiling as if in need of guidance. "As I said, I'm a low-level tech. Sure, I catch glimpses of what gets encrypted onto our servers, but not all of it. I certainly haven't seen anything about an attack on America."

"I must have that information, Mr. Erdem. A lot of lives could depend on it."

Erdem brought himself back down to earth and stared at Bishop. "If what you say is true, it's more likely that these so-called plans have been wiped. If they didn't want Wulf having it, they wouldn't risk someone else obtaining it."

Bishop's heart sank, the Turk's conclusion a logical one. "And there's no other way to attain it?"

Silence lingered for a moment, until finally the other man spoke. "I didn't say that exactly."

Bishop stepped closer to him, their chests almost touching. He waited for a group of patrons to walk past and lowered his voice further. "What are you talking about?"

Erdem clucked his tongue. "There may be a way to do this. It'll cost you, though. I'm not going into this without being paid properly this time."

Bishop considered his own blackmail. Nothing stopped him from marching him to the Anca Syndicate and telling them that Erdem had helped Wulf rob them blind. However, it came with risks. As much as he preferred the stick, maybe the carrot was the smarter play. "I can arrangement payment."

Erdem smiled. "Okay then, let's talk..."

25

Bishop followed Erdem up the fire escape, their footsteps echoing inside the tight confines until they reached the top. At the upper floor, a battered door greeted them. The Turk shoved it open, bathing them in the afternoon sunlight. Both men shielded their eyes for a moment, allowing their vision to adjust.

What awaited them was a box office seat to the extensive landscape that was Istanbul. In one direction, the modern buildings stood rising into the sky, while beyond, the great city sprawled outward, its history carved of stone and brick. Closer to them wound the metropolis's industrial belt, a gray expanse of factories and warehouses stitched together by scattered office blocks.

Being a weekday, the air buzzed with the sound of manufacturing. Machines whirred inside the various structures, trucks rumbled down the tight roads, and factory workers moved like ants in a maze, their purpose too small to notice from so high up.

Erdem gestured for Bishop to join him at the edge, and

they both crouched low. The young man pointed at the structure opposite, an immense complex of concrete and steel.

"That's where the Anca Syndicate is based."

Bishop examined the exterior. It was quiet. Much quieter than the activity around the block of factories. At first glance, it appeared abandoned. Graffiti lined the walls, a mix of crude tags and the occasional piece of street art. Something, however, did not add up. The windows were intact, and cameras were affixed at all the entry points.

The perfect disguise.

"Two stories?" Bishop asked.

Erdem nodded. "The action takes place on the upper floor. At any one point, there are maybe fifty personnel working at the operation."

"Quite the setup. Not exactly a mom and pop venture, is it? Who funds all of this?"

Erdem shrugged. "Themselves, I suppose. From the hacked data that's sold. I told you, some of the stuff is—"

"Yeah, I get it. A treasure trove. How do they pay you?"

"In cash. No names, no records."

Bishop took out a pair of binoculars and studied more of the building, confirming that it was indeed well secured. "And the bottom floor?"

"That's where all the servers are stored."

"And where we'll find the plans?"

"That's right." Erdem nervously bit the top of his thumb. "Think of the entire network over there as one huge computer. They're the hard drive of the operation. Everything that gets hacked is funneled into the servers. If the attack plans were deleted, odds are they were moved into a separate storage server."

Bishop peeled the binoculars away from his eyes. "Like a

giant recycle bin."

"Exactly."

"If that's the case, how long have we got until the data's lost for good?"

"Seventy-two hours." Erdem considered the question further. "If they wiped it as soon as they discovered Wulf had stolen it, that means we have to retrieve the files tonight. Otherwise, it'll be gone forever.

Bishop set himself down on the rooftop, the low wall of the ceiling shielding his view and any other onlookers. He pulled out the packet of cigarettes Abella had gifted him and slid one free. He offered one to Erdem, who shook his head. The Turk sat as Bishop ignited the tip of the cigarette, the swirl curling in the air.

"This is your ballgame, Mr. Erdem. How do we proceed from here?"

Erdem brought his hands together. Whether he was a religious man, Bishop was unsure. What he did know was that Erdem had a deeply contemplative side to him. Perhaps it was why Wulf had selected him for the original infiltration.

"I can't remotely access the network like Wulf did. Even if I was good enough to do it, being able to infiltrate the deleted server would not be possible."

"Why?"

"The firewalls." Erdem placed his hands in his lap. "Because of the time allotted it takes for the wiped data to vanish from the system, there are layers of extra protection. I simply don't have the proficiency to retrieve it before getting found out."

Bishop took a drag of his cigarette. "What's the alternative?"

"We take the server."

"Take the server? As in physically rip it out of the wall and wheel it out of the warehouse?"

"That's right."

Bishop puffed his cheeks and blew out a plume of smoke. "A heist..."

"We may not be robbing a bank, but it won't be that much different. The syndicate has armed guards on site."

"I'm guessing not the typical guards who take a two-week course to earn their badge?"

"No." Erdem shook his head. "There's also a security system locking everything down."

"Do the hackers operate twenty-four seven?"

Erdem nodded. "We can't use the cover of night to protect us."

Bishop frowned and tapped some ash next to him. "If we could transport the server out of there without getting ourselves killed, do you have the expertise to extract the data from it?"

"I can extract it, but it'll still need to be decrypted. I lack the ability to break it."

"Who can do it?"

Erdem pondered, coughing from the Russian tobacco smoke lingering around them. "I know someone as good as Wulf. Possibly better."

"Would he help us?"

"He might, if he's suitably compensated."

Bishop drew in more of his cigarette until it burned down to the end of the filter. "Very well, a heist it is."

"We'll need more manpower. You and I alone won't be able to pull this off by ourselves."

Bishop stubbed the cigarette. "I'm way ahead of you, Mr. Erdem."

26

NEW YORK, NEW YORK

"Now let's take a look at yesterday's baseball action. It was a quiet Monday with just the six games on the slate. In the NL, the Cubs took on the Cincinnati Reds and won at home eight to two, while the Cards shut out the Brew Crew, eight to nothing. Over in the AL, we had a road victory for the Mariners. They defeated the Anaheim Angels five to one. Oakland got it done against the Rangers with a solid performance seven to one. And the White Sox and Minnesota sealed wins against the Indians and Detroit, respectively."

"I watched that Twins game. A real close contest against the Tigers."

"Absolutely. But let's shift our focus to the teams that matter. After a well-earned day off, both New York clubs return to the schedule today. The Yankees will square off against the White Sox, while the Mets take on the Pirates. The Bronx Bombers are thirteen games clear of Boston in the AL

East. It shouldn't be too long until they clinch the division. As for the Mets..."

Miguel turned down the volume of the radio sitting atop his US Mail cart and made a turn at the corner. The route was a common one. So familiar, he could have done it blindfolded. As always, he would start the morning on Pine Street, then move over to Pearl, swing across to Broad, and then loop back onto Wall Street, passing several of the banking and stock exchange buildings as he went.

He checked his watch. 8:20 a.m. He was ahead of schedule, the mail load lighter than usual. He trundled the beaten old cart farther down the sidewalk and parked it outside the local deli. Patrons rushed in and out, most in crisp suits, ready to face another day in the New York business district. He waited in the queue like everyone else as the baristas behind the counter ping-ponged backward and forward to get through the morning rush.

"Miguel!"

Louie, the store owner, smiled at him when he reached the end of the line. There was no need to ask Miguel for his order. He knew it as well as Miguel knew his postal route. It was a dance they performed every day, each step as automatic as breathing. The proprietor of the cozy but busy little haunt prepared his hot drip with milk and three sugars, pouring it into a Styrofoam cup and placing its lid on top.

"Just the way you like it." Louie slid it across the counter.

Miguel reached for some cash from his wallet, handing a fiver to him.

The old Italian man whipped out some bills and coins to pay the change. "How is it out there at the moment?"

Miguel put the money away and grabbed his cup. "Clear skies."

"Enjoy it while you can. It won't last."

Miguel chuckled. He understood his home all too well, having lived there for all fifty-five years of his life. Before he knew it, they would be deep in fall. Then winter would roll in, making his job much more precarious. At least there was a single constant. He could always depend on one of Louie's hot coffees. "I'll see you tomorrow, Louie."

"I'll see you then."

Miguel navigated through the ever-burgeoning line of people eager for their morning brew, then grabbed his cart from beyond the door. He was on the final stretch. Down Wall Street, onto Old Slip, and back to Pine. He set off again, passing the tall buildings and the office workers on the sidewalk rushing to get to their desks. Even though he was invisible to them, they never crashed into him.

He turned up the radio, letting the voices of his favorite sports program fill the air. The hosts were discussing the upcoming Yankees game and the times they had crossed paths with the players on a recent road trip. It was his go-to show.

He entered the apartment complex on the corner of Wall Street and Old Slip, the doorman standing at the entry in his crisp burgundy uniform.

He opened the door and doffed his cap. "Good morning, Miguel."

"Hi, Reg. How's your day?"

"No complaints on my end."

Miguel held up his cup. "Do you mind?"

The doorman shook his head. Reg never minded him bringing in his coffee, but he felt it proper to ask all the same. He switched the radio off and passed by him, stopping at the row of mailboxes. With the pace of a man who knew the name and number of every resident, he filed the letters into the respective slots, moving at the speed of a Las Vegas blackjack dealer.

He wheeled the cart to the door, which Reg opened for him again.

"How do you think we'll go tonight?" the man asked.

"With Mussina on the mound in the Bronx?" Miguel laughed. "No problems."

"I'll see you tomorrow, Miguel."

He gave the doorman a wave on the way out as his cart clattered over the bump in the path. Turning left onto Old Slip, he soon returned to Pine Street. His final destination loomed before getting back to the depot. With a last sip of his coffee, he drained the cup and tossed it in the trashcan at the corner.

The building stood as one of the more modern along his route, the windows gleaming in the sunlight. He checked his watch. 8:47 a.m. Still well ahead of schedule. He stretched out his left leg, his weary muscles pulsating from the fatigue.

With a shrug, he pressed on toward the office building and entered the lobby. He passed by the same familiar faces he saw every morning, the men and women arriving for the start of their day to get in some work before they officially clocked on.

"Hello, Miguel," the two security guards at the elevator greeted him, their words almost spoken in unison.

"Vic. Steve. Hi," he said to them.

Vic, the elder statesman of the pair, had been at his job nearly as long as Miguel. Steve had been by his side for about six months. Miguel doubted Steve would be around that much longer. Some people like him were content with their roles, while others saw their future elsewhere. Miguel understood. The man was still young. He remembered the feeling.

"Eighth floor?" Steve asked.

"Please."

The guard rang up an elevator car with a push of the button. While they waited, the trio talked baseball and football as they always did. When the doors slid open, it was back to business. Miguel shuffled his cart inside, and the elevator ascended. The doors opened promptly, and he entered the reception area of level eight.

Through the glass windows, office staff worked at their cubicles. Before it, sitting at a long desk on her own, was Angie hard at work. She nestled the phone between her head and shoulder while rattling away at her computer.

Miguel stopped and opened his cart, pulling out three wads of mail, placing them in front of her and the coffee mug next to her keyboard. She smiled at him, though remained focused on her call. Normally, they would chat for a few minutes, asking about each other's daughters. Instead, he gave her a brisk wave and headed back to the elevator. Before his ride arrived, a droning sound filled the busy atmosphere.

He furrowed his brow. It was as if someone had cranked up the AC. But it was not that. The noise amplified in intensity. The floor shook, the reverberation pulsing through the handle of his cart. He relinquished his hold of it and turned his attention to the window, gazing out at the street and the tall buildings beyond.

He glanced upward, the sound becoming louder again. Even the glass started quaking. From out the corner of his eye, he spotted Angie putting down her phone. She stood, her coffee almost tipping from the edge of her desk.

"Miguel, what is it?" she asked.

A dark shadow swept over the block as if night had temporarily fallen. Then a streak sliced through the air, the noise turning into a deafening roar.

Miguel snapped his head farther upward at the twin buildings of the World Trade Center, their oblong shapes towering in the sky.

An object hurtled at the North Tower.

A plane?

Surely not, it was too low.

Before he could process the thought further, a blinding orange fireball erupted from the side of the tower. The sound was brutal, like a fist had come down from the heavens and slammed into the structure. Debris exploded from it as if it had been struck by a missile, raining down jagged fragments of steel, glass, and concrete. A shockwave rippled through the streets below. Even from such a height, Miguel could hear the screams.

He froze. What had he just witnessed? An accident or something deliberate? Raw terror overwhelmed him. Whatever it was, was beyond anything a regular old mail carrier could have ever imagined. More of the office staff joined him at the window, their eyes filled with disbelief, their voices frantic. Somehow, in that moment, the world Miguel knew had changed forever.

And he had a front-row seat.

27

WASHINGTON, DISTRICT OF COLUMBIA

Jeffrey Phibbs put his phone in his pocket and returned to his seat. At the polished mahogany table inside the dining hall of the St. Regis Hotel, he sat, picking up the linen napkin from next to his plate and placing it over his lap.

He met the man's gaze across from him. "My apologies, Senator. It was just the office. I've got some meetings this afternoon that I had to rework."

Donovan Brent held up a hand, pausing mid-chew, his mouth still full of the eggs benedict he had chosen for his breakfast. He savored the rest of it and smiled. "Don't worry, Jeffrey. I realize how busy it gets out at Langley. I worked on that Senate Intelligence Committee for what, six years?"

"Sounds about right."

"I'm surprised you even managed to keep this appointment on a Tuesday."

"It's been too long since we've had a proper chat. Besides,

I'm on the clock seven days a week. I can always carve out a couple of hours for you."

The distant honking of horns and the hum of traffic outside the doors seeped into the otherwise refined setting.

The former official frowned. "Don't work yourself into a premature grave. Heading up the agency is an important job. But you're no good to anyone burned out."

Phibbs picked up his knife and fork and resumed slicing into his omelet. "An occupational hazard."

Brent, a man Phibbs had considered a mentor in his early days before becoming the chief of the CIA, stared across at him. Concern lingered in his steady blue eyes. It was the kind only someone with decades of experience in their field could carry. "I know it's not my place to say, but I will anyway."

Phibbs shoveled some of his breakfast, intrigued by what was about to be said. The eggs had, of course, gone cold since taking his call.

"Have you ever considered retiring?"

Brent's question nearly made Phibbs choke. He slowly chewed what he had and clanked his cutlery down, dabbing the sides of his mouth with his napkin. "Do you think I'm doing a bad job, Senator?"

"Not at all." Brent shook his head. "I'm far from the hustle and bustle of DC these days, however, even from my distant post at the university, I can tell you're steering a tight ship."

"Then why would I retire? I'm needed at the agency."

"I agree. You're the best who's out there. If they had to replace you, they'd be hard pressed to find someone close to being as qualified. That doesn't mean you shouldn't look out for number one. I've seen people in your position come and go. A point arrives when you've got to pass the baton. Not just for you, but for your family. And your sanity."

Since Phibbs had taken the reins in 1993, time had passed him by in a blur. Before he had known it, the twenty-first century had arrived and he had breezed past Allen Dulles' record as the longest-serving director of the CIA. He had always trusted Brent's counsel. It had proved invaluable more often than not. Retiring, though, would be a bitter pill to swallow. Perhaps one day he would sit down with Nicole and discuss it. As much as he relied on Brent's guidance, it was his wife's counsel he depended on most of all. "Retirement will happen eventually, Senator. Until then—"

The snappy, hurried tap of footsteps echoed behind him. O'Brien, the head of his security detail, appeared from the shadows, having been standing near the door. The other two, who had been stationed in plainclothes at a nearby table, also mobilized, their fingers pressed against the electronic buds in their ears.

Before he could ask what was happening, his phone rang. Brent put his fork on his plate and raised an eyebrow.

"I'm sorry, Senator, you'll have to excuse me again." Phibbs rushed off to the alcove near the lobby, his security detail following him and taking up defensive positions around him.

He flipped open his cell and brought the device to his ear. "This is Phibbs."

A rush of voices sounded all at once, overlapping with one another before someone cut through the background noise. "*Sir, this is Rivers.*"

The CIA's deputy director was flustered, his panicked voice laced with other phones ringing around him, printers whirring, and televisions blaring.

"What's going on?" Phibbs asked.

"*There's been an incident in New York. The North Tower of the World Trade Center has been struck.*"

"Struck. By what?"

"*We don't know at this stage. It may be a light aircraft. We're working to put together the reports on the ground.*"

Phibbs peered beyond the window where burgundy curtains framed the sunlight streaming in. "What's the weather like in New York this morning?"

"*Uh, stand by.*" Muffled words filled the phone line until Rivers returned. "*Seventy degrees, clear skies, little to no wind.*"

It was exactly what Phibbs feared. "Have any of our stations picked up transmissions from anywhere around the world?"

"*Sir?*"

"Has anyone taken responsibility?"

"*We're still trying to determine if this was an accident or an attack. As it stands—*"

"We have to assume, at this stage, that it may not have been an accident. At least until we have confirmation. I'm returning to Langley. Get all relevant parties on the horn. Let's start mobilizing our assets."

"*Yes, sir.*"

Phibbs clamped his phone shut and went back to his table, where Brent had already stood, likely detecting something was amiss. "I'm sorry, we'll have to reschedule, Senator."

"What's happened, Jeffrey?"

The sound of distressed patrons rippled from the far end of the dining hall, the mass of onlookers mingling around a TV in the corner. Phibbs strained to make sense of the chaos.

Through the crowd he glimpsed the vision of the tall pillar that was the World's Trade Center's North Tower now alight.

"Check out the news."

Before they could say their goodbyes, O'Brien and his remaining security detail whisked Phibbs out of the hotel and into his armored car. The driver laid rubber and set a route for Langley.

O'Brien switched on the TV inside the cabin, and Phibbs focused his attention on the CCN coverage. It was the same station that had been playing in the hotel. The vision centered on the North Tower. Smoke billowed from the upper floors. The headline at the bottom of the screen read: BREAKING NEWS — PLANE CRASHES INTO WORLD TRADE CENTER TOWER.

The talking heads rambled on, discussing the images, accompanied by the distant wails on New York's frantic streets and the screams of emergency services sirens either on site or heading to the scene. It ticked past 9:00 a.m., and Phibbs rang HQ, receiving more information from Rivers and his team. More intel had come through that it had been a commercial jet, not a light plane.

Eyewitness accounts began to flood in on the news, one talking to the CNN anchors near the feet of the World Trade Center. His voice trembled, recounting the details of the impact into the North Tower.

Suddenly, another explosion erupted on the screen. For a moment Phibbs thought a section of the North Tower had ignited, but as the TV helicopter swung around, it became clear. The blast had come from the South Tower. The anchor and eyewitness noted the same thing, their voices heightening at the carnage of the second strike.

"Oh my God..." Phibbs uttered, the magnitude of the disaster sinking in to everyone else in the back of the armored car.

They knew it.

He knew it.

Confirmation.

"*Sir, are you seeing this?*" Rivers asked him on the other end of the line.

Phibbs stared at the TV, his hands trembling ever so slightly. The time ticked over to 9:03 a.m. His career at the agency flashed before him. The never-ending meetings, the detailed reports, every shred of intel that crossed his desk. A lump formed in his throat, and his heart pounded, threatening to tear its way out of his chest.

"I saw it, Rivers. Begin activating our counterterrorism protocols. America is under attack."

28

ISTANBUL, TURKEY

The hotel room was much busier than when Bishop had left it. Instead of it being empty, a group of five larger-than-life individuals awaited him and Erdem. All had aged since Bishop had seen them last. Some for the better. Most for the worse. There were fresh scars to match the old ones. Something, however, had not changed.

The determination in their eyes.

Erdem froze at the doorway, appearing taken aback by the welcome. For a moment, Bishop wondered if he might bolt. That thought quickly disappeared. Two things stopped him. One: The Turk realized he was already in too deep. And two: If he fled, one of Bishop's invitees would have gone after him, the escape lasting only mere seconds.

"You can come in, Mr. Erdem," he said. "None of them will bite. Not much anyway."

A round of chuckles broke out in the now tight confines of the hotel room.

Erdem eased the door shut and joined Bishop's side. "Who are these people?"

"You told me we needed a team for our heist. Here it is." Bishop gestured to the first man sitting on the left half of the sofa. He was bald, even more so than Bishop, though twenty years younger. Muscles stretched at the seams of his tight green t-shirt, a spark of mischief in his eyes. "This is Hirsch."

Bishop continued to the shorter man next to him. Stockier, but just as muscular. A scar ran down the side of his face past his ear. His head was shaved with a buzz cut. Unlike Hirsch, his stare was harsh, as if he chewed metal shavings for breakfast. "He's Mildren."

His attention drifted to the lone woman in the room. She propped a foot on the armrest next to Hirsch, red hair spilling over her shoulders. She wore a tank top, revealing her toned figure and curves that would make any man look twice. The sassy expression Bishop remembered was still there. Half-smile, half-dare. "She's Rampling."

"And these fine gentlemen are the Wong brothers. Quinn and Trent."

Quinn had jet-black hair. Trent's was bleached and slightly longer. Their eyes were dark, revealing men who had seen many things over the years.

Bishop focused his attention on Erdem. "These are the people who are going to help us retrieve the server and ensure we, and you, get out of there in one piece."

Erdem turned, evading their curious gazes. "Can we trust them?"

"I trust them more than I trust you."

The Turk went to speak. Bishop held up his hand to stop him in his tracks.

"I used to deal with men and women like them every day.

I know their capabilities and sent them places where most would've had no chance of ever returning. They never let me down. I'll put it simply. They'll get the job done. And act as insurance."

"What do you mean?" Erdem asked.

"If I discover you haven't been truthful with me since our first meeting, they'll find out. And when they do—"

It was Erdem's turn to raise his hand. "I understand, Mr. Bishop. We won't have any issues on that front."

Bishop held back a sneer of satisfaction. What he had told the kid was true, just minus the finer details. In reality, Hirsch, Mildren, Rampling, and the Wongs had been former assets of Bureau 61. Though the defunct branch of the CIA dealt mostly with solo ops into hostile territory, sometimes more firepower was required. For that, you needed specialized tactical teams. Handpicked operators who worked in groups, who could slip behind enemy lines, do their job, and vanish. No loose ends.

Like all Bureau 61 operatives, they were hired off the books. Mercenaries, in effect. Though loyal to the United States. Just not officially. Plausible deniability had to be upheld. If their adversaries captured them, they would be viewed as merely a ragtag group, unconnected to the US government. No names or records.

The five in the room with him were some of the best. Hence why he had wanted them. Before leaving Seattle, he had sent a coded SMS to those he knew were still plying a mercenary trade in Europe. He had transmitted another message when he had boarded his flight from Venice to Istanbul, just in case he found something.

And indeed he had in Ali Erdem and the Anca Syndicate.

He stepped to the center of the room, and all their eyes met his. It felt like a father looking at his kids. Dangerous kids at that.

"When I contacted you, I must admit I wasn't sure if anyone would turn up," he began. "I knew you were in the region—"

"Yeah, about that, boss," Hirsch said. "How did you nail us down so quickly?"

Bishop shrugged. "You're very good at what you do. Never forget that I'm better."

Laughter filled the space, and Rampling slapped Hirsch playfully on the shoulder from behind.

"Thank you for coming."

"We wouldn't have missed it," Quinn chimed in.

"What's the op?" Rampling crossed her arms. "It must be big."

"It is." Bishop brought them up to speed, starting with Harvey Wulf's message to him in Anchorage, through to his escapades in Venice, and finally his meeting with Erdem and his information on the Turkish hacker group. "Our new friend here believes the data with the attack plans on it lies on a particular server inside the warehouse. It's our mission to go in there, extract it, and get the intel to the CIA before anything goes down."

"And who's going to decrypt the data if this guy"—Mildren jabbed a finger at Erdem—"can't pull it off?"

The Turk stepped forward. "I know someone who can help. He lives right here in Istanbul."

"You'll take care of them," Bishop said.

Mildren nodded.

"Which then brings us to retrieving the server," Bishop went on. "The hacking group works on a twenty-four-hour schedule. That means we'll be going in there when they're staffed. The warehouse has two levels. They operate on the upper floor, while the servers and equipment are kept on the lower floor. That's our target."

"What kind of security are we looking at, boss?" Trent asked.

"Mr. Erdem?"

"At any one time there are seven guards on site," Erdem said. "Patrols are undertaken both inside and outside the facility. There's also an office on the top floor, with access to all the surveillance cameras and security systems."

"Do we get to kill anyone?"

Bishop snapped his head to Hirsch, who grinned at him. "I want zero fatalities if we can help it. Complicating matters with the Turkish government isn't why I'm here. However, if we find ourselves in trouble..." He trailed off, his message loud and clear to the group. "Mr. Erdem, please continue."

"Right." The Turk clasped his hands behind his back. "As it stands, I still have access inside the site. When I return to work tonight, I'll upload a virus into the security software. It'll deactivate the alarms and demagnetize the electronic door locks. I'll also rig up dummy visuals to the cameras."

"First things first," Bishop said. "We neutralize the perimeter guards, then hit the facility from the two side entrances. Mr. Erdem will draw up a blueprint for us. Once we're inside, we nullify anyone who gets in our way. Then we take the server."

"Sounds like a piece of cake," Rampling said.

Bishop readied to address the team again, but before he could say anything, a chorus of buzzing and a collection of ringtones filled the room, including his own. Everyone reached for their devices. As Bishop slid his from his pocket, Mildren pointed at the TV behind him.

"Put the news on! Now!"

Bishop pivoted and flicked it on, bathing the dark space in light. He flipped through the channels until he found a local news network. The New York skyline filled the screen. Black smoke poured from the Twin Towers of the World Trade Center, both buildings ablaze. The headlines and other text graphics were in Turkish, but the image spoke louder than any words could.

He was too late.

29

LANGLEY, VIRGINIA

The operations center inside the CIA's new building pulsed with urgency as Phibbs stepped through the doors. Wall-mounted screens blazed with live news feeds from all the major networks, while intelligence reports scrolled across similar displays from CIA stations around the globe.

Analysts typed away at their workstations, their eyes fixed on the monitors, while at the other end of the room another group of operators fielded calls filled with relevant information from the other primary agencies and institutions. The teams worked in tandem, putting together the puzzle. For now, the picture was frustratingly incomplete.

On the drive back from DC, Phibbs's deputy director kept him informed in real time while every piece of news crossed his desk. Chaos did not even begin to cover it.

His gaze fell upon one of the news feeds where choppers circled the Twin Towers of the World Trade Center, both buildings spewing smoke and debris into the air, choking

New York's once clear skies in a dark blanket of haze. Above the screen, on the wall-mounted clock, read the time: 09:29.

At the heart of the operations center, other groups of CIA personnel sat in clusters around laptops and sprawled paperwork. His deputy director appeared from the corner, snapping his cell phone shut.

"Sir."

Phibbs patrolled behind the analysts hard at work, glancing at their monitors. "What's our sitrep, Rivers?"

The man followed him before they came to a stop at the head of the table. "Where do you want me to begin?"

"Let's start with the planes. Have the FAA given us an ID on them yet?"

Rivers nodded and rotated a lonely laptop, tapping the trackpad to wake the screen. "Flight 11, a 767, out of Logan International Airport in Boston departed at 7:59 a.m. and struck the North Tower at 8:46 a.m. Flight 175, another 767, left the runway at 8:14 a.m., hitting the South Tower at 9:03 a.m."

"What were their destinations?"

"Both LA."

"So, they were fully fueled."

"Yes, sir."

Phibbs rubbed his temple. "Have they given us anything else?"

"All hell is breaking loose at Air Traffic Control Command. I spoke with the FAA chief five minutes ago, and they're just starting to figure it all out now. He claims they lost the transponder to Flight 11 before the first attack, while Flight 175 went dark shortly after takeoff. As it stands, they're coordinating with NORAD to track other flights still in the sky."

"Good. Have they been able to nail down any other potential hijackings?"

"They're yet to ascertain that."

"They'd better be quick. There can't be any doubt about it. This is a highly coordinated operation. Who knows how long it's been in the planning."

"Yes, sir."

Phibbs found his attention drawn to the images on the TV screens again, the rolling coverage of the towers almost nauseating on the many monitors. "How are the emergency services faring at ground zero?"

Rivers cleared his throat. "Not good. Apparently the heat is unbearable. According to the last report that came in, the fire teams are having trouble reaching the affected floors. Stairwells have been blocked, and elevator shafts have been destroyed."

"So, anyone above the blast zone has been cut off." Phibbs took a breath. "What about the sprinkler systems?"

"Some are intact. Others aren't. The firefighters are doing their best to get everyone out."

"Up all those floors..."

"The hoses can only go so far up. And as they do, the water pressure decreases."

Phibbs leaned over the table and closed his eyes for a moment, absorbing everything. His job, a living hell, now especially, was still easier than that of those currently scaling the twin buildings. They were the true heroes.

He opened his eyes and ran his finger over the trackpad to bring up more real-time intel. The data scrolled quicker than he could read it. "What about Washington? The airspace, the government sites and officials?"

"The FAA hasn't closed down the airspace yet but are

considering grounding all flights until they can sort this mess out. Emergency protocols are in effect in DC. Government buildings are being evacuated as we speak. The President's still on the ground in Florida, while the VP is in the bunker of the White House. The Speaker has been moved to a secure location, and congressional leaders are being taken out of Washington."

Phibbs nodded. "Make sure we're liaising with the NSA. I want to know who did this. Whatever they need, give it to them."

Rivers hurried off and picked up one of the many phones at his fingertips. Phibbs paced the room, rounding a table. The time clicked over to 09:34. Beyond the glass walls, the same frantic movement unfolded in the adjacent offices, the burden of stress lining everyone's faces. There was something else, too. An expression he no doubt wore himself.

Shame.

How could this have happened on their watch?

His watch.

They were supposed to be the line that stopped things like this from happening. They were the keepers of the peace, fighting in the shadows to protect America's citizens. Phibbs's shoulders tensed at the thought. Fighting in the shadows. Where had he heard that before?

"Oh my God..."

The voice came from the table, where a pair of women sat with their laptops. One froze, her hands quivering. Phibbs approached and put a hand on the back of her chair.

"What is it?" he asked.

She took a moment to compose herself. "We're getting reports from New York. The networks have footage of people jumping from the towers. They're not making it available to the public yet."

Phibbs glanced at one of the TV feeds and the buildings still ablaze. He could not fathom what it must have been like to be trapped above the impact zone, cut off from any escape with the inferno closing in. What choice did they have?

His stomach churned, the cold eggs from breakfast threatening to rise. He stepped backward to gather himself, the glare of the screens, the ring of the phones, and the overlapping voices becoming one.

Shaking off the sensation, he walked to the other side of the room, where a staff member sat in front of a monitor displaying the flight paths of every aircraft across the continental United States. Hundreds of them above the heads of the millions of Americans sitting in their homes glued to their TVs.

On a nearby screen, images from the floors of the Wall Street Stock Exchange flashed by, with the headline: WALL STREET CLOSED.

The SEC and NYSE had made the right decision. Now was the wrong time to focus on money with the World Trade Center burning down the block. Whoever had orchestrated the attacks had done exactly what they had intended. They had struck at the very heart of global capitalism, making a monumental statement. One that would be remembered for generations to come.

His phone vibrated in his pocket, and he fished it out, flipping it open, immediately recognizing the caller ID. Aaron Quade, the director of ExoCipher. He answered it.

"I wondered how long it would take you to call." Phibbs was not in the mood for niceties. "How did we not see this happening?"

"Mr. Phibbs, we have terabytes of intel streaming in from around the world every single day and—"

"Quade, now is not the time for excuses," he snapped. "You run the biggest SIGINT operation on the planet. The CIA relies on the data you provide. I'm struggling to understand how a terrorist op of this magnitude never got picked up. You need to—"

"Sir!"

Phibbs put the phone to his side and peered past the clock, now reading 09:37, toward Rivers, who held a handset of his own.

"It's the Pentagon!" he said. "It's been hit!"

Phibbs let go of his cell, the device clattering to the floor, his call to Quade left hanging. As he thought about the man who headed up ExoCipher's operations, he remembered Quade's role as the deputy director of Bureau 61, the archaic branch of the CIA consigned to the history books. His thoughts then drifted to its prickly leader.

John Bishop.

He had cautioned Phibbs this was coming.

Despite the technological marvels Quade had at his disposal, it was a grumpy retiree with few resources who had warned him. The weight of the words spoken by Bishop echoed in his mind.

"Who's going to do all your dirty work now, Phibbs?"

30

ISTANBUL, TURKEY

Everyone had claimed their own corner of the hotel room. The Wong brothers sat on opposite sides of the bed on their phones, facing away from each other in almost perfect symmetry. Their lips moved faster than the words coming out of their mouths.

Hirsch stood next the door on his own cell, his back pressed against one wall, a foot propped against the other. Mildren remained on the sofa, hunched over, a hand cupped over his ear to block out the noise of the others, speaking to someone on the other end of his phone. Rampling paced near the dining table, texting rapidly with one of her contacts. Then there was Erdem. Silent, standing next to the TV, his gaze fixed on the news.

Bishop had positioned himself on the balcony, staring through the glass door, unable to remove his attention from the haunting images of the burning towers on the screen. His throat tightened. He swallowed, attempting to dislodge the lump that had formed. Despite his efforts, the guilt did not go away.

Was he the one who had flown the planes into the buildings? No. Had he done everything in his power to avert the disaster? Yes. None of that, however, seemed to matter. All his efforts to uncover the plans of the attack had failed.

It had been for nothing.

He was a slow, out of practice, incapable of keeping up with the pace of a world which now moved much quicker than any he used to once live in. He clenched his hand at the sound of the engaged tone on the other end of the line. No matter who he called, and how many times, he was unable to reach those who mattered, whether in the US or a CIA contact around the globe.

He was alone again. Even with his former Bureau 61 team by his side, he had been severed from the world.

One that was burning.

He flipped his phone shut and turned to face the city. The cars on the road below moved to their normal rhythm, the occasional honk from an aggressive driver a reminder of how far away he was from New York. Bishop might as well have been on a different planet. He could only imagine the panic back home. The chaos and fear taking place as reality sank in. The first plane could have been seen as an accident. The second erased any doubt. America was at war.

One that no one saw coming.

Bishop, the man he was, the person he had been trained to be, could not help but think of the repercussions. Once the dust settled, grief would follow. Afterward, stronger emotions would surface. The public would demand blood. Someone, anyone, would have to pay. He imagined this must have been what it felt like after Pearl Harbor. And everyone who studied history knew what happened after that.

The globe, already in turmoil, was thrust into disarray when the United States officially entered the conflict. Not only did they confront Japan but joined the war against the savage force that was Nazi Germany. The call went out to the American people, and they answered, unleashing the country's industrial might. A power never before witnessed in human history. Within just a few years, they had turned the tide, upending the world order and reshaping it at their own will.

Bishop reached into his pocket and withdrew a packet of cigarettes, lighting the tip of a Russian smoke and filling his lungs with the unforgiving taste.

That's exactly what this was. Those who had planned the attacks wanted to shake up the current order. A calculated assault on democracy and capitalism at the home of the free world. It was ideological warfare.

Bishop again called one of the many numbers he had already attempted. This time, it rang.

Several seconds passed until finally, an answer.

"*Boss?*"

It was the voice of his friend and former deputy director of Bureau 61.

"Quade."

"*Hell. Where are you?*"

"Turkey."

"*Turkey?*"

"I've been following some leads. I guess I was too late."

There was a brief hush across the phone line. "*Are you seeing all of this over there?*"

"Yeah." Bishop inhaled more of the smoke and pivoted on

a heel. His mercenary crew remained scattered inside the hotel room. "The TV's locked on to a local station."

More silence filtered through.

"Are you still there, Quade?" Bishop asked.

"*I just spoke with Phibbs. We, uh... A few minutes ago, there was a third attack. Not sure if you've got the info, but the Pentagon was hit, too.*"

Bishop's cigarette dangled from his lips. He snatched it before it tumbled to the balcony floor. "Another plane?"

"*Seems like it.*"

"How much did it take out?"

"*Unsure yet. Might have been a wing of the building. It appears the FAA are going to close all continental airspace.*"

"That's a lot of planes to bring down."

"*They don't have a choice.*"

"No, they don't. Has anyone taken responsibility?"

"*No.*"

Bishop sighed. "You know why I'm calling you, right?

"*I have a general idea.*"

Bishop took another drag of his cigarette. "When I set out to find the information Wulf intended to send to me, I knew it was going to be big. But this... This is bigger than anything I could have thought possible. It was planned and synchronized. Designed for maximum impact. We're talking potentially years of preparation. How the hell could this have gone unnoticed?"

Quade sighed. "*I had Phibbs ask me the same questions. Perhaps you were right, John. Maybe SIGINT isn't the answer to all our prayers. In this instance, SIGINT failed.*"

Bishop tightened his hand around his cell. "I'm the first to voice my concerns about the flaws of SIGINT. But this is more than the failure of a system. It's a monumental blunder of all methods and processes."

"*And because of that, I will likely be sitting before many senate hearings in the coming months and years.*" A phone sounded in the background. "Look, boss, I've got to go. I, uh, I know you'll be feeling like hell out there at the moment. Don't beat yourself up too much. You couldn't have stopped this."

The call ended, and Bishop flicked the cell shut. He finished the rest of his cigarette and tossed it at his feet, stamping out the last ember with his shoe. He ambled toward the door where the team inside had come together, their cells abandoned, their gazes again refocused on the TV.

Bishop entered. He moved past the sofa and stood between Quinn and Trent Wong. "What's going on?"

"One of the towers just fell," Rampling said.

He focused in on a replay to find the South Tower collapsing on itself, as if it were being imploded from within. The house of cards crumbled, debris shooting in every direction, destruction spreading across countless surrounding blocks.

A deeper hush fell over the seven individuals standing in the room, the occasional glance moving from one person to the other and then back at the TV. Erdem sat alone, perched on the arm of the sofa, his boyish face unreadable while he listened to the Turkish talking heads.

Bishop stepped forward and stood in front of everyone, their eyes meeting his. "I asked you here today, because I wanted to stop this." He gestured to the screen. "Regardless, we now need to focus our attention on the mission ahead."

"What mission?" Erdem appeared from the pack. "This is over. You intended to infiltrate the warehouse because you wanted the plans to these attacks. What's the point now? It's done."

The others seemed to weigh up his words, turning their attention to Bishop for his rebuttal.

"I've just received word that another plane has hit the Pentagon," he said. "Done or not, Mr. Erdem, we at the very least need to go in there and get whatever we can extract. If that leads us to the mastermind of this whole operation, then all the better. We're still on. Draw up the plans. I want to move within the hour."

31

COMMERCIAL FLIGHT — NEW YORK TO MIAMI

Tyler awoke from his slumber, his head heavy on the headrest. His eyes cracked open, and a momentary dizziness took hold. For a moment, he wondered where he was.

Then he reached out for his armrest, the steady vibration of the aircraft engines reverberating through him. New York was behind him, Miami ahead.

He shuddered, thinking about the small back room that waited him at his parents' house. Placing his seat in the upright position, he crouched, looking forward to his beach vacation in Monterrey.

Three days in Miami wasn't that long, was it?

Just enough time for Dad to complain about the Braves never being able to capitalize on their talent.

He stretched, stifling a yawn, the usual hush on a journey of such length appearing to be absent in the air. The conversations of the surrounding passengers were full of noise and vigor. Tyler tuned them out, his hangover now hitting him like a ton of bricks. The constant back and forth of the other cattle-class patrons was only exacerbating the thud within his skull.

He stood, a little unsteady on his feet, his wayward steps betraying his fatigue and the remaining alcohol in his system. He shuffled to the rear lavatory and waited for someone to depart, ducking inside when the coast was clear. His bladder emptied rapidly. He then checked out his reflection in the mirror. It was not a pretty one. His eyes were bloodshot and his face pale. The sleep he'd had out of New York had done nothing for his scruffy red hair either.

Tyler lathered his hands in soap and washed them, throwing some cold water on his cheeks for good measure. It was lucky he was on vacation, because his disheveled image was certainly not one becoming of his position.

A knock echoed on the door, and he gathered himself, flushing the toilet and unlatching the lock. He stepped back out into the cabin, where an impatient man stood waiting. Tyler apologized and offered a weak smile.

His stomach grumbled, and he turned, spotting a flight attendant in the rear section in a tizz with the refreshments cart. "Sorry, excuse me. I know I would've missed the breakfast service, but is there any chance I'd be able to get a coffee or a bite to eat?"

She glanced at him with a crooked brow and reared up her shoulders. For a fleeting second, Tyler wondered if she was going to snap at him.

"I didn't snore all the way from New York, did I?" he asked, attempting to lighten the mood.

Her hardened features softened, and she shook her head. Without a word, she pivoted and poured him a coffee into a paper cup, handing it to him with some packets of sealed chocolate chip cookies.

Tyler smiled. "Thank you."

She nodded, and he set back off again to his seat. He remained in the aisle, gripping the headrest to keep himself upright while he enjoyed some of his drink. It was not anything extraordinary, but it was hot and filled the right spot.

Around him, the chaotic blur of conversations carried on, the tension inside the cabin palpable. A theme, however, appeared, the same series of words spoken over and over again.

Terrorist. Accident. Buildings. President. Bombs.

Tyler decided to sit, his gaze drifting to the husband-and-wife duo next to him. Both were in their mid-fifties and had not stopped talking when they had boarded. The constant chatter was now gone, their faces as pale as his.

"Is something going on?" Tyler asked them. "What's with all the hubbub?"

The woman looked at her husband and then back at Tyler. "We don't know exactly."

"Some rumors started coming out of business class about ten minutes ago," the man said.

Tyler peered at the curtain dividing him and the passengers who had the money to pay for more comfortable seats. "What rumors?"

"We only caught bits and pieces of it."

"Sir, this is important."

"Um, well, from what we've gathered, there's been an attack in New York."

Tyler's first thought was of his sister. "What?"

"Yeah, like a bomb or something going off in some buildings."

"You're sure?"

"No. But that's what we've heard."

Tyler sipped his coffee, his attention again drawn to the thin blue curtain. If information had come from the ground, he wondered if perhaps someone had used one of the air phones in the business-class section. Maybe there was some truth to the rumors.

He wrenched himself up, his legs steadier this time. Either the coffee had instantly worked or the shot of adrenaline pulsing through his system had sparked him to life. He proceeded to the curtain and peeked his head inside, the dialogue amongst their business-class passengers just as engaged as those in economy. Of the dozen men and women there, they were all clustered around one gentleman sitting in his seat playing with his air phone.

Tyler had been right.

He narrowed his eyes, his focus getting lost beyond them where a flight attendant was attempting to assist an agitated passenger. The man, in his late thirties, sat rigid in a sharp suit-and-tie combo, his posture tense and his cheeks red. From such a distance, Tyler struggled to make out his words. Though, it did not take a rocket scientist to know none were pleasant.

Just as Tyler was about to enter the section and render some help of his own, a voice burst from the PA.

"Ladies and gentlemen, this is your captain speaking. We've received word of an escalating situation in US airspace. Air traffic control has instructed us that we're to divert from our scheduled route. Unfortunately, that means we'll be making an unscheduled landing in Atlanta. At this time, we

don't have any further details. Rest assured, your safety is our top priority, and the flight crew is here to assist with any of your needs. We should be on the ground within the next thirty minutes. Once we land, we'll have more information for you."

If the passengers were not animated before, they certainly were now. The businessman rose from his seat, his annoyance only escalated at the announcement.

Tyler brushed his way through the curtain and approached the flight attendant's side. "Sir, please calm down," he said to the passenger.

"Who the hell are you?" The man glowered at Tyler. "I don't intend to calm down until I know what's going on here! And why the diversion? I've got things to do—"

Tyler clamped his hand on the man's shoulder, pushing him down onto his backside. His glare at the businessman was as cold and commanding as he could muster, silently disclosing that he was to shut up for the rest of the trip or else. The man grunted in frustration and reached for his newspaper on the empty seat beside him. Tyler nodded to the flight attendant, and they moved down the aisle, clear of the confrontation.

"Thanks," she said.

"Any time."

"Unfortunately, we only had the one air phone working. And then that stopped operating. Everyone's losing their mind."

Tyler glanced across at the commotion continuing to take place. "He makes a good point. If people don't find out exactly what's happening, rumors and hearsay will turn this panic into a full-blown riot. I realize the captain said he had no more details, but I consider that hard to believe if there's an 'escalating situation' taking place."

"I'm not sure what to tell you, sir."

Tyler reached into his pocket for his wallet. "I'm going to need to ask a favor. I'd like to see the pilots."

"That's out of the question."

"I'm afraid I have to insist." Tyler revealed his FBI ID and badge. "Special Agent Jack Tyler."

At that moment, the woman's frantic demeanor melted away, his identity appearing to reassure her. She inclined her head to the cockpit, and he followed her. With the slightest of knocks, she opened the door, revealing the interior of the aircraft's command center. Inside, two pilots sat next to each other at the controls, spooked by their sudden arrival.

"What is it, Kathy?" the captain asked, a noticeable layer of sweat beading down his face.

"This is Special Agent Tyler from the FBI," she said. "He's requested to see you."

Tyler stepped forward, briefly lost in the view of the clouds. "All right, gentlemen, I need you to tell me everything you know."

The pilots exchanged a glance, the look unsettling Tyler immediately. Their throats seemed to tighten as they prepared themselves, bracing for the magnitude of the truth. Whatever they were about to reveal to him was no simple tale.

32

ISTANBUL, TURKEY

Rampling pounced, striking first on the unsuspecting guard. The butt of her M4 Carbine crunched into the back of the minion's skull, her speed almost blinding in the shroud of night. Bishop grasped him by one arm, while Rampling took him by the other, the pair dragging him across the rough tarmac surrounding the warehouse. They tossed him behind a rusted old forklift, its once functional chassis now an abandoned relic. They gagged him and tied his limbs, stripping him of his sidearm, just in case he regained consciousness before their mission had been accomplished.

On the far side of the building, the Wong brothers would execute a similar move, dispatching their target and hiding him from sight.

Two down.

Rampling signaled to the warehouse and the side door tucked down the alleyway. They remained out of the camera's view and waited. Now it was up to Erdem. The success of the operation rested on his shoulders. He was a wildcard, a third of Bishop's age. A man he had still not decided to trust. One way or another, this assignment would determine his real motive.

Fifteen minutes earlier, the Turk had entered the building, swiping his ID to gain access. It was agreed that he would begin his night shift in the usual manner. Unbeknownst to his colleagues, his task would be more covert, assisting Bishop and his band of mercenaries to breach the facility instead.

The key to the infiltration proceeding smoothly lay in the security center on the upper level. Under his cover as a loyal employee to the Anca Syndicate, Erdem would enter the office and give the guard his coffee. The Turk would then depart, but not without leaving a virus in one of the computers. Once gone, it would present the guard with dummy visuals on all the camera feeds. Next, he would take the alarms offline and demagnetize the outer doors.

Bishop leaned slightly into the alleyway and took his phone from his pocket, waiting for the call.

"Has he done it yet?" Rampling asked.

Bishop shook his head, frustration simmering within. It had been nearly twenty minutes since Erdem had gone inside. Bishop considered the reservations he had about everything. What if Erdem had been found out? Or worse. What if he had been the villain the whole time, having betrayed Wulf and now doing the same to Bishop?

He shoved his doubts aside and visualized the next part of their plan once they were in the facility. With the doors released and the cameras out of commission, they would have to neutralize the inner perimeter guards. Rampling and Bishop would be required to take care of one, the Wong brothers the other. That left two more and their supervisor in the security office. The poisoned coffee would deal with the latter, the remaining two nullified when they presented themselves.

That would leave the server clear in their sights. By that stage, Erdem would meet them downstairs, pulling the plug and replacing it with a dummy. With the tech on a trolley, all that would be left to do was walk out of there.

Bishop's phone vibrated. He checked the screen. The SMS read only one word: DONE.

He pointed ahead, relief washing over him. "Go."

They hurried through the alleyway, Rampling leading the charge with her rifle held steady. Bishop followed with a Beretta 92FS sidearm in his grasp. His mind flickered back to his last mission in the field before taking up a desk job at Bureau 61 HQ. Decades had passed, yet his heart still raced, the familiar rush of adrenaline a recognizable ghost from his past.

Rampling reached the door first. She glanced over her shoulder at Bishop, and he readied himself, swinging it open.

Sure enough, the magnetic lock had been rendered useless, and no alarms sounded, just as Erdem had promised. Rampling fanned her rifle into the dull lighting of the warehouse. No one was home.

They entered, the hum of dozens of servers filling the space with an eerie energy. The heat radiating from all the machinery gave the space an unsettling feeling as if the place were a steamy jungle instead of a technological wonderland. The duo proceeded forward, ensuring their steps made no noise on the polished concrete floors. Following Erdem's map, they kept to the edge of the warehouse, moving in the direction of the main server room.

Rampling gripped his shoulder, and they stopped. Footfalls. A single set. Just up ahead. She gestured a hand signal for them to split up. Bishop nodded. He went left of the storage racks beyond. Rampling went right.

Bishop crept onward, spying the guard striding away from him. Ideally, he would have a silencer affixed to his Beretta so that he could deliver a soundless death knell. But they were not there to kill. Not if they could help it. Rampling appeared on the other side of the rack, ready to take the other man down.

Then the target shifted in the other direction.

It was up to Bishop, his mind again taking him back to places like Moscow, Havana and East Berlin. He shook himself from the nostalgia and stepped out from the cover of the storage bin at the base of the rack. He closed the distance, little by little, until he was almost on him.

Bishop threw an arm over his shoulder and jerked him backward, sweeping out his leg in a single motion, sending him crashing to the floor with a brutal thud. He landed on top of the guard and slammed his elbow into the man's temple. His eyes rolled, and his neck lolled. At that moment, it was 1975 and the Cold War was back on.

Rampling emerged from the shadows and helped Bishop to his feet, checking out his handiwork. "You've still got it."

Bishop grunted and motioned onward. They leveled their guns all the way to the door, which Erdem had instructed them to head toward in the pre-op briefing. Rampling took point, and Bishop covered the rear. At the top of a short corridor, another section opened up. At one end was a metal staircase to the upper level, and down the other the hardware of the facility.

Hundreds of cables dangled like veins, linking the operation above to the necessary equipment below. It almost gave the warehouse an organic feeling, as if stepping into the brain of a giant sleeping machine.

They continued, wary of getting caught in the labyrinth by the unaccounted guards. At another tall tower of storage racks they came to a halt, a faint rustling sound materializing from the other side through the drone of the machinery.

Rampling checked around the corner and turned to Bishop with a smile. "Come on."

Bishop trailed her to find the Wong brothers at work, their rifles slung over their shoulders, hauling two unconscious guards into a storage bin.

Bishop did the math. "That's all of them."

"Do we get paid extra for taking most of them out for you?" Trent asked.

Bishop patted him on the shoulder and passed them by. "Come on, we've still got plenty to do."

He made a beeline for the server aisle and stepped through the gauntlet, the noise of the incessant cooling fans and humming electronics almost deafening him on entry. They stood like black monoliths. Tall. Proud. Holding more secrets than anyone could imagine.

Erdem's map had been clear. He walked to the fifth one on the right side, the outer casing indistinguishable to the others around it. He put his hand on it, and the server's heat pulsed through him.

A sudden burst of footsteps echoed beyond the server banks, followed by the sound of guns being cocked and readied. He spun and rushed over to Rampling and the Wongs who were preparing themselves. From the top of the stairs, a team of at least ten guards appeared.

They were not hackers; instead, the group was armed

with assault rifles, their sights squarely set on the foursome who had found their way inside the warehouse.

"More guards?" Rampling muttered.

Bishop's thoughts drifted to Erdem. Where was he?

"Dammit!" he cursed. "He *was* the traitor all along!"

33

Nesim Demir nibbled at his kofte as he sat alone on one of Istanbul's most premier rooftop bars and restaurants. The food was brilliant, the view of the city and the skyline even better. Normally, the place was packed. Tonight, however, only a handful of tables were occupied, matching the sparse foot traffic on the streets below. No doubt the news from America had people indoors, unwilling to pry themselves from their TVs.

He could understand that. He was not heartless, but he had his own thing to do. Too many weeks of planning were on the line. It was not his first visit to the bar. In fact, he had been there multiple times in the last month. Was it because of the food? The atmosphere? Not exactly.

Two months earlier, when Demir had been scrolling the local online message boards, he had come across something unexpected. The forum, mostly frequented by teenagers searching for work, was a word-of-mouth hive of information. Most of the discussions centered on which companies were looking to hire, where to go, and when to show up. Mundane stuff, really.

Then he had found something darker. Juicier.

A thread on the working conditions of the various restaurants, cafés, and diners throughout the city. What the facilities were like, how management treated their employees, and what they got paid. It was a different world to what he knew.

He had never been the kind of fifteen-year-old who would rush home after school to knock out his homework so that he could slave away at a part-time job waiting tables, packing shelves, or serving at a cash register. He did not need grades to prove his worth or require payment from the man.

Demir took another bite of his food and wiped his hand with the napkin next to his plate. He then reached down to the bag at his feet and unzipped it, sliding out his most trusted companion. His laptop. Pushing his food aside, he flipped on the computer and booted up the operating system. A plethora of different applications and programs materialized on the desktop.

To the unsuspecting eye, his screen would have been an indecipherable jumble. It wasn't exactly *Solitaire* or *Minesweeper*. He smirked and placed his fingers on the keyboard, typing a rapid cascade of strokes, the jangle likely an annoyance to the other paying customers.

Continuing to work, he glanced at the waitstaff moving around the other tables. Children. Mid to late teens. The pay was a joke for such a glamorous establishment. The food was not cheap, and the drink prices were among the highest in the city.

From the shadows of the kitchen, another figure appeared. Older, fatter, and walking with an arrogant swagger. He had his top shirt buttons undone, revealing his jet-black chest hair and thick gold chain. What little hair was on his head was slicked across in a desperate comb-over. His name was Murat Yildrum. A decrepit individual.

How did Demir know all of this? The online message boards. When it came to Yildrum's establishment, many things became evident. He paid his staff poorly, treated them badly, and even physically assaulted them, sending them home with gashes and bruises. If they were boys, that was.

Then there were the women. Yildrum's sexual abuse of his female employees was rampant. Why had no one done anything about it? The answer was fear. They were teenagers, worried about their future job prospects.

Online spaces. They were a beautiful thing. The anonymity they offered gave people the freedom to speak the truth without reprisal.

Of course, the anonymity was only an illusion. Demir could dismantle someone's digital persona in minutes. He could tell them all their interests, their family connections, their pet's names, even their passwords.

Demir smiled. With his algorithms, he had gained access. It was almost too easy. Naturally, he could have accomplished all of this in his apartment away from prying eyes. But where was the fun in that? After the weeks of preparation, he wanted to savor the victory.

With the single tap of a button, it would all be done. There would be no fireworks. No applause. No medals pinned on his chest. Just the quiet satisfaction of knowing that he had done it.

Then there was the money.

His gaze remained fixed on Yildrum, the man's smarmy smile playing on his lips as he moved from table to table, hovering around the patrons like a filthy house fly. Demir held back for a moment until he finally decided to do it.

Click.

Nothing changed. At least not yet.

In the coming minutes, Murat Yildrum's life was about to come crashing down. His bank accounts would be drained and business reduced to rubble. Then there was the report to the police. A complete compilation sent to the local authorities on the full extent of his abuses.

And his victims? Those who had suffered at his hand? Within a month, they would receive a check in the mail with their names on it. Where it came from would be anonymous. In truth, it would be Yildrum's money, now lost to him. Small consolation for all the scars. Regardless, Demir was sure they would be appreciative.

Then there was his cut.

Demir would, of course, take a portion for himself, as he always did. For his troubles.

He closed his laptop and finished his meal, tossing the napkin on his plate. With the computer once again stowed in his bag, he stood and paid the server, leaving a hefty tip for the staff. On the way out, he passed Yildrum, their eyes locking one last time.

He traipsed down the stairs and out of the bottom floor exit onto the street. He reached the station in a matter of minutes, hurrying down more steps into the Istanbul Metro, boarding the next train service home. The carriage was threadbare, the passengers sitting in hushed contemplation, either reading or listening to music on their headphones. Demir sat in an available seat and closed his eyes momentarily, allowing a quiet sense of satisfaction to wash over him.

The train lurched to the next station, the rhythm of the

journey matching his mood. Calm and controlled. He counted his stops while it weaved a path through the heart of Istanbul. He only had five until he reached home.

Eventually, he arrived and departed the train, and climbed yet more stairs to the street. He entered the lobby of his apartment building and rode the elevator all the way to the seventh floor. The fresh scent of wax lingered in the air. A clear sign that the janitor had just finished their rounds. The cleanliness was a welcome change from his old digs.

Demir walked to his door and inserted the key into the lock, opening the familiar space shrouded in shadows. He flipped the switch on the panel.

Nothing.

A busted bulb?

He sighed and stepped across the living area, fumbling his way to another switch. With a swipe, the light in his kitchen blinked on.

Something else to add to the shopping list.

Demir returned to the door and closed it, setting his laptop on the dining table. He stifled a yawn and proceeded to the sofa to rest.

The lights winked out again.

His posture stiffened. "What the hell..."

A sudden clatter echoed from behind, and he spun around. From the dim light filtering from the window, a moving shape appeared in the darkness. Before he could brace himself, the figure pounced.

34

Gunfire burst from the weapons of both groups, the clatter of rounds echoing inside the cavernous warehouse. Bishop dove behind a storage bin beyond the entrance of the server room, risking a look at the scrap. The extra guards had materialized, flooding from the upper level without warning, quickly taking cover at any barricade they could to launch their assault.

As bullets flew, Bishop's mind raced. Someone had tipped off the Anca Syndicate. There was no other explanation for the additional security personnel on duty. What was in question was whether Erdem had underrepresented their forces deliberately. It seemed more likely than not.

Bishop cursed under his breath and broke from his cover, getting a shot away at an errant guard straying from the bottom of the staircase. His round hit the mark, sending his target staggering to the floor in a collapsed mess.

He considered the server room behind him. Erdem had ceased to be a factor with their element of surprise gone. All they had to do was tear it out of the wall and hightail it. The challenge was doing so with their lives intact.

A bullet ricocheted off a steel beam above his head, jolting him from his thoughts. He shuffled to Rampling's side. While he did, the rear door to the warehouse opened and another team of guards stormed in, their weapons blazing up the faint light inside the facility.

"We're pinned down here, boss!" She pivoted with him to unload on the new wave of at least half a dozen guards pushing toward their position. With the Wongs holding the other flank, Rampling was indeed correct. They were boxed in. "I think it's time to play our ace in the hole."

Bishop squeezed off more rounds with his Beretta, missing one of their assailants by mere inches. "I believe you're right." He took out his phone and opened it, sending off a quick SMS.

Behind them, the brothers dropped another guard. Unfortunately, the enemy was relentless, their numbers much too great. It would not be long until they were directly on top of them. The pair shifted, taking up alternative positions to consolidate their defense.

The group of four tossed spare ammunition between them to ensure their resistance stayed strong. Suddenly, a new sound broke through the hum of the servers and the blast of the automatic weapons.

A deep, pulsing roar.

Even the guards paused, glancing upward, despite being indoors. Before they realized what was going on, it was already too late.

A barrage of high-caliber bullets ripped through the rear of the warehouse, tearing into the approaching six guards. They were bamboozled. One by one they dropped with an overwhelming firepower none of them saw coming. Bishop crouched low, taking in the carnage, picturing the helicopter outside, its machine guns screaming with Hirsch at the controls painting targets through the outer wall.

His insurance policy had paid off, but it had not solved their problem of the guards continuing to advance from the upper level. He and Rampling turned their attention to those preying on them at the staircase. Trent and Quinn had taken two more down, yet they still outnumbered them.

Bishop fired off another volley from his sidearm, forcing a guard to hide behind a stack of pallets. He emptied his magazine and ejected it, tossing it to the concrete floor.

"Any ideas?" Rampling asked.

Bishop slapped a fresh magazine into his gun and glanced at their dangerous position, their hold on the server room precarious at best. They had an avenue of escape. To take it, though, meant leaving without the server. He spotted the outline of something in the gloomy light to the right of the storage racks, creating a gauntlet between them and the guards. "I might. I'll need you to cover me."

"You got it."

The brothers nodded, too, acknowledging his plan, and they all readied their weapons. Bishop braced himself and prepared to make a break for it. Rampling discharged the first shot. The others followed.

Bishop hoofed it, surging to his feet and dashing across the warehouse. His allies took the brunt of the incoming fire. A barrage shadowed him nonetheless. Somehow he beat the assault, his legs moving faster than he thought possible.

He neared the object in the shadows, and its outline formed the shape of a forklift. Unlike the one outside, this one was fully operational. At least, he hoped it was. He threw himself into the seat, grasping the steering wheel to keep himself from sliding out the other side. Through the faded light, he caught Rampling's gaze. She flashed him a cheeky grin, instantly understanding his game plan.

She tapped the brothers on the shoulders, signaling them to fall back. They followed her order, and Bishop started up the forklift with a twist of the key in the ignition. It buzzed to life, and with a shift of the lever he sent it forward, spinning the wheel to the right. The racks loomed ahead. He aimed for the main support column in the center and increased speed. Not intending to be in the driver's seat when it made contact, he leaped, hoping the landing would not be a rough one.

His hope was in vain. He came down on his shoulder, jarring his arm in the process, the pain searing down the left side of his body. The air in his lungs whooshed out, but it did not stop him from rolling to a halt and flipping over to take in his handiwork.

The forklift's line stayed true, slamming into the central support column of the racks. It collapsed in a chain reaction: pallets and crates crashed down in a thunderous boom. The guards under it were doomed. Too slow to react, they found themselves buried under the weight of wrecked steel and storage.

Bishop attempted to stand, groaning from the agony flaring through him. Nothing was broken, just battered. Rampling rushed over to him to help him upright while the Wongs made sure the enemy had been taken out.

No one survived.

His stunt had worked.

"Where did you learn to think on your feet like that?" Rampling asked with her tongue in cheek.

"From a past life." Bishop winced and stumbled to the

debris. "Tell Trent and Quinn to get the server to the chopper. Hirsch should have landed by now."

"What about us?"

Bishop stared out at the staircase, noticing a path through the carnage. "Erdem."

She arched an eyebrow and nodded, hurrying off to give the brief to the others. They finished scouting the destruction, finding no more threats.

Ramping returned, joining Bishop's side. He took the lead this time, climbing the stairs and stepping over the twisted remnants of the destroyed racks. At the top, the office floor was littered with the stunned faces of the hackers, frozen throughout at their cubicles, no doubt dumfounded at the scale of the private little war which had taken place.

Rampling and Bishop swept the area, their weapons raised. No one spoke or moved, none eager to become collateral damage.

"Erdem!" Bishop yelled out, his voice echoing across the technological haven of computers. "Where is he!"

One hacker pointed to a room. Bishop recognized it from the map Erdem had drawn up. The security office. He pushed on with hobbled yet determined strides. Rampling followed close behind. Bishop slammed the door open. The security supervisor was slumped unconscious in his chair, his mug broken, the coffee dripping off the edge of his desk onto the floor.

Bishop pivoted sideways to find Erdem huddled next to the wall, his knees pulled to his chest and his arms wrapped around them like a naughty child who had been told to sit in the corner and think about what they had done.

"You!" Bishop pointed his gun at him. "Get up!"

Erdem did so slowly, while Bishop wrenched him the rest of the way with his hand clasped around his neck.

"You son of a—"

"I didn't know!" Erdem shot back, almost whimpering. "Not before it was too late." He motioned to the incapacitated guard. "Look! I poisoned him like we agreed. I hacked into the security system and I got you inside the building. Listen to me. I swear, someone else told them you were coming. I didn't rat on you!"

Bishop glanced back at the debilitated guard. Somewhere in the mess of words was the truth. Unfortunately, he did not have the luxury of time to untangle it. Maybe Erdem was being honest. Maybe not. The odds leaned toward deception.

Still, Bishop needed him. For now.

He wrapped his grasp around Erdem's collar and forced him into the waiting hands of Rampling, who stood at the door.

"Let's go, Mr. Erdem," Bishop said. "We're going to see your friend, Demir."

35

ATLANTA, GEORGIA

Tyler cut his way through the flood of passengers streaming from the plane and across the air bridge, merging on the other side in the terminal. Chaos met him beyond. Shouting. Confusion. Fear. Their flight had been one of the countless grounded in the Hartsfield-Jackson International Airport since the FAA had closed down all US airspace.

He cast a sideways glance at the airline staff stationed behind the counter, who, to their credit, had shown up to face the music. Within seconds, they were bombarded by anxious passengers demanding answers. When would they complete their flight? Was there alternate transportation? Were hotels available until the skies reopened?

Right now, none of that mattered to Tyler. He took his phone from his pocket, while putting his carry-on bag at his feet, having found a patch of floor inside the terminal. He activated his phone, and a series of alerts greeted him. Missed calls from several of his contacts. Most were from his parents, likely worried, knowing he was in the air. He scrolled his contact list, finding Kate's number. She had been all he could think about since the pilots had made him aware of the situation in New York.

The World Trade Center. The North Tower.

Tyler had never asked her where her office was inside the building.

Was it on one of the upper floors? Was it where the plane had struck? He hoped it was closer to the bottom and that she had made it out before it had collapsed. Those and many other questions had swirled inside him for hours as his airplane circled Atlanta, waiting for an available slot to land.

He tapped Kate's caller ID and brought the phone to his ear, straining to hear over the noise of the crowd. A dial tone sounded for a moment before her voice filtered through. Relief filled him.

It was, however, short-lived.

"You've called Kate Tyler. I'm not able to answer right now, so please leave a message."

Tyler clenched the device in his hand and attempted to contact her again. Straight to voicemail. The third time produced the same result.

What else could he do?

"Hey, Kate, it's Jack. I need you to call me. Please, just... yeah, call me when you can."

His stomach twisted at the thought of her buried beneath the rubble of the collapsed buildings. What little he had eaten threatened to come up all at once.

He breathed and scrolled to his parents' number. His mom answered straight away, her voice shaking with every syllable spoken. She was relieved to hear his voice, thankful that he had not been on one of the hijacked planes, even if he was in Atlanta and not with them in Miami.

Then Kate's name came up.

Like him, they could not reach her. His mom's voice rose with the stress of the moment. Tyler's dad took the phone from her, and they chatted briefly. He was always the voice of calm, but even his tone wavered. Tyler guaranteed he would do all he could. Even though that was very little, feeling just as useless as them.

When he got off the phone, he tried his brother. A man he had barely spoken to of late. Why, he could not say. Perhaps he hoped the day's events might be enough to break up the radio silence between them. As always, the calls went unanswered. Not even a reply to his messages.

He put the phone away, leaning against the wall next to the window. Beyond, rows of aircraft sat idle on the tarmac. A high-price graveyard mirrored in every city across America.

The collection of noise around him turned into one very loud, unrelenting drone, his fatigue and apprehension brewing to create a hurricane within. Through the din, a few words cut through. He lifted his head, scanning the sea of bodies, where at an opposing gate a group had gathered to watch the news on the mounted wall TV.

Tyler picked up his bag and walked through the crowd, fighting the tide, until he reached the other side. The CNN network showed live images where the Twin Towers of the World Trade Center had once stood. Smoke and debris hung in the air like a wound refusing to close. At the bottom corner, the time ticked just past 11:00 a.m.

The anchors outlined the timeline of the acts of terror,

their voices professional, though heavy with the weight of what they had witnessed during the morning. From the first plane strike to the second, followed by the Pentagon attack and then the collapse of the buildings.

Something else caught Tyler's ear, but he struggled to hear it through the ruckus. Another aircraft? Flight 93? Was that right?

He shook his head, wishing everyone would just quieten down. He looked out at the images of devastation in Manhattan and reached for his phone, trying Kate again. Straight to her voicemail.

He tapped through his contact list, landing on a number he called more than any other. He pressed the green button, and a ringing sound filled his ear.

It rang. And it rang.

Then an answer, *"Jack?"*

Monica Brunelli's voice was like a siren sound in the pandemonium. He pushed back against the throng, desperate for a space of his own. It suffocated him, a relentless surge. Eventually, he made it to the far side.

"Yeah, Monica. It's me!"

"Where are you? Are you okay?"

"I'm fine. I just landed in Atlanta."

"Atlanta?"

"They rerouted me here before I could get to Miami." Tyler paused. "How is it up there?"

"Most of the FBI building has been evacuated. Some of us have had to stay behind to man the command center so that we can coordinate our field offices and liaise with other agencies. It's bedlam, Jack. I've never seen anything like it."

"No one has." Tyler strained his ears to listen to what was

going on in the background in DC. "What's this I hear about a Flight 93?"

"We're only getting preliminary information, but it sounds like the aircraft was forced down in a Pennsylvania field. From what we've been able to gather through the FAA, it appears to have been hijacked like all the others. This time, though, the passengers resisted."

Tyler straightened, his back arching farther upright. "Those brave people."

"We're not sure what the target of the plane was, but we're getting whispers out of NORAD that it may have been heading to DC."

"Finance. Military. Government. Makes sense." Tyler bit his bottom lip. "The planning and effort that must have been involved... Do we have the identity of the hijackers?"

"Not yet."

A hush fell over the conversation, and Tyler closed his eyes.

"Hey, Monica..."

"Yeah."

"It's Kate. She was in the North Tower this morning."

"Oh, Jack." Her pain bled across the line. If the woman could have embraced him, she would have. "*Have you—*"

"I've tried calling. She's not answering her phone."

"I'll contact our people on the ground in New York. I'll make sure they do everything they can."

"Thanks." Tyler grasped his carry-on bag tight. "I've decided to head there myself."

"From Atlanta? But how? I can't imagine they'll open the airspace anytime for a while."

"If not a plane, then train or car. One way or another, I'm

going to find her. After I've done that, I'll return to DC. I don't think the moment's right for a vacation."

Brunelli sighed. *"Be safe out there, Jack."*

"You, too. I'll see you soon."

Tyler clamped his phone shut and turned toward the exit through the mass of stranded passengers. Getting out of the airport would be a mission in itself, let alone the seven-hundred-mile trek to New York City.

36

SAKARYA PLAIN, TURKEY

The helicopter's rotors thrummed in the night sky, the flight from Istanbul a turbulent one with the unexpected gusts in their path. Bishop held on to his harness, while Erdem sat beside him in the passenger cabin. Across from them, Trent Wong and Ramping kept their sidearms low but ready, angled at Erdem just in case he did something stupid.

Few words had been spoken since they had left the warehouse. With the server strapped down, the next phase of the mission was clear to everyone. Soon they would deconstruct the information they had risked it all to obtain.

After leaving Istanbul, Bishop had received an SMS from Mildren telling him he had taken care of everything. At least one of their plans had gone off without a hitch that night.

He glanced at Erdem. A part of him wanted to open the cabin door and toss him into the dark for his treachery. The other part tried to believe he'd had nothing to do with betraying them to the Anca Syndicate. Perhaps he was getting soft in his old age. Once upon a time, he would not have hesitated. But then there was the nagging possibility that Erdem might be telling the truth. If that was the case, how did the hackers know they were coming?

Had they been onto Erdem from the very beginning and made him believe he was still safe after finding out that he had helped Harvey Wulf? And by doing so, set a trap for him, which Bishop and his mercenaries had unwittingly got themselves ensnared in?

He continued to ponder and turned his attention to Rampling, whose eyes were fixated on Bishop. Gone was her whimsical joviality, instead replaced with something else. Concern. Bishop evaded her gaze and looked past her to the cockpit. Hirsch was at the controls, focused on the sky with Quinn Wong next to him. The chopper pilot had done well. It had not been the first time his skill had got him and others out of a tight spot.

Everyone on his team had performed a stellar job. At that moment, it felt like he was back behind his desk at Bureau 61, directing operatives around the globe. And though the position was never an easy one, the familiar sensation was almost comforting. Maybe he had not lost his edge after all.

He took in the view beyond the side window. The lights of Istanbul were long behind them, swallowed by the dark sprawl of agricultural plains beyond the outskirts of the city. The helicopter had charted a course east, and by his internal chronometer, would soon be closing on their landing zone.

Bishop drew a breath, returning his focus inside the cab. A light sheen of sweat formed above his brow. He dabbed it with the back of his hand, finding Rampling still watching him. He could tell she wanted to reach out to him with her more feminine side. Ever the dutiful soldier, she restrained herself, knowing he would not have welcomed it. He despised appearing weak.

The helicopter began its descent, the landscape below slowly coming into focus. Moonlight bathed the contours of the farmland with a natural glow that stretched across the plains. Though Bishop was no expert on the area, even from such a height, he could make out the crops, both corn and rice in abundance.

Structures took shape, some quite impressive, evoking the charm of Tuscan villas. Others were more rustic, little more than log cabins, their wooden facades sagging under the weight of time. Most were likely abandoned to rot with neglect.

Hirsch brought them low over a cornfield, then glided toward a flatter, grassier expanse. Eventually, a house appeared over a slight crest. It was no cabin, but it was still old, the timber weathered and worn by relentless summers. It at least stood firm, much like a nearby barn on the same property. A bit farther away was a lake, its glow almost green.

He tugged at the controls and hovered over the abode, easing the chopper down beside a white van which was already on site. The dense grass absorbed the impact, and Rampling slid the door open. She jumped, offering Bishop a hand. He took it, his legs initially unsteady. It did not take him long to get acquainted again with the hard earth. The pair set off for the dwelling, leaving the others to handle Erdem and the server.

Though Mildren had been using the property as a safe house for his private mercenary operations, there still seemed to be a stale odor hanging in the air. It was the kind of scent that only came with a place long forsaken.

Bishop and Rampling stepped over the battered floorboards, following the light down to the narrow hall to the back room. Bishop crossed the threshold first to find Mildren standing, his broad shoulders filling the space with a threatening menace. On the opposite side of the room sat a figure in a chair with their hands and feet bound with rope, their head covered by a black bag.

Bishop winked at Mildren and approached the seat, yanking the bag away. The gagged individual recoiled, squinting from the light of the dangling bulb overhead. As his vision adjusted, he attempted to speak.

Bishop removed the gag and threw it on the floor with the discarded bag. "Good evening, Mr. Demir."

"Who the hell are you!" he spat, ridding the fabric threads from his tongue with a vicious splutter.

"My name's Bishop."

"Is that supposed to mean something to me?"

His ferocity caught Bishop off guard. He had guts for someone who had been captured from his apartment, thrown in the back of a truck, and for all he knew, was about to be killed. "I guess not."

"If this is about the hack on Yildrum?"

Bishop shook his head. "This has nothing to do with your prior work. At least not in the way you think."

Demir crinkled his brow.

"I've been told your skills with a computer are second to none."

"By who?"

A clatter echoed from the down the hall. Rampling

stepped out of the way, allowing Trent to shove Erdem inside, making him the center of attention.

"Erdem?" Demir's gaze darted between him and Bishop. "What's this about?"

"See!" Erdem said. "If I'd been the one who tipped off the Anca Syndicate, wouldn't I have warned Demir that you were coming after him?"

Bishop frowned. The man had a good point. Right now, however, was not the time to discuss it. "Get him out of here."

Trent took him by the shoulder and dragged him along the floor, the Turk stumbling over the scraped and dented timber.

Bishop pivoted around. "You're here, Demir, because I require your expertise."

Any trace of fear in the man's demeanor evaporated, replaced by an unshakeable arrogance. "I'm listening."

Bishop glanced behind to Rampling, who wheeled the server inside the room and set it down between everyone.

"We believe the plans to the attacks on the United States lay in these hard drives," he said. "I'm told they're heavily encrypted. I want them, and you're going to get them for me."

"What would you want with plans of an attack that's already taken place?" Demir asked.

"My people still don't know who orchestrated it. I've got no doubt there will be plenty of information on there that'll be useful."

"Fair enough, I suppose." Demir struggled against his bindings. "It's going to be difficult without my equipment, though."

Bishop nodded at Mildren. "My colleague here took the liberty of packing all your computers into the van before your trip from Istanbul."

Demir glared at him. "I guess you've thought of everything, haven't you?"

"You'll be assisted with anything you—"

"Wait, a minute. Who said I was going to help you?"

Silence fell over the tiny room.

Bishop crossed his arms. "You want to be compensated, I assume?"

"Well, I'm not doing it for free."

"I'll ensure you're well paid."

"Who's picking up the bill?" Demir asked.

"Me."

"That's not good enough."

"It'll have to be."

Demir shook his head. "Then I don't work."

Bishop held himself back from lunging at him and strangling the man. "Fine, I'll put it to you another way. The US government will provide the money. However, I want to make it perfectly clear, while the cash might come from them, it's me you do this job for."

Demir considered it and nodded. "Music to my ears."

Bishop turned to leave the room.

"One more thing," Demir said.

"What?"

"I'll need Erdem."

"Why?"

"Because I don't trust these jarheads to not break any of my equipment."

Bishop sighed. "Done."

"Then it would seem we have an agreement." Demir smiled and extended his hand, his bindings keeping him firmly restrained.

Bishop snatched Mildren's knife from his belt and cut

through the rope, grasping Demir's hand to shake on it. With the formalities completed, he left the room with Rampling in tow.

"Do you have authorization from the US government to make that deal?" she asked.

Bishop chortled. "I most certainly do not."

37

ATLANTA, GEORGIA

"I'm sorry, sir, but we have no more vehicles available."

Tyler grasped the edge of the counter inside the rental agency. His fingers dug into the worn laminate, while his forearms tightened in frustration. The flustered clerk frowned with an apologetic gaze.

"Are you sure you haven't got something out the back?" he asked. "I'll take an Edsel."

She furrowed her brow, his out-of-place attempt at wit sailing over her head. The question itself was ridiculous anyway. It was not a supermarket. There were not extra cars sitting on some shelf in the rear.

"I apologize," he said. "It's just you're the last agency I've tried, and everyone has told me the same thing."

"Ever since the first planes started landing, we've been overwhelmed by the demand."

"Of course." Tyler peered past her to the TV in the corner. Footage of Ground Zero in New York still played, as haunting now as it had been when he had initially touched down. His thoughts returned to Kate. If he'd had to guess, he must have called her at least twenty times. He had also rung her former roommates who had not been able to get on to her or find her in her new apartment. "Well, thanks for your help anyway."

Tyler left the reception area and passed the massive queue of people who were about to be just as disappointed as him. A sideways glance told him what he already knew. Everyone had somewhere to be. They understood the seriousness of what was unfolding and were aware that no one would be flying out of Atlanta anytime soon.

It was time to try a different tack. With his carry-on over his shoulder and his larger case rolling behind him, Tyler departed the terminal, walking outside to the taxi rank. Another line of drained travelers greeted him, most probably heading to a nearby hotel to hole up until the chaos settled.

Tyler joined it and started doing the math in his head. The fare would be outrageous. So much so that he gave up calculating. How he would pay for it, he did not know. That was a problem for later. To his surprise, the queue moved at a decent pace, each cab filling with passengers and departing into the dense traffic crawling from the terminal.

Beyond the airport, the roads in and out choked with gridlock, the beating sun and Tyler's frustration curdling only to darken his mood. The professional composure he exuded wore thin the more he thought about his sister. She should have been at home in her apartment. He should have been in DC in the operations center, with Monica and the FBI brass coordinating the hunt for the bastards who had done this.

His aggravation boiled over, and he stepped out of the

line, marching to the front, ignoring the chorus of complaints coming his way.

"Hey, what do you think you're doing?"

"Can't you see there's a queue, buddy!"

"Get back to your spot!"

Tyler wheeled his bag to the car's side and tapped on the driver's window. The man promptly slid it down and pushed his sunglasses down his nose.

"Where you headed?" he asked.

"New York," Tyler said.

The driver smirked. But it was not one of amusement. "Yeah, that's going to happen, buddy."

Tyler revealed his FBI badge. "I'm a special agent in Washington. I have to—"

"I don't care if you're the President of the United States. I can't drive you halfway across the country for a fare that I won't get paid for on the return trip."

"Then at least drive me to Charlotte. I'll figure out how to travel the rest of the way from there."

The cabbie shook his head. "No can do. I'm out of hours anyway. I've already done more than I should. Every one of the other drivers will tell you the same. I'd suggest getting out of the way so these good people can get to where they need to go."

With that, he slid the window up and turned his attention to his customers on the other side of the car. Tyler trudged from the road and back onto the sidewalk, where the crowd of swelling passengers continued to stream from the entrance.

The harrowing sense of being stranded gnawed at him. His head thumped, the persistent throb that no amount of liquids had been able to ease. As he considered his next move, the roar of a loud engine filled the air. A bus. A Greyhound bus passed by the taxi rank, departing the airport and pulling out onto the road.

Tyler raised an eyebrow, recalling where he had seen the ticket office. With a renewed sense of purpose, he set off down the exterior of the terminal building. Naturally, the bus terminal was just as busy as everywhere else. Flashing his credentials again, he shoved his way through to the front of the line. There was no time for decorum. Not now.

He slapped his badge on the counter. "I'm Special Agent Jack Tyler. I know it's a lot to ask, but I need to get to New York. Do you have any availability on the next bus out of here?"

The clerk checked her computer, the crack of the keys echoing inside the small booth. "I can book you on the four p.m. departure."

Tyler glanced at his watch. Three hours. Still a long wait, but better than nothing. "I'll take it."

He pulled out his wallet and paid the fare, collecting his ticket and offering the clerk a grateful smile. After stepping away from the counter, a wave of relief washed over him.

Until he remembered...

He slipped out his phone and dialed Kate's number again.

Of course, it went straight through to her voicemail.

"Hey, Kate. Don't worry, I'm coming for you," he said, closing his cell shut and thrusting it back in his pocket.

The question was, would she be there when he arrived?

38

SAKARYA PLAIN, TURKEY

The abyss filled Bishop's view, the darkness surrounding him. He sat on the rickety old chair on the balcony and inhaled the smoke from his cigarette. The Russian tobacco he had grown far too fond of in the past day burned between his fingers, the sparks dancing in the night upon the former farmland property.

"You're not going to make me to beg, are you?"

Bishop glanced up to the sound of approaching footsteps from inside the home. Rampling emerged from the wired door and shut it behind her. The hinges corroded to near uselessness gave no resistance, slamming hard against the timber frame.

He reached for the packet sitting on the rusty steel table and opened it, sliding one out for Rampling. She took it gladly, and he tossed his lighter to her. With a flick of her finger, she lit up her cigarette and drew in a long breath.

"Oh my." She coughed before quickly adjusting to the severity and taste. "I swear I can feel my lungs shrinking."

"Yeah, I wouldn't have too many of those," Bishop said.

"I'll listen to your advice when you take your own."

Bishop grunted in response. She passed him and took a seat next to the table pressed against the exterior wall. The pair sat in silence, the only sound that of them expelling smoke from their cigarettes.

"We haven't got to talk much since you invited me out here for this little outing of yours," Rampling said, breaking the stillness.

"I suppose dodging all that gunfire might have something to do with it."

"Yes, well, if there was one thing I knew to expect when I signed up was that there would be plenty of fireworks."

"You wouldn't have had it any other way."

"You've got that right." Rampling chuckled. "How are you feeling anyway?"

Bishop was taken aback by the question. When she had worked for him as an operative at Bureau 61, their relationship had been strictly professional. Such questions had no place in that realm. Things were different now. He was no longer her boss. And she was older. Gone was the fearless, headstrong twenty-something-year-old who knew she could take on the world and win. Now, replaced with someone just as confident, but with a sharper edge, her cerebral side more pronounced.

"I've seen the worst attack on American soil since Pearl Harbor. Thousands of innocent people have died, and by the time this is over, America will probably be at war."

Rampling puffed a small haze of smoke between them. "I

didn't ask for a pulse of the nation. I wanted to know how *you* are."

"I'm not sure what you're getting at—"

"I saw you on that helicopter, holding on as if your life depended on it. It made me think of Libya. Remember when we flew over Tripoli? You told me choppers felt like a second home since Vietnam after practically living aboard them. Tonight, that didn't appear to the case."

Rampling was too smart for her own good. It was exactly what he had feared when he had left Anchorage. For eight years, he had been alone. Well, mostly. And now in the big wide world, he was forced to rely on the interpersonal skills he had all but forgotten.

He tapped some ash in a grimy mug he had found in the safe house's kitchen. "I'm not sure what you want me to tell you."

"I can see you're hurting, boss. That much is certain. The others have noticed it, too. They're just too macho to say anything."

"Perhaps they know well enough to mind their own business."

"You're probably right." She nodded. "Unluckily for you, I'm not like them. This is the twenty-first century. We talk about our feelings now."

A shudder ran down Bishop's spine at the thought.

Rampling leaned closer to him across the battered table, its legs groaning from the shift in weight. "I know when you recruited me in '89, it wasn't because you needed another killing machine. You wanted someone who could take the enemy apart on a personal level."

"Of course. But I paid you to dissect them, not me."

She shrugged. "Force of habit."

"I hope your other skills haven't gone to waste since we stopped working together."

"Now you're changing the subject."

Bishop evaded her gaze and enjoyed more of his cigarette. He toyed with the packet—another tell she would likely pick up on. He placed it back on the table and let his hand drop to his lap.

"Perhaps we could talk about what you've been up to since you left Bureau 61," she said.

He rolled his eyes. "I didn't ask you on this mission as a therapist."

"Who said anything about a therapist? We're just talking."

Bishop pressed his fingers to his temple, the cigarette remaining firmly wedged between them. His thoughts drifted beyond the fields of Turkey, back to the falling snow of Alaska. He could see his boot prints trailing through the white blanket covering his riverside property. He smelled it, too. Damp and clean. The gust of the trees wafting a stiff breeze over his home. His shoulders sank at the memory of the old paper birch. Its leaves long since fallen, and winter having taken possession of the land.

"Boss?"

He snapped out of his reverie, the Alaskan landscape fading into a mist, once more finding himself in the darkness of Mildren's safe house. Rampling watched on, the concern from the helicopter again etched across her face.

"I..."

Before he could say anything else, footsteps pounded within the house, getting ever closer to them. The door burst open, and Mildren appeared.

"We've got something," he said.

Without another word spoken, Bishop and Rampling stubbed their cigarettes in the mug and hurried indoors, following Mildren down the hallway to the makeshift computer setup which had been assembled by the two Turks.

Demir sat at the desk with a trio of monitors flickering in front of him, while the computer towers hummed beneath him at his feet. Erdem stood behind him, careful not to stand on the many cables sprawled along the floor, connecting the setup to the server. Both turned as the others entered.

"What have you got for me?" Bishop asked.

Demir ushered him closer with a wave. "I've managed to break down all the encryption sequences."

Everyone squeezed into the room and peered over the man's shoulder.

Bishop shoved Erdem aside to see what they had found. "And?"

"It's all here." The arrogance Demir had displayed earlier had disappeared. His joviality had suddenly taken a turn into something much darker.

On the screen, he pulled up flight manifests, addresses of safe houses on US soil, financial records, passport details, flight training information. Bishop did his best to process the flood of data while each line and image scrolled by.

The names of the hijackers were all in Arabic. None were familiar to Bishop. However, there was a word that appeared constantly that stood out in the data collected by the Anca Syndicate.

"Al-Qaeda..." Bishop muttered. He knew them well. A terrorist organization formed out of the ashes of the Soviet-Afghan War. Though they were only in their infancy when Bureau 61 was operational, in the years since they had claimed responsibility for the bombings of the US Embassy in Nairobi in '98, and the attack on the *USS Cole* just last year.

"I should've known. This has Bin Laden's fingerprints all over it." Bishop locked his fingers together, resisting the urge for another cigarette. "This is comprehensive."

Demir nodded. "The assaults on the World Trade Center and the Pentagon—"

"What about the plane that went down in Pennsylvania?" Rampling asked. "It obviously had a target of its own."

Demir swiped across the screen with his mouse and brought up more intel, most of it in Arabic, but some translated into English. "They were going for the White House."

The room fell silent, heavy with the reality of their discovery. Bishop closed his eyes and leaned against the back wall. If he had been in private, he likely would have berated himself for not getting to Wulf sooner.

"I know it seems like the perfect time to feel sorry for yourselves," Erdem said, his confidence restored since being freed from his chains. "But there's something else you need to see."

Bishop opened his eyes. "What?"

39

LANGLEY, VIRGINIA

The time ticked past 6:00 p.m. Phibbs had not eaten since breakfast. The only fuel he'd had was coffee. Far too much of it. He had already told Nicole he would not be home for dinner. When she had asked when he might be back, he could not give her a definite answer.

Perched on the edge of the conference table, he gazed at the massive screen affixed on the far wall of the CIA operations center. Intel streamed in from all over the world, the blur of words having become a haze. His tie lay next to his side; he had ditched it while loosening his shirt's top button much earlier in the afternoon.

Everyone appeared just as disheveled as he felt, their attire ruffled and eyes hollow. At no time in modern history had the United States experienced a day such as this. On the various TV feeds, the news ran nonstop. Talking heads analyzed every detail of what had happened, and experts offered speculation as the coverage continuously replayed old vision and showed new footage as it became available.

Each time it repeated, the wail of New York's emergency services' sirens rang like a bell in his head. Not only had many lost their lives who called the Twin Towers their office, but also the ones who had gone in to save them. Though the final toll had yet to be counted, there was little doubt that when the dust settled, the dead would number in the thousands.

For the moment, a calm descended over the room. While his analysts worked minute to minute trying to unravel details of the attacks, Phibbs pored over their reports and fielded calls from his contemporaries at the NSA and the FBI. He had spoken with the Secretary of Defense and even the Vice President. The conversation with those higher in the chain had gone as he had expected. Tense and far from pleasant.

"Sir, would you like another coffee?"

He snapped from his daze. One of the admin staff stood before him with a mug in her hand. She had only started two weeks ago, and he had forgotten her name already.

"That'd be good. Thank you."

He took it from her grasp, and she moved on, offering a cup to his deputy director. Rivers politely waved her away and picked up a phone next to a nearby analyst. The man had done a fantastic job under the circumstances. Perhaps, sooner rather than later, he would be the one sitting in Phibbs's chair.

He thought back to the discussion he'd had with Senator Brent at breakfast. Just nine hours earlier, the notion of walking away from this seemed unthinkable. Maybe the advice had been sound after all. Like it or not, there was a real chance it would not be Phibbs making the decision for himself when the vultures came for him.

He lifted his mug to take a sip of his coffee when a buzz vibrated behind him. He glanced over his shoulder where his cell sat plugged into the charger at the power outlet. The official line to his office had rung off the hook all day. His personal phone had at least remained relatively dormant, his contacts having the decency to know that now was not the time to reach him.

Phibbs yanked the cord from the port. No caller ID. He recalled the last instance he had received such a call. With a quick flick, he opened the cell.

"Hello."

"This is Bishop."

"John..." Phibbs walked from the room, making his way to his office. "I hope you haven't called me to tell me you told me so."

"You know me better than that."

Phibbs frowned. Whatever Bishop was, he was not vindictive. "Where are you?"

"Turkey."

Phibbs closed the door and went over to his chair. "And here I was thinking you were still in Italy."

"I see you've been talking to Teresa Abella."

Phibbs sat down. "She passed on everything to us you wanted her to. Seems like you've got yourself into a bit of a wild goose chase over there. Unfortunately, we haven't been able to do much in the way of digging into Erik Olsson's past. Our resources have been stretched rather thin, as you can imagine."

"He's irrelevant now anyway." Bishop took a breath. *"I've found it, Phibbs."*

"Oh?"

"*All of it. The whole box and dice. Harvey Wulf was right. He obtained the information from a hacking group in Istanbul. They call themselves the Anca Syndicate. They specialize in hacking assets in the Middle East. When Wulf got out of there with some of their goods, he discovered the plans to the attacks. While what he had was destroyed, I managed to track the original source.*"

Phibbs sensed what a potential game changer this was. "Who did it, John?"

"*Al-Qaeda.*"

Phibbs closed his eyes. Their suspicions had been right. The terrorist front's name had surfaced too often in recent years, and had only got bolder with the success of their latest attacks. But to have accomplished something of such magnitude was beyond anything their intel had prepared them for.

"*I'm sending you everything I have. It should appear on your computer any second now.*"

"My computer?" Phibbs furrowed his brow and shifted his mouse to wake up his desktop monitor. As promised, a data packet transmitted directly to him. "How are you doing this—"

"I have my ways," Bishop continued. "*Listen, Phibbs, this is nothing short of the declaration of holy war. There were nineteen hijackers, all tied to Al-Qaeda. Some are from a terrorist cell out of Hamburg, Germany. It's all there. I'm sure your people are going to have a hell of a time sorting through it.*"

Phibbs opened the first of the files. One by one, the faces of the hijackers filled the screen. He stared into their eyes. They looked like ordinary men. Behind the facade, however, was something else. Hatred. Cold and calculated.

He took note of the targets, the planning involved, the web of connections from the Middle East to the United States and the various terror cells scattered across the world. Buried amongst it was the target of the plane downed in Pennsylvania. The White House.

Phibbs leaned back, the scope of what Bishop had uncovered settling over him. It was enough intel to keep his analysts busy for years to come. And he had done it all on his own. Without even needing to be asked. "John, I don't know what to say. You've—"

"*Don't get all mushy with me, Phibbs. My stomach couldn't cope.*"

Phibbs managed a smirk, or at least the closest approximation to one he had mustered all day

"*Listen,*" Bishop went on. "*The fight isn't finished. We might not have managed to stop the first wave, but it doesn't mean we can't prevent the second.*"

Phibbs's attention flicked from the screen, tightening the cell phone in his hand. "What are you talking about, John?"

Bishop took a long, raspy breath. "*There are plans for a fifth attack. This isn't over. Not by a long shot.*"

40

SAKARYA PLAIN, TURKEY

Bishop snapped his phone shut and placed it in his pocket. Now came the waiting game. Beyond the balcony, Mildren's van and Hirsch's helicopter sat looming in the shadows of the exterior lights. Like sentinels in the night, they remained quiet in the darkness, the silence of his surroundings almost overwhelming.

As had often happened in recent days, his thoughts returned to his tenure as the head of Bureau 61. The sleepless nights, the impossible assignments, the burden of sending men and women into the unknown to stop catastrophes before they struck. Now, he was placing that faith in someone else's hands, trusting that their skills could help avert disaster. He hoped Phibbs was up to the task.

He turned to the door, where the muted sounds of the mercenary team spilled from the spartan living area of the safe house. Normally they would have been much more boisterous, the room filled with laughter and good-natured ribbing. Tonight was different, the mood subdued. They recounted stories of past missions. Ones shared together, and others that caught them up on their lives post-Bureau 61.

Bishop imagined similar reflections were taking place all over the United States. Stories had a way of soothing the soul. They reminded people that even at rock bottom, the world was able to heal itself. Would that happen this time? Bishop did not know. What he was certain of: September 11 would go down as a day no one would ever forget. They would remember the exact moment when they switched on their TVs and saw those towers ablaze, the grip of helplessness and fear overwhelming them, along with the terrifying uncertainty of what came next.

In the past, it had been individuals like Bishop who shaped turning points such as these. They were the hard calls only certain people could make when the world teetered on the edge. Suddenly, he felt just as vulnerable as he had when Bureau 61 had been disbanded. He had lost his purpose once again. There was nothing left for him to do.

Or was there?

He opened the door and moved inside the house. Rampling, Hirsch, and the Wong brothers fell silent, looking at him expectantly. He could see the same emotions he carried swirling within them. He nodded to them, an acknowledgment for all that they had done. Rampling, ever the keen observer, studied him that little bit more. She obviously saw something the others had not.

He pushed on down the hallway and stepped into the hacking center haphazardly built from Demir's equipment. Mildren remained standing watch over the pair with an attentive eye as they yanked cables from the ports, unplugged hard drives, and killed power from the outlets.

Bishop stood at the threshold and put his hands on his hips. "And what do you think you're both doing?"

"We're packing," Demir said, coiling some blue ethernet cable. "My work here's complete. Now I'd like to be paid. I hope you've got my money."

"We're not done here."

Demir tossed the cable on the desk. "I did what you asked. We had an agreement."

"And now I'm changing that agreement."

"You can't—"

"I can do whatever I damn well please, Demir." Bishop nodded to Mildren, whose menacing stature filled the room, his finger resting snug against the trigger of his gun. "I hold all the aces here."

Demir glanced at Erdem and then back at Bishop. "What do you want?"

"I need to learn everything about the Anca Syndicate that there is to know."

"Why?"

"Because as far as I'm concerned, they're just as guilty as those who carried out the attack. We know for a fact that they had hacked that information from sources within Al-Qaeda. If they were proper global citizens, they would've handed that intel over to the CIA."

"At the very least made them pay for it, or blackmailed them," Erdem added, his thoughts appearing to align with Bishop's.

"Exactly. They were sitting on a gold mine and did nothing about it. Quite the opposite, in fact. They buried it. When they discovered Harvey Wulf had stolen the intel, they sent an assassin after him to ensure that the information never reached anyone who could do anything about it before it was too late. They even went to the effort of ensuring there were no copies. And when they found one, they destroyed that, too."

Demir's mind appeared to race, his head bobbing at Bishop's reasoning. "You think there's something more to this..."

"Maybe. There's only one way to find out."

"What would you like me to do?"

"To do what Harvey Wulf did." Bishop went over to a monitor and rested a hand on it. "You're going to hack the hackers. You'll work your way into Anca Syndicate's network and find the smoking gun I'm after. We need to know why they were so desperate to keep these plans for themselves."

Demir rubbed his hands together, the earlier glint in his eyes returning, no doubt savoring the thought of another challenge. "Wulf had the advantage of Erdem being on site to help him, paving his path inside the system. We can't do that this time."

Bishop released his grip on the dormant screen. "Back in Istanbul, Erdem claimed you were even better than Wulf. Was he mistaken?"

A sly grin appeared on Demir's lips. "No."

"Then I have to believe there's a way for you to do this remotely."

"It's not impossible..."

"But?"

"But it may cause us some problems."

"What kind of problems?"

Demir paced the room, his mind appearing to formulate a plan. "They'll know I'm doing it."

"The hackers?"

"They'll be able to trace us," Erdem interjected, breaking up the exchange.

Bishop's eyebrows rose at the realization. "And you wouldn't be able to stop them?"

"No," Demir said. "Not if you want me to do what I'll have to."

"In other words, we could have some very unsavory visitors rock up on our doorstep."

Demir nodded.

Bishop mulled over the Turk's explanation. If the Anca Syndicate were as powerful as they seemed, then the guards at the warehouse would be the least of their worries. "Leave that problem to me. Anything else?"

Demir chuckled. "There's always something else."

"Of course. Money." Bishop returned to the door and leaned against the rotting wooden frame. "Do what I ask and I'll ensure you get double what we initially agreed to."

"Make it triple."

Bishop considered it for a moment. "Very well. Get to work, gentlemen."

41

LANGLEY, VIRGINIA

"This is our guy. Omar Al-Tezmi."

Phibbs stood at the head of the conference table, framed by the glow of the wall-sized monitor behind him. Gone was the lulled and despondent atmosphere inside the CIA operations center, the staff within once again focused on the task at hand.

He had ordered all the TVs switched off and temporarily assigned all non-essential personnel to the secondary center, cutting down the noise from earlier. No calls. No chatter. No distraction. The table, surrounded by the CIA's best and brightest, fixed their gazes on the screen where a file photo filled their view.

Like the nineteen hijackers who had been responsible for the previous attacks, Omar Al-Tezmi looked unremarkable. Just another regular Middle Eastern man. His face was blank, his stare unreadable. Bishop's intel, however, revealed a much different story.

"Five attacks. Al-Qaeda has planned five for September 11. Three have been already been carried out to maximum effect. One was thwarted, thanks to the courageous men and women of Flight 93. Preventing the fifth...is on us." Phibbs clicked a button on the remote in his hand, minimizing the photo and revealing a page of translated text. "Al-Tezmi arrived in Atlanta twelve months ago. Within a week he was working as a busboy in a downtown restaurant. From everything we've been able to pull together, it appears that this op will be a solo job."

A phone rang on the side of the room. Rivers got up from his seat and hurried over to answer it.

Phibbs clicked to the next slide, continuing the presentation, revealing an overhead map of the Hartsfield-Jackson International Airport. "Al-Qaeda counted on the FAA grounding our flights after the first attacks. And in doing so knew that passengers would be stranded at various locations, thousands of miles away from their destination. So, what better target than the biggest aviation center in the continental United States?"

He advanced to another slide of the roads in and out of the airport, including restricted routes closed to civilian vehicles. "This is where Al-Tezmi plans to enter." He pointed to a service road heading for a runway. "According to the intel, the terminal is the primary target. If he can't reach it for whatever reason, his fallback is the air traffic control tower."

Phibbs took a step forward and hunched over the table, gazing into the eyes of his team at their level. "Whichever way he plays it, the outcome is catastrophic. If he hits the terminal, we'd be looking at mass casualties. If he takes out the tower, we lose our ability to manage the skies across a major stretch of the Southeastern United States." He stood upright. "Mr. Burfoot. How's the evacuation coming?"

"I spoke with our liaison at FBI operations five minutes ago," the man said, scanning the notes in front of him. "They're coordinating with the Atlanta Police Department to begin the evac. All passengers on site, and non-essential personal are being shipped out as we speak. They're being assisted by the local bus companies and have even pulled school buses to speed up the process."

"Good. And the roadblock?"

"Every road surrounding the airport has been locked down except for the one required for the evac. The National Guard is working with the APD to take care of it. If this Omar Al-Tezmi tries anything, he's in for a rude shock."

"Which brings us to the mode of destruction." Phibbs stepped back to the screen and pressed the remote, bringing up a schematic of a semi-truck. "It seems he's got his hands on a motherlode of ammonium nitrate."

"I've been in contact with several agricultural firms. All have done inventories for us," Klisters interjected from the other side of the table. "Sure enough, one has about ten thousand pounds missing. They've audited their manifests, and it turns out over the past nine months, ammonium nitrate has been gradually going unaccounted for in multiple warehouses. It would appear some crafty accounting has taken place to hide the theft."

"That's what we're searching for, people, a semi-truck full of ANFO," Phibbs continued. "Just because we've locked down the airport doesn't mean we should let our guard down. If he detonates this anywhere, he'll make the Oklahoma Bombing look like a picnic. Burfoot, tell me what the Feds and the APD are doing to ensure every government building within in the Atlanta Metro area is prepared for the worst."

The man nodded. "Everyone's aware of the situation, with personnel stationed where possible. All government officials, including the mayoral team, are being evacuated from their homes and moved to safety. The APD have called in the state police for backup, and the Atlanta branch of the FBI is on the hunt for any suspicious vehicles. Every truck entering the city will be searched before it's allowed through."

"Excellent."

"Sir!" Rivers popped his head up from his phone call. "The Feds are sending a team into Omar Al-Tezmi's residence. We've got live audio."

"Let's hear it."

Rivers tapped the keyboard at his fingertips, and the speakers in the ceiling of the operations center crackled, filling the room with a buzz of static.

"We're in position. Breach in three, two, one. Go!"

A door closed, and a clatter of boots stormed across wooden floorboards.

"Clear right!" a voice said.

"Clear left!" shouted another.

More footsteps bounded inside the home.

"The living room's clear!"

"So's the kitchen! Moving up the stairs!"

Doors and cupboards banged opened, slamming against drywall. *"The bedroom's clear. No sign of Al-Tezmi."*

More doors thudded. *"I'm in the bathroom. All clear, too... Wait!"*

"What is it?"

"Can you hear that?"

"What?"

"A phone ringing. It's coming from next door. It hasn't stopped since we arrived."

Phibbs ruffled his brow, mirroring the others at the table.

"Let's move!"

Hurried footfalls went back down the stairs and across the lawn to the neighbor's house. The ringing landline phone became clearer.

"Perhaps someone just isn't at home," Rivers muttered, Phibbs having thought the same thing.

"I have blood here!" came the call across the transmission. *"Under the door!"*

"Breach now!"

The door banged open.

"I've got a body here!"

Phibbs glanced over at his deputy director, feeling slightly embarrassed for going against the instincts of those with boots on the ground.

"Civilian. Male. Appears to be a chest wound," the man informed everyone. *"Caucasian. Mid-fifties."*

"Any sign of a bomb? Are they wearing a vest?"

"Negative. Appears to be a good old-fashioned homicide."

Everyone in the CIA operations center leaned in their chairs, catching the exchange of the FBI team on the ground, relaying updates to their command. Eventually, Phibbs signaled for Rivers to cut the transmission. He had heard enough. Their person of interest was not at home. Could the neighbor be linked to Al-Tezmi? Potentially.

Phibbs decided it would be up to those in the field to determine. It was an anomaly compared to what was currently on their plate. They had one individual to stop, and that was Omar Al-Tezmi.

"All right, people, our target is still out there," he

announced, his voice cutting through the brief stir of conversation. "We all know our roles. We're to continue liaising with the domestic agencies and the Atlanta Police Department. I want us to keep poring across the intel John Bishop has brought us to see if there's anything we can dig up that might help us take Al-Tezmi down. We need that truck."

The team rose from their chairs in near unison and dispersed, some taking their posts at the phone and computer banks, others heading to the outer offices.

Rivers approached Phibbs and darted his eyes sideways at those around them. "I hope we get this right. If we don't, we'll be out of here on our asses."

Phibbs snorted. "That's if we're not already."

42

INTERSTATE-85, GEORGIA

Tyler drifted in and out of an uneasy sleep. With the fall of night having come and gone, the switched-off cabin lights plunged the Greyhound bus interior into darkness. The only illumination came from the headlights of cars traveling the other way, their ghostly flares flickering over everyone's faces.

He peeled his cheek from the glass, the harsh bump in the highway pulling him from his micro-nap. Stretching his neck and back muscles offered little relief from the cramped position. He had thought the window seat was a win at first. But it came at a cost. The man next to him was heavyset, his bulk spilling over the armrest onto his side.

Tyler shifted as much as he could, trying to claim some more room. It was in vain, the lack of legroom making his situation laughable at best. He straightened and scanned the rest of the bus from front to back. It was quiet, those around him either asleep or staring blankly through the windshield past the driver at the void ahead.

Most had headphones in their ears, lost in their music or perhaps tuning in to a local AM station, clinging to what news they could find to keep them in sync with the outside world. One thing united them. They were exhausted. The day had been one that no one would forget. And with the bus bound for New York, chances were everyone on board had been touched by it in some way.

His hand unconsciously slid into his pocket, the maneuver an awkward one considering the tight space. The man beside him glanced at him, clearly noticing the stray fingers. When he saw Tyler was only reaching for his phone, he looked away. Tyler flipped the cell open and inspected the glowing screen. The battery was a tad above fifty percent. It was a good thing he had charged it before leaving the airport.

It brought up the series of calls made. He had spoken to Monica Brunelli again when he had left Atlanta and also had another conversation with his parents, telling them he was on his way to New York.

The bus peeled off the interstate and descended a long offramp. For a moment, Tyler tensed, wondering what was happening. Then he remembered the driver's announcement that there would be a toilet stop about two and a half hours into the trip. He checked his watch. Sure enough, it was 6:27 p.m. Right on schedule. The green signs with Lavonia plastered on them pointed the way.

In the opposite direction, the white and yellow glare of the oncoming headlights shifted to the strobe of blue and red. The vehicles closed, their shapes sharpening into police cruisers. Everyone inside the bus rose, a ripple of unease permeating throughout, still twitching from the harsh reality of what had taken place that morning. Tyler counted them as they passed. One. Two. Three.

The bus rumbled on until it came to a halt in the small town's main street between a rest stop and a diner. The brakes hissed, and the engine cut off. Then the PA crackled, and everyone organized themselves, pulling out their headphones and shuffling in their seats.

"Welcome to Lavonia, ladies and gentlemen," the driver said. "*We'll be stopping here for a short time. Take a few moments to use the bathroom facilities provided. Stretch your legs and have a smoke. You can get a bite to eat and a coffee at the diner over the road. Make sure you're back in fifteen minutes or you might find we'll be gone when you return.*"

One by one, the passengers filed off the bus, their quiet courtesy catching Tyler off guard. He had been on many trips across the country in his time. Usually, there was always someone pushing ahead of others. Not this time. Perhaps another symptom of the day. A wave of guilt washed over him, having done the exact opposite earlier, his lack of decorum jumping those queues very unbecoming.

They all dispersed. Some went for a leak in the restrooms, others lit up their cigarettes, while the rest wandered to the diner in search of comfort food and a drink. Tyler went to the bathroom first, before queuing for a coffee. As he stood, he dialed Kate's number again. Just like every time before, it rang. And rang. Then went to her voicemail.

He sighed and put the cell away. Another police cruiser raced past, its red and blue lights streaking in the night. It followed the same route as the others, heading south onto the interstate.

Tyler narrowed his eyes. Suddenly, a fifth police vehicle approached. This time, however, there were no lights. They sped into the parking lot and screeched to a standstill. Tyler got a good look at the markings. The Georgia State Patrol.

The driver and passenger doors flew open, and an officer burst out from each side. They marched to the front of the line and grabbed coffees from the server, evidently having pre-ordered them by phone at the station house.

Tyler broke from the queue and intercepted them before they could return to their car. "Sorry, Officer, a moment if I may?"

The younger one appeared ready to suggest he take a hike, clearly in too much of a hurry to answer any questions. Tyler flashed him his FBI badge, stopping the attitude in its tracks.

"I'm Special Agent Jack Tyler, based out of DC. Can you tell me what's going on?"

The officers glanced at each other before the most senior one stepped forward. "All state units have been given orders to head to Atlanta."

"Why? What's happened?"

"Nothing yet. From what we've been told, we're to assist in preventing a potential terrorist attack on the Hartsfield-Jackson Airport."

"The airport? I was just there."

"They're evacuating it now. But they need backup throughout the city to lock down all the other vital buildings and infrastructure."

Tyler glanced at the bus, and beyond to New York, waiting at the end of the journey. He thought of Kate. Then of his parents. Guilt swelled inside him. His sister was one person. His blood. But what if this was the beginning of something larger? The potential devastation caused by another terrorist attack was incalculable.

Would his mother ever forgive him for turning around? Could he ever forgive himself?

"We've got to go," the older officer said.

Tyler held up his hand. "You wouldn't be able to give me a lift, would you?"

"To Atlanta?" The cop checked the information board above the bus windshield. "Aren't you going to New York?"

"Not anymore."

The officer looked at his offsider, and they shrugged at each other.

"Have you got any bags?" the younger cop asked.

Tyler found the bus driver at the diner and convinced him to help him with his luggage. Retrieving the items from the compartment, he jogged to the police cruiser and tossed them in the trunk, sliding into the rear seat.

With the lights flashing, they flew out of the parking lot and sped onto the I-85 back the way Tyler had come. He pulled out his phone and tried Brunelli's number. Just as he thought she was not going to answer, a faint voice filtered through from the other end.

"Jack?"

"Yeah, Monica, it's me."

The background noise was fierce, even more so than earlier. Phones rang incessantly, and people raised their voices in a chaotic cacophony. It sounded like a war room.

Tyler cut straight to the point. "What's going on in Atlanta?"

43

SAKARYA PLAIN, TURKEY

Demir and Erdem chattered with each other in their native tongue. Though Bishop could speak more than just English, he was proficient at some languages better than others. Turkish was not one of them. Their fingers flew across their keyboards, line upon line of code flickering on the trio of monitors. One thing was evident. They were throwing everything they had into breaching the Anca Syndicate.

Trent Wong stood watch over them, the glow of the screens casting shadows over his face. Bishop gave him a subtle nod, a silent command to tell him to stay alert. He exited and walked down the hallway. The living area, once occupied by the others, was now empty, the old worn furniture idle again to collect the falling dust.

His team had migrated to the balcony. Bishop made his way through the door to find everyone but Quinn Wong puffing away on cigarettes. The man and his brother were a rare exception among the group who wore the vice as badges of honor.

Bishop inhaled the acrid secondary smoke hanging in the air. As he approached, their conversation came to a halt. Like soldiers on a battlefield, they waited, ready to receive their next orders.

"Erdem and Demir have made it clear that, given what they're attempting, it's likely the Anca Syndicate will trace their activities to this location. If the work takes as long as I suspect, there's a real chance we'll end up with company out here. What that entails, I'm not sure."

Everyone kept their gazes fixed on him, not a single glance straying.

"Mildren has been good enough to allow them to operate here. He's aware of what might come. I need to know where the rest of you stand. You came to Istanbul to complete a job, and you did that. I can't ask more of you. If they come at us with serious resources, we'll find ourselves in a full-scale siege situation. If anybody would like to back out now, I won't think any less of you."

The hush continued across the balcony, broken only by the faint chorus of insects chirping in the fields around the safe house.

Rampling took a deep drag of her cigarette and exhaled. "None of us are going anywhere until the job's done."

Bishop studied the four people before him, a determination seared into their faces. They were hardened warriors who were unable to take a backward step. He should have expected as much.

"Very well. Then it's time to get organized." Bishop turned to Hirsch. "The machine gun on your chopper is a M240H, isn't it?"

He nodded.

"Remove it."

Hirsch raised an eyebrow. "What? Why?"

"Because we have to plan for a hostile force. Your ride in the sky has the potential to be a sitting duck. One RPG and you're out of action. If we're going to win this, it won't be in the air."

Hirsch gave a knowing shrug, then tapped Quinn on the shoulder. The pair headed off for the helicopter parked behind the white van and got to work.

"Mildren, you told me you had some supplies to show me."

The man motioned for Bishop to follow, leading him and Rampling across the field to the barn. In the gentle breeze of the evening, the old timber frame creaked, its bones so frail that it seemed ready to collapse at any moment. Weeds and yellow tufts of grass blanketed the ground, while throughout were the skeletal remains of the stables that had once stood inside, the wood warped and rotted.

There was a loft above their heads and a narrow staircase leading up to it. Though rickety, it would offer a fantastic vantage point to survey the surrounding fields.

As Mildren led them onward, the hard-packed dirt beneath their feet gave way to something more solid. Each step created an echo, the hollow sound rising from below. Bishop glanced at Rampling who had noticed the change of terrain, too.

Mildren stubbed his cigarette and kicked away a layer of soil with his boots, revealing a stainless-steel sheet just below the surface. He walked over to the barn wall and uncoupled an old pulley line. He brought the hook to the center of the plate and slipped it through a fabricated hole. Returning to the wall, he gave the rope a heave, and it snapped taut, yanking the sheet sideways across the ground.

Mildren revealed a massive cache of weaponry underneath. Bishop did not know where to look first. The small arms were neatly assembled to the left. Glocks, various Berettas, and even a few CZ 75s, relics of the Cold War that had seen better days.

He crouched, the worn joints in his knees crunching in his effort to get a closer view of the assault rifles. Among the collection were some modern M4 carbines, along with older Heckler and Koch G3A3s and AK-47s. Beyond were a row of shotguns. Mostly former Soviet and Turkish surplus.

Nearby were crates of grenades stacked. Some were American, gone unused in Desert Storm, others were Soviet F1 lemon grenades, more artifacts from a bygone era. There were also packs of plastic explosives. Their age was questionable, but they would still do the job. Tucked amongst the chaos was a FGM-148 Javelin, an impressive modern RPG.

On the opposite side were two Mosin-Nagant sniper rifles stacked next to combat attire and night-vision gear, all remnants of the Soviet-Afghan conflict. More crates containing every conceivable type of ammunition needed for war were piled high beneath.

Bishop stood, joining Rampling who appeared equally impressed. "What were you planning to do with all of this?"

Mildren shrugged. "My clients have certain needs."

"I can imagine."

Rampling tossed her cigarette to the ground. "So, do you think we have enough here to put up a decent defense?"

"Possibly." Bishop paced around the excavated burrow. As well armed as they now were, they could easily find themselves outmanned. And while the mercenaries under his command were some of the most elite, even the most skilled fighter had their limits.

"Wait! You haven't seen the jewel in the crown." Mildren led them past the cache.

Bishop and Rampling followed, curious as to what else he might have in his possession. They made their way to the corner of the barn where a crude compartment had been built from fresh timber. Palings enclosed each side, the raw wood unpainted. Mildren stepped to the front and unlatched a makeshift door, swinging it open to reveal what lay inside. At first, Bishop struggled to make out the shape within.

More light spilled in, revealing the exterior of the object painted in desert camouflage. There, resting idle, sat another leftover of the Cold War. It crouched low and menacing, a narrow turret jutting forward, housing a 73mm smoothbore cannon. The silhouette was unmistakably Soviet in design.

"Is that a BMP-2?" Rampling asked.

"No, a BMP-1," Bishop corrected her, recognizing the infantry fighting vehicle. "Does the cannon work?"

"No." Mildren shook his head. "The machine gun does, though."

"These were amphibious. Can it still go in the water?"

"There's some rust, but not enough to stop it from going for a swim."

Bishop brushed his hand over the cold steel, the old Russian vehicle a sight to behold. "Good. Let's get ready."

44

ATLANTA, GEORGIA

The lights of the city shimmered on the horizon, the abyss of the interstate yielding to form the greater metropolis of Atlanta in the distance. Tyler had ridden high in the backseat the entire way, his eyes fixed on the road ahead. Though the journey had been much more comfortable than the bus, his mind had been anything but still. His thoughts swirled restlessly, most of them circling to one person. Kate.

Every call continued to go unanswered. Monica continued to request the FBI's help in New York, but due to the scarcity of resources, they lacked the ability to assist. And then there was the call to his mother, informing her he was heading back to Atlanta.

As he had expected, the reception had been frosty. Beneath the tears, however, he had caught a flicker of understating. He had a job to do. At that moment, it was all hands on deck. If he could aid in preventing another attack, that was where he had to be.

Tyler exhaled as the cruiser veered closer to the city, turning off the highway to the airport. The police officers, who had been kind enough to take him along with them, had remained professional, likely wary of saying too much with a Fed in the back seat. Aside from the occasional radio call from their station house, the silence in the car held.

Traffic flowed by them in the opposite direction. Buses mostly. City transit, long-distance coaches, even some yellow school busses. All were filled with people, their faces pressed to the windows, clearly being shuttled to hotels or whatever makeshift location the city could provide.

The police cruiser stormed toward the checkpoint. Every vehicle ahead of them was going through a vigorous inspection with the National Guard in charge of the scene. When they reached the front of the queue, they went through the same process. They had their IDs checked. Then the car itself underwent a bomb detection sweep. Once satisfied, they were waved through.

The road to the arrivals terminal was choked by Atlanta PD vehicles and unmarked black sedans. On the sidewalk leading inside the building, law enforcement officers swarmed the area. They moved throughout, donned in bulletproof vests. FBI agents stood out amongst them, the bold yellow lettering on their backs almost glowing in the artificial lights overhead.

Tyler's unintended escorts found an available spot and pulled into it. The pair got out of the front and released the door for him, allowing him into the stuffy evening air.

"Thanks for the lift." He retrieved his bags from the trunk, and before he knew it, the officers hopped back in their car, resuming their journey to the city, their taillights fading into the night.

As Tyler stepped onto the sidewalk, he paused to get a lay of the land. He pushed on past the last of the passengers boarding buses and went toward the terminal. Uniforms of all kinds moved throughout, including the black fatigues of the National Guard, all the personnel well-armed.

Tyler could not shake the feeling he was out of place, as if he had arrived at a party uninvited. He walked through the doors and headed straight to the storage lockers to stow his bags. The last thing he intended to do was continue lugging his non-essentials when the world was spinning out of control.

With his possessions locked away, he went over to a cluster of FBI agents meandering about. The hum of intermittent conversation crackled over their radios from various areas around the airport. Tyler wasted no time and flashed his badge, breaking up the powwow.

"I'm Special Agent Jack Tyler from the DC office, here to see the SAC. I was told Murray Hagon is already on site."

The agents exchanged a glance, sizing him up, probably wondering what an outsider from so far away was doing there.

One, sporting a thick handlebar moustache, gestured beyond the huddle. "This way."

He followed the agent into a vast space, which would normally serve as an airline operations hub. They passed through a guarded door, flanked by two Atlanta PD officers, into a hectic discord of activity. The regional FBI field office had taken over, making themselves at home. Laptops were sprawled over all the available counters, phones rang off the hook, and several screens with dozens of split views gave those on hand real-time CCTV surveillance of every square inch of the airport.

They approached a person at the heart of the chaos. He was quite tall, thick black hair, and seemingly able to juggle three conversations at once. Tyler and the other FBI agent waited for a moment to get his attention.

"Sir, this is Special Agent Jack Tyler," the other man said. "Apparently from the DC office."

Tyler ignored the subtle jab, instead extending a hand to the SAC. Hagon passed his offsider a folder and grasped Tyler's hand in an almost suffocating grip.

"I wasn't told someone from Washington was joining us." Hagon frowned, as if talking to him was more of a burden than a necessity. "How did you get down here so quickly?"

"I was heading to Miami for a vacation when my flight was canceled in Atlanta. When I found out what was happening here, I thought you might need an extra pair of hands."

"So, you're not here to take command?"

"Not at all. I work in the Behavioral Analysis Unit. I just want to help."

"Very well." Hagon's demeanor shifted, the defensiveness in his voice melting away with the realization his baby was not about to be snatched from him.

"What are we looking at?" Tyler asked. "I assume you've had no sighting of any suspicious semi-trucks near the airport since you began the lockdown."

"No." Hagon shook his head. "Once the barricades went up, traffic came to a halt. As it stands, the last passengers are being bused out. Once they're gone, we should be able to manage any comings and goings with ease."

"What about the city?"

"Checkpoints have been set up throughout. So far,

searches of trucks have revealed nothing out of the ordinary. But that won't stop us until we find him."

"If you find him..."

"What's that?"

"It's likely Omar Al-Tezmi has gone to ground. He'll have noticed the airport has locked down. He'll also be aware the greater Atlanta metro area has a ring of steel around it. So, unless he's feeling particularly daring, I doubt that we'll see that semi-truck on the road. Al-Tezmi will be anything but predictable."

A queue of waiting agents formed beyond them, each holding cell phones or files in their hands, ready to inform Hagon of any developments.

"As you can tell, we're pretty busy here, Agent Tyler," he said, appearing to not want to give his theory any credence. "Perhaps you best resume your vacation—"

Tyler fought back his urge to scowl. It was not the time for some egotistical turf war. "I'm here now, sir. You might as well take advantage of my expertise."

Hagon considered his offer, sweeping the room before setting his eyes on the bank of phones where other agents were fielding calls. "I could use someone to coordinate with DC. You can speak their language, so..."

"Of course." Tyler stepped aside to give Hagon space to work with his staff. While answering phones was below the scope of his normal duties, at least he got to remain in the heat of the action.

45

SAKARYA PLAIN, TURKEY

"How are Trent and Quinn doing in the southern field?"

Bishop leaned into the helicopter while Hirsch completed his handiwork in the cockpit. The mercenary had landed the chopper closer to the boundary of the property near the front gate.

"They should be done within the next twenty minutes," Rampling said, with a binder in one hand and a pen in the other.

"Good." Bishop gestured for the binder, and she passed it to him. He looked over the checklist and the rough aerial sketch of the potential battlefield, displaying the house, the barn, the three access roads, and the small lake tucked beyond the dwelling.

Leaving Hirsch to continue his work, Bishop led Rampling back to the house. They traipsed up the tiny steps to the balcony where the M240H machine gun from the helicopter had been mounted. The weapon was stable, the chamber bristling with ammo, and the belt-fed rounds spilling over the side into stacked crates.

Rampling gave the gun a firm shake. Satisfied, she lingered, gazing out into the darkness, appearing deep in thought.

"What is it?" Bishop asked.

She moved to the house's facade, tapping her fingers against the rotting wood. "If someone does come here and they breach the perimeter, what's to stop them torching the whole place? Like the chopper, we're a sitting duck. One RPG and we got up in flames."

Bishop nodded. "I've already given that some thought."

"And?"

"I don't think they'll hit the house point-blank."

"How do you know?"

"Because they'll want to know exactly what we're doing in there." He motioned inside. "More specifically, what Demir and Erdem are up to. They're diving deep into the Anca Syndicate. And I trust that whatever secrets they unearth will be enough to keep them alive so they can tell them what they've found, perhaps even who they've told."

Rampling puffed out her cheeks. "I hope you're right."

"When am I not?"

The woman chuckled softly, and they stepped inside the house. She tailed Bishop down the hallway to the rear room, where Demir and Erdem remained hard at work. Mildren was back on watch and turned as they entered.

"How's everything coming along?" Bishop walked up behind the pair at their computers. "Any luck getting into the network?"

"We're in. Have been in for a while." Demir hammered at the keys with a speed Bishop had only ever seen Harvey Wulf achieve. "The problem is staying in."

"So, they know then?"

"Oh, they know. Right now, they're putting firewall after firewall up to try and lock us out. While I hold them off, Erdem's taking everything he can."

"Nothing like a good old jailbreak, is there?" Rampling quipped.

Bishop stared at the stream of code racing down the screen, a blur of numbers and commands. While gibberish to him, it was a second language to them. "Have you found anything yet?"

Demir pointed to Erdem's monitor. "There is something that might interest you."

Bishop shifted closer to Erdem and rested a hand on the back of his chair. The younger man brought up a string of files. Names, details, photos. Bishop recognized some of the faces glaring at him from their earlier op at the warehouse. "The hackers?"

Erdem nodded. "Every single one of them."

"How did you get that info?" Rampling asked. "I can't imagine that kind of stuff is just lying around on one of their servers."

"You're right, it isn't. To make matter even more difficult, when we worked together we used nicknames to protect our real identities in the outside world."

"Then how did you assemble this list?"

"I pulled their images from the warehouse's CCTV security system. All of them. I then cross-checked them with the Istanbul Police Department database, getting a facial match.

What you're looking at here are their official driver's licenses. And of course, their real names."

Bishop raised an eyebrow. "You hacked into the local police computers."

"Child's play, even for me."

Bishop wondered if Erdem was trying to atone for his betrayal, or did he genuinely want to help, having been innocent of the events at the warehouse?

"This is the first step to uncovering who controls the Anca Syndicate," Demir said. "Now that we know who the hackers really are, we can deep dive into their bank accounts. I believe once we're in, we'll find a money trail and—"

"Wait a minute," Bishop interjected. "Erdem, didn't you say you were paid in cash?"

Erdem nodded. "I did. But my compensation is chicken feed in comparison. The hackers are making real money. The amount you'd need a truck for. They're likely being paid through legitimate business accounts, maybe several, to mask their activities. The more we dig, the more of the web we'll unravel."

"It'll take some doing." Demir kept his eyes on the monitor. He grabbed a second mouse, and started operating both displays in perfect sync. "The question is, how far do we go? We might end up in places hard to explain, not just to Turkish authorities, but authorities in territories abroad."

Bishop glanced at Rampling and Mildren, the trio used to working in realms they were not welcome. "I'm paying you to get to the bottom of the Anca Syndicate operation. Whatever it takes, do it. I trust you'll cover your tracks sufficiently enough to avoid any trouble."

Demir tossed a mouse aside and returned his attention to the keyboard. "I'll do my best."

Bishop and Rampling left the room and re-entered the dark hallway.

"You're putting a lot of faith in those two, boss," she said.

Bishop leaned against the wall, glancing over his shoulder at the Turks, pondering the risks ahead. "Let's hope it all pays off."

46

ATLANTA, GEORGIA

The night had grown late. Tyler had been awake for nineteen hours, the weight of his lack of sleep clawing at him. The sting of the hangover had long since faded, but with every minute that passed, the fatigue threatened to take hold of him.

Ringing phones inside the makeshift FBI operations center blended into a restless melody as the frantic movement of people around him dissolved into a blur of color. The cold air from the airport AC nipped at his skin, sending a chill throughout his body. Only the caffeine pulsing inside him kept him tethered to the waking world.

He shook his head, trying to steady himself. He paced the room, passing Special Agent in Charge, Hagon, who remained busy with his team of offsiders, constantly bringing him fresh intel as it became available.

He clenched his hands thinking about Kate, refusing to accept the reality that stared him in the face. Not without proof. But what would that proof look like if she had been in her office when the North Tower collapsed? He squeezed his eyes shut, a lump forming at the back of his throat. How many other families out there were enduring the same torment? How many were trying to come to terms with such brutality so close to home?

Since arriving in Atlanta, Tyler had been on the phone with DC, getting the flood of new information from Brunelli at FBI HQ. The hijackers' names, the commandeered flights, the coordination of the attacks. Every detail had been synchronized to near perfection. They had sacrificed their lives so that they could take the lives of others.

To what end?

When everyone processed the loss and grief, America would retaliate. Maybe that was the point. Al-Qaeda wanted war. A holy war.

More death.

More barbarity.

Tyler had believed he had seen it all in his brief career. Now he realized how wrong he had been. Everything was about to radically change. The way people traveled, security in the airline industry, and then there was the paranoia that was bound to follow, creeping into every corner of people's lives.

If something as devastating as today could unfold so easily, the public would demand assurances and guarantees that it would never happen again. What would the government's response be? The very freedoms and liberties the nation was built on would be tested like never before. What would the American people be prepared to sacrifice to ensure their safety?

Tyler opened his eyes, his gaze finding the TVs. Some

were tuned to the mainstream networks, others to cable channels such as CNN and Fox News. All had shifted away from the relentless replays of the morning's attacks, now broadcasting live footage beyond the gates of the Hartsfield-Jackson International Airport.

Word had gotten out.

At least, partially. Most of the network anchors and reporters on the ground were left to speculate about what was actually happening. So far, the authorities had said nothing of substance to any of them. How long it would be until there was a leak, was anyone's guess.

But they could make an educated deduction. The sheer presence of police, FBI agents, and National Guard at the airport, along with beefed-up security throughout the city, spoke volumes. It had become a big waiting game.

For everybody.

"Agent Tyler!"

The voice of an agent he had worked with since he had arrived carried across the operations center, snapping him from his daze. She raised a phone in the air, signaling he had a call. He walked over to her and took the receiver.

"It's Special Agent Brunelli," she said.

With a nod, he thanked her and lifted the receiver to his ear. "Monica."

"Hey, Jack. How you holding up?"

"I'm fine," he lied. "Just trying to make sense of it all here."

"I've been reading the reports coming in from down there. They've stopped hundreds of trucks all over the Atlanta. They've even scoured the depots, making sure every vehicle is accounted for. It doesn't sound like so much as a car has tried to break through the barricades at the airport."

"Omar Al-Tezmi won't come here. I doubt he'll be driving his truck anywhere in the city. He knows we're onto him." He jerked his head to look at the TVs. "Hell, it's all over the news."

"Do you think he's going to hold off?"

Tyler checked his watch, the time ticking just past 9:40 p.m. "Everything has been calculated. If I had to guess, these terrorists would love nothing more than to finish the day with some fireworks."

Brunelli paused for a moment on the other end of the line. *"Then what's Al-Tezmi going to do?"*

"That's the question, isn't it? It's our job to get inside the minds of people like this to figure out what they're thinking." Tyler leaned back against the desk. "Sitting here won't achieve anything, will it?" He was wasting his time. "I've got to go, Monica."

"What—"

Before she finished speaking, Tyler slammed the phone on the cradle and turned. With a quick yank, he pulled the charger cable from the outlet and freed his cell, placing it in his pocket. As usual, Hagon was swamped by his staff. A lot could be said for his micromanagement style, but Tyler was not there to make any slights to his leadership.

Tyler pushed in front of the other agents. "I need a car."

The chatter came to a stop, and Hagon rose his brow. "What for?"

"I'm going to do what I do best. You don't need me answering phones. You don't need me here at all, do you?"

Tyler let the question hang in the air. He had bet Hagon was eager to get rid of him.

"I suppose not." Hagon fished some keys from his pocket.

"Here, take mine. It's parked out front. Press the fob, you'll find it."

Tyler nodded his thanks and made a swift exit. The time had come to do what he was trained to do. To get into the heads of the bad guys.

47

Tyler pulled the car up to the curb of the suburban street. Atlanta PD cruisers lined both sides of the road, while beyond, yellow crime scene tape crisscrossed not only Omar Al-Tezmi's house but also the perimeter of the neighboring property. Tyler switched off the ignition and yanked out the keys, stepping from the vehicle.

The police officers grouped around their cars, tuned in to the constant crackle of radio traffic spilling from inside. Units across the city checked in, confirming their positions and feeding updates to command. Atlanta was not just on alert, it had become a fortress.

Tyler passed by the gathered cops, earning sideways glances from them. He stopped at the perimeter where an officer raised his hand to block his path. Before they could say a word, Tyler took out his badge and showed it to him. They checked it over and nodded, passing him some gloves and shoes covers to enter the scene with.

Tyler ducked under the tape and onto the neatly trimmed lawn, flanked by sparse garden beds. To other neighbors, it was just another house, owned by another man. The past few hours had shattered the illusion. From across the road, curious eyes flicked from behind shifting curtains, the once serene community transformed in an instant.

Tyler hurried up the steps and put on the shoe covers and gloves, entering Al-Tezmi's home. It was quiet. Eerily so. A few forensic examiners moved throughout, dusting surfaces and scouring for clues, bagging anything of interest. Tyler started his own investigation downstairs, scanning the living room, dining area, kitchen, and laundry. It was fastidiously tidy.

There was little in the way of storage, no photos on the walls, and barely any furniture. The absence of possessions made the place easy to keep clean. It felt more like a movie stage than a home. As if no one had ever lived there.

The examiners glanced up from their work while he passed by them, no doubt just recognizing another investigator doing his job. He let them be and climbed the stairs, checking the bathroom and bedrooms. Like the rest of the house, it was bare but functional. Al-Tezmi lived simply. No frills. No indulgences.

Tyler's mind drifted to the man who had called it home for the past year. Somewhere along the way in his native country, his faith had been warped. Instead of embracing the Quran's call to live in peace with others, he had used the text to allow himself to be turned into an instrument of evil.

Tyler stood in his bedroom, recalling the image of Omar Al-Tezmi faxed down from DC. He was only twenty years old. His brain not even fully formed. Malleable. Just like all those before him. Shaped and twisted into a weapon.

He stayed in the house, searching for something that might hint at Al-Tezmi's next move. Or at the very least, his current whereabouts. He had left no clues. The man well trained in the art of the game. Still, everyone made mistakes. Even those who were careful.

Tyler turned to the window and eyed the neighbor's house. It had a similar two-story build, perhaps slightly bigger.

He went back downstairs and walked by the examiners, returning outside. He crossed the lawn and ducked under another stretched reel of crime scene tape, entering the other front yard. More forensic techs were coming and going, lugging their kit bags and evidence from the homicide. Tyler tossed the old gloves and shoe covers and asked for a fresh set. He took the new ones and pressed on.

The house was messier than Omar Al-Tezmi's. It felt lived-in, the air carrying the unmistakable scent of cats. Fur, litter, kibble. The owner's body lay sprawled on the floor near the door, his blood having spattered over the threshold outside.

A plainclothes officer stood over the corpse, notepad in hand. He was seasoned, closer to Tyler's father's age than Tyler himself. He produced his credentials and viewed the scene.

"I'm Special Agent Jack Tyler. Behavioral Analysis Unit."

The man eyed the badge with a crooked brow. "Detective Thomas Lambert. Atlanta PD. I wasn't aware the FBI was—"

"I'm not here to take over your investigation. I'm just observing. What can you tell me about the homicide?"

Like Burfoot back at the airport, the detective appeared to exhale. Tyler recognized the guarded expression. Territorial. He had seen it in law enforcement officers all over the country when he had worked in regional field offices before his move to DC. He did not blame them. If he were in their shoes, he would want to protect his work, too.

Lambert flicked his notepad closed. "Oliver Nial. Fifty-six years old. A single knife wound across the neck was all it took."

Tyler stepped over the pool of blood surrounding the corpse, which was pressed face-first into the wooden floorboards. "Any sign of a struggle?"

"There's a lot of bruising."

"Forced entry?"

"No. He appears to have opened the door willingly."

"Like he was just greeting a neighbor?"

"Exactly."

Tyler nodded. "Have you found the smoking gun that the murderer was Omar Al-Tezmi?"

"My people are checking over the prints left behind as we speak. It shouldn't be long until we have conclusive evidence."

The detective obviously had the same thought as he did. It was too much of a coincidence that the dead neighbor lived next door to a potential terrorist with a link to the nineteen hijackers from earlier in the day.

But why would he kill him? What purpose did it serve?

"How long has he been deceased?" Tyler asked.

"Anywhere between twenty-four to thirty hours," Lambert said.

"Really? So, the homicide took place yesterday. Either in the afternoon or evening."

"That's what the examiners believe."

Tyler brushed his chin. "Do you mind if I look around, Detective? I'll make sure not to get in the way."

"Knock yourself out."

"Thank you." Tyler began a sweep of the house, mirroring the same routine as he had followed next door. Downstairs first, then up. Books and railway memorabilia filled the cupboards and shelves. It gave the home a distinct personality that Al-Tezmi's lacked.

He checked the bathroom. It could have used a good clean, the buildup of mold along the tiles hard to ignore. He then moved to Nial's bedroom. It was even messier. The bed was unmade, and his clothes spilled out of an overflowing laundry basket.

Tyler circled the bed and approached the closet. He yanked it wide open to peer inside. It was more organized than the other parts of the room. The left side was filled with sweaters, pants, shirts and polos. The other was lined with a row of identical tan-colored overalls. He reached for one and pulled it from the hanger. Two patches adorned the chest. His name, Oliver, and the corporate logo. The Squeaky Cleaning Company.

Tyler pursed his lips. He took out his phone and dialed. The line barely rang before it was picked up.

"*Hello, Jack,*" Brunelli said. "*What's—*"

"I want you to do some checking for me, Monica."

She was a professional like him, not taking the bluntness in his tone personally. "*Shoot.*"

"Oliver Nial, our homicide victim, worked for The Squeaky Cleaning Company. I need a list of their contracts and every location he serviced."

"*I'm on it.*"

Within seconds, she began making a series of other calls to the corporate entity that was The Squeaky Cleaning Company. Management. Payroll. Supervisory. Tyler waited, the hum of activity filtering across the line. Papers shuffled in the background. Voice blurred.

Finally, she came back on.

"Jack?"

"Yeah," he said.

"The business holds contracts in over thirty locations throughout the Atlanta metro area."

"And Nial?"

"He was a janitor. He worked at three of them. Two shopping centers and..."

"And?"

Brunelli paused for the slightest of moments. *"The CNN Center."*

Tyler lowered the phone, his eyes straightening on the uniform and his hands ruffling it in his grasp. "Oh my God..."

48

SAKARYA PLAIN, TURKEY

"Two left."

Bishop offered Rampling his packet of cigarettes, and she gladly took one without hesitation. He claimed the last for himself and scrunched the empty pack, tossing it at his feet. He struck a flame, sparking the end, and handed the lighter to his colleague. Within seconds, smoke curled between them.

Silence.

A hush before the storm, perhaps.

Bishop rested against the back wall of the safe house, his arms crossed, scanning the fields beyond. Rampling sat beside him. They had barricaded the perimeter of the dwelling with whatever they could salvage. Upturned furniture, rusted forty-two-gallon barrels, piles of bricks from the barn, even planks of wood stripped from the house itself, leaving it a skeletal husk.

Rampling adjusted her night-vision goggles. The

predawn darkness had only deepened with the moon slipping behind the trees, as if retreating from the battlefield. Perhaps it knew something they did not. Bishop joined her, scouting the edge of the property for any potential threat.

Nothing.

Every member of the team was similarly equipped. Night-vision gear, dark fatigues, and enough weaponry and ammunition to make a stand. The task was simple: buy time for Demir and Erdem to do their work and stave off defeat should someone show up and knock on their door.

Bishop took a mental stock of everyone on the property. The Turks remained at their desk, dismantling the Anca Syndicate and uncovering their secrets. The Wongs, Hirsch, and Mildren were scattered throughout the grounds, ready to unleash from the shadows should the time arrive.

"Maybe they're not coming," Rampling said between puffs.

"Half our luck," Bishop muttered, tapping some ash on the ground.

The same chorus of insects that had buzzed nonstop since their arrival filled the field around them. But now, Bishop could swear they had got louder. Perhaps he was just getting paranoid. Or maybe his senses were improving, his sight and hearing sharpening after decades of being in hibernation.

He chuckled at the notion.

Rampling smiled. She lifted her goggles and met his gaze. "I don't think I've ever heard you do that before."

"What's that?" he asked.

"Laugh." She nodded. "I knew you had it in you, but you were never one to let your..."

Bishop raised a brow as she trailed off, her eyes suddenly evading his. "You were saying?"

"You always put a wall up so that others could never see the real you." She faced him again. "I get it. To someone like you, enjoying something, or at least expressing it, probably feels akin to weakness."

The faint curl in Bishop's lips vanished. He grunted. "The psychoanalyst in you is showing again."

"Sorry. I can't help myself."

A hush fell over them once more, and they continued to smoke in silence. Bishop glided his night-vision goggles back on and stared at the end of the property. The rabbit-proof fence met the grass at the field's edge, the twisted wires barely hanging on, sections sheared clean from splintered timber posts.

"My wife died in a plane crash."

The words left Bishop before he could stop them. For a moment he regretted the slip, cursing to himself for letting something so personal out in the open. Rampling turned to him, her smile gone, replaced by the half-opened mouth of shock at his revelation.

"You wanted to know why I had trouble on the helicopter." Bishop tore the goggles from his head and placed them down next to him. "Fear of flying."

Rampling rested her arm on her assault rifle. "I never knew you were married."

"I wasn't. Not when I was with Bureau 61. Back then, I was wed to the job." He paused, surprised he was still talking. "When they shut us down, I returned to Alaska. Low and behold, within a week of being home, I met the girl I took to prom in a supermarket."

"Childhood sweethearts, huh?"

Bishop nodded, the image of Pat on the high school dance floor flickering in his mind. "The last time I'd seen her was the day I shipped off to Vietnam. Between the Army, being an operative in the field, and heading Bureau 61, I'd never set foot in Anchorage again until eight years ago. We got chatting. She told me she'd lost her husband three years earlier. One thing led to another, and before we knew it, within six months we were married, living by the water."

Rampling remained silent, letting his story sink in and giving him the time to finish pouring out his heart.

"In 1997, a friend came to visit her from Oregon," Bishop continued. "They hadn't seen each other since they were kids. The woman stayed with us for a week. We had dinners together, went shopping. All the stuff you do when catching up. One day, they booked one of those joy flights. You know, one of the twin-prop planes to get the views of the mountains and the city. I wasn't interested in going. Besides, I had wood to chop for the winter."

Bishop drew a steadying breath, the memories of the day flooding back to him like a nightmare clutching at his soul. "The investigation found alcohol in the pilot's system. Not much, but it was enough to call it pilot error. He botched the landing. Debris littered one end of the runway to the other. And the bodies..."

His throat tightened. "The investigator said Pat and her friend wouldn't have lived long enough to feel any pain. I believed him. She was...there was nothing left."

He stopped himself, the rest of it caught somewhere between a whisper and a memory. Rampling's hand found his shoulder.

"I'm so sorry, boss."

The warmth of her touch was comforting. Not like what

he had shared with Pat, but what a daughter might offer her father.

"When I got Harvey Wulf's message, I knew I'd have to confront it," he said. "I'd never been afraid of boarding a plane in my life, but when I got on that flight to Seattle, I knew."

"*Crow's Nest to Kingpin.*"

Quinn Wong's voice crackled over the radio, stopping Bishop in his tracks. Bishop unclipped it from his belt and brought the device to his mouth to respond to the man sitting in the barn loft.

"Kingpin receiving."

"*We've got some action heading our way. I've sighted three vehicles driving toward the main gate. They look to be four-by-fours. A dozen men. All armed.*"

"Any other sightings?"

"*Negative.*"

Bishop crinkled his brow. "Kingpin to Ironclad."

"*Ironclad receiving,*" Hirsch responded from the front of the house.

"Do you have a visual yet?"

"*Negative. No, wait. Positive confirmation. Three four-by-fours, thirty seconds away from the main gate.*"

Bishop put a hand on Rampling's shoulder, a silent acknowledgment of what had just been shared. A moment neither would forget. He collected his night-vision goggles and rushed through the back door, cutting through the house past Demir and Erdem, making his way to the front.

Hirsch sat behind his machine gun, the firing line between the sturdy makeshift materials ahead of him providing cover, but also a decent view of the gate. He exchanged a knowing look with him. Bishop had been right.

This was much bigger than a rogue group of hackers stirring up trouble in Istanbul. There was much more to it. And now the threat had arrived on their doorstep.

Bishop set his goggles in place and narrowed his eyes to the west. Dust kicked up from the road, and exhaust spewed from the rear of the vehicles. "Here they come."

Beyond the parked helicopter, the four-by-fours appeared. They rolled in, filled with soldiers, weapons in their grasp, prepared to open fire. They neared the chopper, and Bishop moved to Hirsch's side. Together, they glanced at the ground where a line of wire lay connected to a detonator switch.

"You ready?" Bishop asked him.

"Just say the word, boss."

Bishop squinted, the ghostly green glow of the battlefield crisp and clear through his goggles. One vehicle drove past the helicopter. Then another. The third disappeared behind it, likely very close.

"Now."

Hirsch flipped the switch. A millisecond passed, and an explosion erupted from the chopper. The plastic explosives inside it detonated in a blinding flash of orange, lighting the night sky as if it were midday.

Debris spewed from every direction in the ruptured craft, the rotors spinning through the air, showering the enemy vehicles with metallic shrapnel. One crashed into what remained of the helicopter. Another tumbled sideways, and the third flipped end over end.

When the dust settled, the duo on the balcony took in the devastating aftermath. The four-by-fours were nothing but smoldering wrecks, and the personnel they had carried were spread-eagled over the ground.

Hirsch smiled, the silence of the farmland settling around them once again. Bishop waited, not nearly as confident as his mercenary. He stepped closer to the balustrade and shifted his gaze skyward, a slight noise emanating from the abyss.

"*Crow's Nest to Kingpin.*"

"Kingpin receiving," Bishop answered his radio. "What is it, Quinn?"

"*We've got a bogey in the air on approach. A chopper.*"

Hirsch's grin faded.

The battle was far from over.

49

ATLANTA, GEORGIA

Tyler swung the car into a gap on the curb outside the CNN Center building amongst the dozens of police cruisers already there. He killed the engine and hopped out into the haze of red and blue lights surrounding the block, painting the scene in a pulse of hectic energy. Uniformed police officers formed a barricade around the exterior, stopping anyone from getting in while allowing those from inside out.

Tyler made a beeline for a cluster of cops in his path, quickly flashing his badge. "I'm here to see Chief Cooper!"

The young minion checked his credentials and pointed him closer to the entrance, where more senior officers stood near a parked vehicle. The oldest of them turned at the commotion as Tyler approached.

"Tyler? Special Agent Jack Tyler?" he asked, having overheard him.

Tyler showed him his badge. "That's me. I drove here from Omar Al-Tezmi's house as quick as I could."

"Chief Lewis Cooper." The man extended his hand, and he shook it. "We just received word from the FBI SAC that you were on the way. You were right on the money. When our units started arriving after the alert came through, we got confirmation from inside the building that some of the staff were being herded upstairs by a man of Arabic appearance."

"Do we have a positive ID on Al-Tezmi?"

The chief of police nodded. "The description matches the one the Feds gave us. He was also wearing the uniform of The Squeaky Cleaning Company and used Oliver Nial's swipe card to access the site twenty-two minutes ago."

"How many people has he taken hostage?"

"Unknown. We're getting snipers into position in the adjacent buildings now." Copper pointed upward at the other structures surrounding them. "We'll have eyes on him shortly."

"Any idea if he's rigged with explosives?"

"We're uncertain at this point. The CNN staff member who got away told us he was carrying a rifle of some kind. That's all we have on him so far."

Tyler nodded, trying to understand Al-Tezmi's game plan. He checked his watch. 11:27 p.m. "Do we know what he did right after signing on with the swipe card?"

"No. That building's full of my people. Not only are we evacuating everyone, we're also sweeping it for anything suspicious. More weapons. Explosives. Potential accomplices."

Around him, the chief's staff barked into their radios, while fragmented updates came through the static-riddled channels. Tyler caught key phrases, giving him an idea of what was happening. The snipers were in position, while evac teams were working methodically. Some inside refused to leave, wanting to cover the story. Tyler shook his head. Typical journalists.

He glanced at the top of the CNN Center to see if he could catch a glimpse of Al-Tezmi. Of course, from such a low vantage point, it was next to impossible.

Tyler stepped aside, allowing Cooper to stay locked in a conversation with one of his deputies. More people rushed from the entrance, their faces red from the rapidness of their withdrawal. Traffic began to clog the streets, the passersby and the CNN employees outside turning into a legion of rubberneckers, drawn to the unfolding chaos.

Tyler narrowed his eyes. What was Al-Tezmi playing at? Hostages on a rooftop. This was not the MO of someone linked to the earlier attacks of the day. Rapid radio chatter fired again. Tyler returned to Cooper's side.

"This is Command receiving Foxtrot One," the chief answered.

"We're in position, Command."

"Have you got a visual on Al-Tezmi?"

"Confirmed," the sniper said. *"He's wearing the tan coveralls as described in the brief. Matches the physical description. Dark hair. Early twenties."*

"How many hostages?"

"Ten. Correction, eleven. The lights have just gone out. Stand by, switching to night-vision mode." There was a pause. *"The suspect is getting the hostages to shut the blinds. Some windows remain uncovered, but we've got an intermittent visual. He's moving them all to the northwest corner of the floor, keeping one, a female, close."*

"Al-Tezmi will want someone near him," Tyler muttered. "He knows there's at least a dozen snipers with their sights on him."

The chief went to the radio again. "Command to Foxtrot One. Is he wearing an explosive vest?"

"It doesn't appear so. The overalls fit tight. No bulk. He's packing an M4 carbine in one hand. A possible small sidearm in the other, but I can't get a clear visual to confirm just yet."

"Roger that, Foxtrot One."

"What are our orders, Command?"

Cooper paused for a moment until going back to his radio. "Stand by and inform me of any changes. If a clear shot opens up, notify me immediately."

"Understood, Command."

The walkie-talkie crackled again, another voice cutting through the constant traffic. "*Team Seven to Command.*"

"Command receiving, Team Seven."

"*We've done a sweep of the underground parking lot, sir. And we—*"

Static filled the airwaves.

"Repeat, Team Seven!" Cooper said.

"*We've found a—*"

Cooper, Tyler, and the other nearby officers standing in the congregation looked at one another. Then they bolted for the building, shoving their way through the knot of CNN employees who had arrived out of the exit. Cameras were being set up and reporters adjusting their earpieces, preparing themselves to go on air.

Tyler reached the entrance first, pushing through to the lobby. Instead of veering for the elevators where more staff emerged, he went for the fire escape, slamming the door open and bounding down the stairs. At the bottom, the parking lot was swarming with police officers scrambling amongst the parked cars.

"This way!" one of them called, motioning Tyler and those trailing to the far end of the concrete jungle.

They reached a section cleared of vehicles and cordoned off with orange cones and draped with tarpaulin to obscure the sight beyond. If Tyler did not know any better, he would say the parking area was in the process of being expanded but still under construction. An officer peeled back the tarp to reveal what lay inside.

A semi-truck.

Tyler walked toward it cautiously. Cooper and the others closed in beside him. How long had it been there? Tyler wondered. He circled to the rear, where more cops had already opened the doors. He propped a foot on the tailgate and peered within. Tangled wires filled the trailer in a deliberate pattern. Rows of ANFO containers lined the floor, with cannisters of gasoline next to them.

"Someone get the bomb squad down here!" Cooper yelled out.

Tyler spotted red flashing in the back of the truck. He leaned in, shifting some wires out of the way to reveal a countdown clock. Nineteen minutes. He then checked the time on his watch.

"11:40 p.m. It's set to blow at eleven 11:59. Still September eleven. Chief, you've got to evacuate this entire area. There's enough ANFO in here to not just level this building but take a chunk of the block with it."

Cooper glanced at a deputy, who hurried off to begin a greater evac. "What's your read on it?" he asked Tyler.

"I'm no expert, but the setup is complex. One wrong move, and we'll go up with it."

"Best to leave it to the professionals, then." Cooper gulped. "What do you think it's doing here?"

"If I had to guess, I'd say Al-Tezmi opted for a plan B. He'd killed Oliver Nial just in case he needed somewhere else to blow the truck up. Knowing the airport was locked down, he brought the truck here before authorities erected the security perimeter around Atlanta. A perfect hiding place and an ideal spot to blow it if things went south."

Before Cooper could speak again, an officer sprinted over to them.

"Sir, I just got off the phone to the bomb squad. The closest team's at the airport. They'll be here in twenty-five minutes."

Tyler and Cooper exchanged glances, the realization setting in.

They'll be too late...

50

SAKARYA PLAIN, TURKEY

The helicopter closed fast. Bishop adjusted his night-vision goggles, zeroing in on the incoming bogey.

"Do you see what I'm seeing?"

Beside him, Hirsch put his goggles over his eyes, tracking the nearing craft. "Hydra 70 rockets. Locked and loaded."

Bishop scanned the field, bringing his radio to his lips. "Kingpin to Gopher, do you copy?"

"*Gopher receiving,*" Trent Wong responded.

"Do you have a visual on the aerial target?"

"*Stand by, Kingpin.*"

Bishop bit his bottom lip as the helicopter drew ever closer to their position. He had hoped it might have been outfitted like Hirsch's bird, with machine guns only. Rockets changed everything. That kind of firepower could put them in a very awkward predicament before they had time to react.

A clatter of another gun firing jolted Bishop. He turned to Hirsch, who lowered his weapon with smoke drifting from the barrel after shooting off a few rounds where the four-by-fours had been taken out.

"I saw one of them move." Hirsch nodded at a soldier, who must have survived the initial explosion.

"*Gopher to Kingpin.*"

"Kingpin receiving," Bishop said, once again lifting the radio.

"*I've got a visual. Standing by to lock on target.*"

Bishop wiped the sweat from his palm onto his leg. Trent had one shot. Miss and he would give away his position. Within seconds, the helicopter would home in and take him out, and then come for the rest of them.

He peered out into the field, spotting Trent break from his foxhole. He swung his RPG over his shoulder, dropped to one knee, and took aim into the sky. The chopper continued to close, the rotor blades thrashing furiously.

The seconds felt like minutes.

"Do it," Bishop muttered. "Do it!"

The helicopter banked hard toward him, the pilot clearly spotting Trent below. Just as it seemed as if it was preparing to unleash its own assault, Trent fired. The launcher kicked against him, and the rocket screamed, a streak of fire bursting through the air.

Bishop followed its path, ascending higher until...

Contact.

The helicopter veered at the last second. But it was too late. The weapon struck true. An explosion tore through the windshield as flames burst within the cockpit. The rotors spasmed and warped, spinning out of control. Then the entire craft detonated, the fireball bathing those on the ground in a hue of orange and red. Debris rained down, the shockwave of the blast rolling across the long grass of the field.

"Yes!" Hirsch yelled out in celebration

Bishop clenched his hand around the radio. "Nice work, Trent."

"*Crow's Nest to Kingpin!*" Quinn called over the static from the barn loft.

"Go ahead, Crow's Nest."

"*I've got multiple contacts converging on the property. More four-by-fours and troop transports.*"

"Where?" Bishop asked.

"*All directions. Front, back and side gates.*"

"How long do we have?"

"*Three minutes until the first wave arrives.*"

"All units, prepare for maximum assault."

Everyone acknowledged Bishop's call via the radio. He gave Hirsch a quick pat on his shoulder as his man fed another line of ammunition into his machine gun. Bishop lifted his goggles and dashed from the balcony, hurrying down the hallway toward the back room.

"How's it coming?" he asked, stepping over the threshold, welcomed by the hum of the computers working overtime.

Neither Demir nor Erdem looked up from their screens, their fingers flying over their keyboards.

"We've traced several of the hackers' payrolls through so-called legitimate companies," Demir said. "The money's been funneled through accounts offshore. It's a complex chain, each one leading to a different point. Whoever's paying them has left a hell of a web to untangle. So far, we've managed to stay ahead of everyone, keeping the banks and the authorities off our tails."

Bishop viewed the monitors, which had several windows

open on them, the list of accounts a blur of numbers that made his head spin. "How much longer do you think it'll be until you find what we're searching for?"

"I'm not sure." Demir sucked his teeth. "We could break through in minutes. Or hours."

Bishop gripped the headrest of his chair. "We're going to have hostile forces on us shortly. I don't need to—"

"I understand." Demir nodded. "We'll just have to work quicker."

Bishop frowned. He was used to being the one in control. Now he was in the thick of it, forced to rely on others. He did not have time to dwell, spinning on his heel and racing out the back door where Rampling had remained, taking up a defensive position behind a stack of bricks.

"Any visual yet?" he asked her.

"No, but I can hear them."

Bishop tilted his head to listen. Diesel engines. Approaching fast. He slipped his night-vision goggles on, mirroring Rampling, while grabbing his assault rifle and confirming he had a full magazine locked into place. He kneeled behind the row of downed forty-two-gallon barrels and dragged the pile of spare ammo within reach.

The noise grew louder, rumbling closer with each passing second. Puffs of dust rose over the crest at the fence line, just past the gates. Bishop hovered his finger over the trigger, bracing for the inevitable.

A four-by-four appeared. Then another. Followed by a troop transport which ambled into view. Bishop did the math. At least twenty soldiers, maybe more, advancing on their position. He gazed at Rampling, who gave him a knowing glance in return.

Bishop resumed his focus to the battlefield, every instinct within him screaming to fire. But he held firm.

Seconds dragged by.

Then the first of the four-by-fours rolled through the gate. The second followed close behind.

That's when the fireworks began. Small explosions discharged beneath the lead vehicle, rocking it from its path in a spray of dirt and flame. Those inside it scrambled and hurled themselves out before it tipped to its side. The second four-by-four crashed into the first, more blasts detonating in rapid succession.

Their plan had worked perfectly. Tripwires strung through the grass, each tied to grenades, turning the path into a makeshift minefield. Crude, but effective.

The two vehicles floundered, the survivors stumbling out, wounded and disorientated. Easy targets. Bishop and Rampling opened fire, taking them out one by one.

Behind the wreckage, the troop transport lurched into view, bottlenecked at the gate. Soldiers jumped out, using the debris of the other vehicles as cover. Bishop dropped one who was not quick enough. Rampling nailed another with a clean shot to the chest.

Gunfire sang from the front of the house, Hirsch, obviously engaging his own wave of enemy combatants. His advantage: the heavy-duty machine gun posted on the balcony, giving him both range and stopping power. The wreckage from the downed helicopter and other vehicles formed a brutal logjam, providing him with a kill zone no one would be able to cross easily.

More rounds rattled from Trent's foxhole, the bleached-haired brother joining the fight, laying down fire from the flank. With bullets raining in from two different angles, the defense had turned into a punishing crossfire, catching the enemy off guard.

At the back of the house, the soldiers, however, grew bolder, charging forward in a desperate sprint. Bishop and Rampling fired on the multiple targets. For every one who dropped, two more emerged and pressed forward.

Bishop's rifle clicked empty just as one of the soldiers edged closer to them. Rampling's weapon ran dry, too. Without a second to spare, both scrambled for fresh magazines.

A bullet buzzed through the air in their direction.

Bishop's pulse skipped a beat.

He had not been shot.

Neither had Rampling.

They peered out to find the incoming soldier crumpled on the grass with an entry wound through his head. Bishop snapped his gaze upward to the barn loft, where Quinn Wong was reloading his sniper rifle, having providing crucial cover for them.

"Nice work..." Bishop uttered under his breath.

He and Rampling clipped new magazines into their rifles and cut down two more enemy targets approaching their position. The defense was holding, and their opponent losing manpower quickly. Meanwhile, more weapon fire flew at the front of the house, Hirsch and Trent maintaining their hold, at least for the time being.

A fresh rumble sounded to the south, beyond the barn. Bishop let off another series of rounds and turned to the disturbance. Two more troop transports rolled into view, their doors swinging open, more soldiers streaming out. Dozens of them. They fanned into a wide formation, the wave pushing toward the house.

Bishop spied one in particular, who was not carrying an assault rifle like the others, but something bulkier. More dangerous.

An RPG.

Bishop widened his eyes at the soldier crouching low and taking aim at the barn. He lunged for his radio.

"Quinn, get out of there!"

Before the last word left Bishop's mouth, the rocket launched, slamming into the side of the barn. Wood exploded, and debris burst from the brittle frame, the detonation swallowing the structure in flames.

"Quinn, can you hear me!" Bishop clutched his radio, his heart racing. "Quinn!"

51

ATLANTA, GEORGIA

The countdown clock ticked past fifteen minutes. Tyler lay flat on his back in the narrow crawlspace in the rear of the truck, sweat covering his brow. He did not wipe it away, instead examining Al-Tezmi's setup. He needed to see it all.

His eyes stung, blinking through the dust and the mix of fertilizer and gasoline fumes in the air. The cocktail was so thick that it was sure to level the building if he could not pull off a miracle. With the bomb squad too far away, this one was on him.

Beyond the tailgate of the truck in the parking lot, a group of police officers stood by, Chief Cooper among them offering barely more than moral support. How long they stayed if things got too real remained to be seen.

He pushed the wires aside, the small flashlight in his mouth clenched between his teeth, casting jittery beams around him. The containers of fertilizer had been wrapped and stacked inside the cargo hold with surgical precision.

While throughout, wires looped and twisted in clumps of confusion, the various colors making it appear like a jungle.

A jungle of death.

He scooted in a little farther, careful to keep Cooper's phone wedged between his neck and shoulder, the speaker function still active.

Then he saw it.

"Symmons, are you there?" Tyler asked.

"*Go ahead, Agent Tyler,*" came the voice of the bomb squad specialist in DC, sitting in the operations center with Monica Brunelli and the rest of the team.

"I've found it."

"*Good. Can you describe to me what you see?*"

Tyler took the flashlight from his mouth and scanned a little closer. "It's a mess. Dozens of wires. Maybe more. Red, green, blue, black. They're all twisted up. Some are just hanging, others have zip ties around them. All appear to be bolted to terminals. There's a relay box here. The timer's feeding into it."

"Okay, that's good." Symmons's tone was calm. Reassuring. Easy when you were half a country away. "*We can work with this.*"

"I think I've got the main detonator here. It's covered with an aluminum cap." Tyler tried to twist it ever so slightly. "It's sealed tight. I could maybe cut it—"

"No!" Symmons said, his voice heightening. "*Ignore it for now. If we hack into it, we'll risk sparking something on the other side. The best bet is to isolate circuits manually.*"

Tyler swallowed hard. "You mean guess?"

"*No, Agent Tyler. We'll work through this. All you have to do is listen and follow my instructions.*"

"I'm all ears." He checked the clock, just ticking under fourteen minutes. "What do you need me to do?"

"*There should be some wires connected to the timer. What color are they?*"

Tyler shimmied backward to check. "Two blue. One red."

"*Is the red held in place by a small screw?*"

"Yes."

"*Cut it as close to the screw as possible. And don't cross-contact it with anything else.*"

Tyler wanted to ask if he was sure. But that would only waste precious seconds. Symmons was a pro. He took his cutters and clenched tight, hovering them over the red wire.

Snip.

He exhaled and tugged the wire away from the timer.

"It's still counting down," Tyler said.

"*That's okay. We've only just begun the process. We need a green one next. It should be running to the center of the relay.*"

Tyler slid farther into the truck again and pointed his flashlight at it. "I've got it."

"*I want you to cut that, too.*"

He took the cutters and did so. "I've done it."

"*Excellent, Agent Tyler.*"

He glanced at the countdown. Thirteen minutes.

He then refocused on the relay box. Something caught his attention in the collection of wires bundled in the darkness beyond. "Hold on a second..."

"*What have you found?*" Symmons asked.

"Stand by." Tyler gently pressed his fingers through the carnage, pushing aside some copper, soldered with another device.

An antenna.

His stomach churned at the discovery.

"Symmons," he said into the phone.

"Yes?"

"There's a transmitter here. It appears active."

"You're sure?"

Tyler ran his hands along the wires feeding it. "Affirmative. There's definitely power leading to it."

Symmons sighed. *"That means Al-Tezmi has it rigged for remote detonation."*

"Then why the timer?" Brunelli asked in the background.

"A failsafe," Symmons said. *"There's every chance Al-Tezmi is carrying a—"*

"Kill switch," Tyler interjected, the realization hitting him like a sledgehammer.

"Foxtrot One to Command!" The voice of the sniper crackled over Chief Cooper's radio, the man and his team scoping out the CNN Center from an adjacent building. *"We have a clean shot! I repeat, a clean shot! Requesting permission to—"*

"No!" Tyler shouted, scrambling out of the truck and hitting the ground inside the parking lot with a thud. "They can't shoot!"

Cooper glanced up from the radio. "They have a clean shot."

Tyler shook his head. "Remember how they said they couldn't get a clear visual on the object in his other hand? It's a kill switch. If we shoot him out, this all goes boom!"

The chief's eyes widened. He yanked the radio back to his mouth. "Command to Foxtrot One. Negative. Do not take the shot. I repeat, do not take the shot!"

A long pause lingered as everyone held their breath.

"Foxtrot One to Command. Snipers holding."

Tyler let out a sigh of relief and got back on the phone. "Sorry, Symmons. We're good to continue."

"Okay. You'll need to go back to those blue wires from the timer."

Tyler climbed into the truck, where the countdown clock had moved to twelve minutes. He put his head back under it and spotted his next target. "I see them. One appears to have a nick at the end."

"I'm glad. That's Al-Tezmi leaving a mark for himself. Cut that one."

Tyler adjusted the tool and sliced it. "Done."

Still alive.

"We're getting closer now," Symmons said. *"Next, you need to find a thick green wire routed to a capacitor junction."*

Tyler tilted his head sideways. "I got it."

"Cut it."

"Roger that."

Snip.

A loud beep sounded, and he furrowed his brow. "What the hell was that?"

"Agent Tyler?"

He peered down at the timer clock. "Oh crap!"

"What is it, Agent Tyler?"

Cooper obviously heard the strain in his voice and approached the tailgate.

"The timer," Tyler said. "It's halved. We've got six minutes left. What the—"

Symmons cursed in the background, while the noise level inside the FBI operations center kicked up a gear. *"It must've been a decoy."*

"Like a failsafe?" Tyler asked.

"*Correct.*"

More of Cooper's men gathered with tense glances, realizing the urgency.

Tyler grasped the phone that much tighter. "Tell me you've got another plan, Symmons."

52

SAKARYA PLAIN, TURKEY

The barn collapsed in moments, flames ripping through the structure with a feral intensity, devouring everything in its path. Bishop tried to spot Quinn inside the inferno or for any sign he had made it out. But the loft had crumpled with the rest of the construction.

"Kingpin to Crow's Nest!" Bishop yelled into his radio. "Do you copy!"

He repeated the call again.

And again.

Nothing.

Beside him, Rampling fired, taking out another advancing soldier from the rear of the house, finishing off the last of the invasion force from behind. Out in the field, Trent Wong turned his attention to the south, where the fresh wave of enemies closed in. Gunfire lit up the night, pounding into his position.

Bishop went to the walkie-talkie once more. "Kingpin to Gopher. What's your status?"

"*I'm pinned down,*" came Trent's voice, ever the professional, even with the knowledge that his brother was likely dead.

"Stand by. Help's on its way. Kingpin to Ironclad. Sitrep?"

"*Still plenty of targets to take care of at the main gate,*" Hirsch responded.

"Do you need help?"

"*That's a negative. Me and my little friend have it covered. Go get Trent, boss.*"

Bishop glanced at the rear fence. The pile of corpses confirming what he already knew. He gripped Rampling's shoulder. "We've got to remove that RPG. Now."

She nodded, and they peeled from their position, mindful of the slim possibility they might get ambushed from behind. They could not ignore the surge from the flank. Bishop zoomed his night-vision sight on them, zeroing in on the one carrying the RPG. The weapon remained slung over his shoulder, while his other comrades pelted the lip of Trent's foxhole with automatic gunfire, dusting him with heavy clumps of dirt.

The man stayed down to avoid being hit, but there was no way to retreat.

Rampling dived behind another barricade of bricks. "He's got maybe two minutes before they're on top of him."

Bishop joined her, wincing as he clipped his side with some stacked timber. He shook off the pain and raised his weapon. "We can't afford to send help if that RPG isn't neutralized."

"We won't have much of a shot. If we don't take him out fast, they'll have us pinned down, too."

"Right." Bishop knew the stakes. He snapped another fresh magazine into his rifle and fixed his eyes on the target. He had to make it count.

"The one who misses owes the other a pack of those Russian cigarettes?"

"Deal." Bishop lined up his shot, the darkness adding an extra layer to the challenge. "Ready?"

Rampling nodded.

Bishop drew a breath and readied his finger over the trigger. "Now!"

Both fired in unison, their rounds shredding through the air. The distance was their enemy, making a clean shot nearly impossible. The soldier with the RPG fumbled, the weapon slipping from his grasp. His closest colleague whirled around, spotting Bishop and Rampling near the house.

"Come on, dammit!" Rampling shouted, emptying her magazine.

Bishop remained calm, shifting the barrel of the gun just enough to track the target's movement.

Then contact.

A bullet slammed into his shoulder. Another into his chest. A third struck his head, blood bursting from the wound. The soldier fell in a heap over his RPG.

The counterattack came quickly. Bishop and Rampling heaved themselves behind their cover, automatic fire chewing at the brick and wood in front of them, while wayward rounds slammed into the side of the house in a hailstorm of destruction.

Bishop unclipped his radio and pressed it to his lips.

"Kingpin to Surprise Package! The RPG is down! Come and join the party!"

"*Roger that!*" said Mildren through the distorted static.

Beyond the barn, the restored BMP-1, its exterior barely visible in the lake, emerged from the water and roared onto land with surprising speed for such an old contraption. Mildren wasted no time charging the Soviet vehicle at the enemy combatants. The deafening clatter of machine gun fire erupted from it, tearing through the bodies ahead of it in a masterpiece of brutality.

The soldiers concentrated on the BMP-1, their rounds clunking into its armor. Bishop cautiously peeked out from their cover, noting the enemies' shifted focus. In the foxhole, Trent took the opportunity of reprieve to resume his attack. Bishop and Rampling joined him, just as one of the soldiers was caught in the path of the BMP-1. Mildren ran him down, the man disappearing beneath the grinding tracks.

Fish in a barrel. One by one, the team picked them off. Hirsch even came along; whatever threat that remained at the front of the house having been neutralized. He hauled his machine gun and slapped it on the ground, firing it into the night.

With the final shots echoing out, silence settled over the battlefield. Only the crackle of the burning barn endured, its flames licking the surface of the wreckage. Mildren climbed out of the hatch of the BMP-1, his face smeared with smoke and grit, while across the field, Trent rose from his foxhole, scanning the stillness. He bolted from his position to the barn. Bishop and the others followed, tiptoeing through the scorched earth.

"Quinn!" his brother yelled. "Quinn!"

Everyone fanned out, hauling away charred beams and

shattered timber. Bishop dove in, kicking aside debris with ash and smoke swirling around him. His boot struck something solid. Metal. He kneeled and uncovered the seared barrel of a sniper rifle. Quinn's sniper rifle. He booted it out of the way and put his hands on his hips to catch his breath. Trent refused to give up, digging ruthlessly underfoot.

Just when it appeared all was lost, a faint shuffle came from beneath a pile of loose boards. Bishop caught it first. He rushed over and dropped to one knee, dumping the seared wood aside with a grunt.

There, under the debris, lay Quinn Wong, barely conscious, his skin smudged with soot and his lungs gasping for air from the smoke inhalation. Trent sprinted toward them, skidding to his brother's side and lifting him gently. The others gathered close, while Bishop exhaled, awed by the miraculous escape from death. Battered and bruised, but alive. He stepped away to let the Wongs have their moment, while Rampling and Hirsch moved in to tend to the injuries.

Bishop turned to the house where Erdem stood frozen on the balcony, staring out at the carnage. His face was pale, his eyes wide in shock. There was something else, though.

Relief.

Bishop rushed toward him, his strides rigid from the injuries done to himself. He followed Erdem to the back room, where Demir remained at his computer. His frantic energy from earlier was gone. He now sat a motionless figure. Quiet. Pensive.

Bishop crossed the threshold and stopped by his side. "What have you found?"

Demir took a moment, then shifted the monitor toward Bishop. "You wanted a smoking gun. Here it is."

Bishop studied the information before him. Though it

was a mishmash of data, code, and bank accounts, the truth was unavoidable. The evidence was all there. He did not speak. Just kept on reading, scanning the screen again, hoping it was wrong.

"You're sure about this?" he asked.

"It's all there in black and white," Demir said.

Yes, it was. It all started to make sense. "It seems I owe you an apology, Erdem. You weren't the villain in this tale after all."

The younger Turk nodded, the man professional enough not to hold a grudge. Not an ounce of bitterness.

For Bishop, the truth only complicated matters, raising questions he was not sure he wanted the answers to. When he returned to the United States, the very intel in front of him would blow everything wide open.

53

ATLANTA, GEORGIA

"Symmons, I need options. And fast!"

Tyler waited for the reply on the other end. Silence. Just the background noise of frantic voices, a few cursing, and a fist hitting a wooden table. It appeared even the best of the FBI's bomb squad could lose their cool. Was there a plan B at all?

"Don't go quiet on me now," Tyler said into the phone. "Monica, are you there?"

There was a shuffle on the end of the line. Movement. Someone finally picked up.

"*Hey, Jack,*" Brunelli replied. "*It's me.*"

"What's going on there, Monica? Tell me they've got another way out of this?"

"*They're...reassessing.*"

"In other words, they don't have a clue." Tyler brought the cell to his forehead. "I didn't find out if Kate was—"

"Don't talk like that. We'll get you out of this. They just have to—"

"Monica, I've got under five minutes. Unless one of those bomb squad guys pulls a rabbit out of the hat, I'm..." He could not say the words. "I guess this means no more mandatory seminars at Quantico."

Silence filtered through the line. A pang of guilt twisted in Tyler's gut. Was this how he was really going out? With a throwaway quip and a defeatist attitude? That was not him. And sure as hell not the way he wanted Brunelli to remember him.

"Sorry." Tyler stared past the tailgate.

Cooper spoke on the radio to his units on the outside of the building. He had sent the rest of his team beyond the potential blast radius.

"You should go, too, Chief," Tyler suggested.

The older man shook his head. "If you're staying here, so am I. Have you got any more ideas, son?"

Tyler pulled his gaze back into the truck and focused. Wires curled around him like veins, snaking to various ports and coiling from junction to junction. He tried to make sense of the chaos, landing on the main detonator covered with the aluminum cap. He reached for it again, twisting it both clockwise and anti-clockwise.

No give.

The thought crossed his mind to cut it, as he had suggested earlier. Symmons' warning then echoed in his head. Sparks. He would only speed up the inevitable.

There had to be another option.

His mind drifted to something he had just said to Brunelli. "Quantico..."

"What was that?" she asked from the speaker of the phone still resting on his shoulder.

The timer ticked to four minutes.

"The seminar, Monica. Do you remember Professor Pasternak's presentation? He cut through aluminum as if it were hot butter. He did it with simple cleaning products. Bleach, ammonia, and—"

"*Hydrogen peroxide!*"

"That's right!" Tyler clicked his fingers and slid himself out of the truck.

Cooper appeared confused at the sudden burst of energy. "What is it?"

"We have to get to the janitor's closet!"

Tyler ran past the cars, including a police cruiser parked in the middle of the underground lot. He stopped near the fire escape, having remembered passing the closed door earlier. Embossed over the green paint was the logo of The Squeaky Cleaning Company.

Slamming it open, he entered, fumbling for a light switch. When he found it, he flicked it on, flooding the small space with a dull jaundice glow. It was not the tidiest of places. Mops and half-empty buckets cluttered the floor, while rickety shelves groaned under the weight of dust-laden boxes. Each had different labels on them.

"*Jack, I've got Professor Pasternak on the line,*" Brunelli said.

"Good evening, Professor." Tyler grabbed a bottle of bleach with his free hand, giving it to Cooper who had caught up to him. "I hope it's not too late to teach some chemistry."

"*What kind of application area are we looking at, Agent*

Tyler?" the man asked, cutting through the pleasantries and getting straight to business.

Tyler found the ammonia and passed it to the chief. "Two inches in diameter."

"*Do you have the chemicals on hand?*"

"Just about." As Tyler shuffled through the room, scanning the labels, his cell phone rang in his pocket. He ignored it and spotted the hydrogen peroxide on the far end of the rack. "Professor, I've got them."

"*You'll need gloves. Please, don't do this without gloves.*"

Tyler rolled his eyes but did as he was instructed, finding an open box. He pulled a pair out and snapped them over his hands. "I'm ready."

"*Now, you'll want a container. Preferably one which hasn't had any other chemical mixed in it.*"

Tyler checked every surface, looking for anything that might fit the bill.

"Here you go." Cooper passed him a plastic measuring jug. "It seems clean."

"Good enough for me." Tyler placed it in the sink. "Okay, Professor, throw some numbers at me."

"*You're going to want to combine two parts hydrogen peroxide, one part ammonia, and a dash of bleach,*" Pasternak went on. "*Not too much or it'll foam like hell and gas you out.*"

"Understood." Tyler dunked in the hydrogen peroxide first. He then gestured to Cooper for the ammonia, which he added next. Then the bleach. As Pasternak had warned, it bubbled and fizzed. "All done, Professor."

"*Now, pour a liberal amount on the application area.*"

Cooper stood aside, and Tyler hurried back to the

parking garage. He shot his gaze to the timer in the truck, which had shifted under three minutes.

"I've got about two and a half minutes to make this work, Professor." Tyler moved inside the crawl space. "Will I have time?"

Silence fell over the line, the absence of sound speaking volumes. He reached the main detonator, his hands steady despite the pressure, and poured. Just like in the Quantico presentation, the aluminum hissed and spat, the smell acrid to say the least.

"*How's it going?*" Monica asked.

Tyler grabbed the phone with one hand while prodding the cap with the other. "Still rock-solid." He turned to the countdown clock. "We'll get an idea if this was all for nothing in two minutes."

He leaned back against the interior wall of the truck and sighed. "You know, Monica. I think if I get out of this, we should go grab a drink sometime. Maybe even dinner."

His cell phone buzzed again. He let it ring out.

"*Are those fumes getting to your head, Jack?*" she asked, undoubtedly wondering what had got into him.

Tyler chuckled and jabbed at the cap once more. It had softened, but only slightly. He glanced at Cooper, who remained waiting at the tailgate. "Chief, I need something I can use to skewer this."

Cooper furrowed his brow in thought until he had a light-bulb moment. He sprinted off toward the police cruiser and opened the trunk.

"What do you like to eat, Monica?" Tyler asked. "I could go for a steak. Mashed potatoes. A side of vegetables."

Cooper returned, breathless, with a screwdriver. He

threw it down to Tyler, who snatched it. He poked at the cap. Hard as rock.

"If you plan to do anything, son, now's the time," the chief said, the timer between them edging just under one minute.

Tyler tried again, almost slamming the screwdriver into the cap.

Suddenly, movement as the tool pierced a small hole through the aluminum.

He poured more of the solution over it and rammed the screwdriver in farther, opening the gap. He bent and twisted at it until finally he caught a glimpse of something inside. "Symmons, are you still with me?"

"*I can hear you, Agent Tyler.*"

"I think I've nearly reached the switch. Are you certain that if I flick it, it's going to defuse this beast?"

Symmons hesitated. "*If it's not rigged like the decoy, then yes. It'll sever the connection between the detonator and the explosive. It'll also take out the antenna for the remote kill switch.*"

The timer dipped under twenty seconds.

Tyler prodded the opening just wide enough for his gloved finger.

Ten seconds.

He tossed the screwdriver aside, his heart pounding and his sweat creating a thick sheen over his skin.

He reached in and closed his eyes...flipping the switch.

Click.

Tyler opened his eyes, the switch now in the opposite position. He pivoted to check the timer.

Frozen at five seconds.

Cooper cracked a smile and shook his head, disbelief

written over his wrinkled face. "Talk about cutting it close." He went for his radio and brought it to his lips. "Command to Foxtrot One. Do you still have a clean shot on Al-Tezmi?"

"*Foxtrot One to Command. Affirmative on the clean shot,*" came the reply.

"Take him down."

"*Received, Command.*"

A single round of firing echoed across the transmission.

"*Foxtrot One to Command.*"

"Command receiving."

"*We got him.*"

Tyler fell back onto the cargo bed, letting out all the breaths he had kept in.

"Monica?"

"Yeah," she replied.

"It's done." His cell phone chimed a third time, and he slipped it from his pocket. "Sorry, give me a moment." He checked the screen, finding an incoming call from Rick, along with two other missed calls from him.

"Hello," he answered.

"*Jack?*"

The voice was not his brother's. It was softer. Feminine. Familiar.

"Kate?" Tyler said. "Is that you?"

"*Yeah, Jack. It's me.*" There was a pause. "*I'm alive.*"

Tyler was not sure what to say, the relief spewing out all at once. "It's so good to hear you're voice. What happened? Were you in the building? Where have you been?"

"*I was in the building. On the thirty-seventh floor. We got out straight away.*" Some sniffles sounded on the other end of the line. Eventually, she pulled herself together. "*I have a friend who got caught under the blast zone. The firefighters managed to get her out, but she sucked in a lot of smoke. I went to the hospital with her and stayed by her side all day."*

Tyler closed his eyes. No wonder no one had been able to find her. She was not listed at any hospital because she was not a patient.

"I'm sorry, Jack, I left my phone in the office, and honestly it was just the last thing on my mind." She paused for a moment. *"When I got home, Rick was there waiting for me. He'd driven all the way from Arkansas in the hope of finding me."*

"Good old Rick." Tyler opened his eyes and smiled. "He's a good guy."

"Yeah."

"Have you rung Mom and Dad?"

"I just got off the phone to them."

"Good. Mum will be pleased."

"She was." Silence permeated between them, until finally his sister spoke once again. *"Hey, Jack?"*

"Yeah," he said.

"Are you okay?"

He looked back at the truck and the defused mess of explosives filled in the back of it. "Yeah, everything's okay, now."

SEPTEMBER 14, 2001

54

SEATTLE, WASHINGTON

Three days after the attacks which would forever be etched into the history books, the sight of business executives from private defense firms, outsourced intelligence outfits, and cybersecurity companies clinking glasses and sipping champagne left a bitter taste in Aaron Quade's mouth.

Sure, the conference had always been scheduled to take place on September fourteenth. And yes, the speakers of the presentations had revised their speeches because of the attacks. But Quade could not help but wonder what those on the outside would think.

They should have canceled the whole damn thing. Or at the very least postponed it for a month or two. Hell, the bare minimum would have been to ditch the champagne and hors d'oeuvres. He hated to imagine what the news services would report if they saw them.

But no. Business marched on. Grief was the backdrop.

After all, what they were discussing was important. The

terrorist strikes would shape the next decade. Maybe longer. Ever since the end of the Cold War, America had been drifting, without a rival to keep it sharp. A reason to wave the banner of capitalism, democracy, and the free world. To remind everyone what the 'right way' was.

Now that opportunity had arrived. Unexpected and brutal. And if Quade knew the people in the room, and he did all too well, they would not let the chance go to waste.

He could hardly blame them.

He plucked a drink from a passing tray, waving off alcohol and sticking to water instead. From the corner of his eye, he spotted a pair of men heading his way. He did not need to look directly at them to recognize them. One was big, packing a few extra pounds. Matthew Hernandez. The other shorter and leaner, moving with a twitchy energy. Benjamin Klauss.

Restrained smiles stretched across their wrinkled faces. Both ran similar private SIGINT firms not unlike ExoCipher, and had been desperate for a government contract like his for years. Usually, their demeanor was frosty. The iciness of men who knew they were good, but not good enough. The warmth they currently exuded sickened him.

"Hello, Quade," they acknowledged in unison.

Quade nodded. "Gentlemen."

"Quite a day, huh?" Hernandez said.

"Indeed," Klauss added. "We were especially awaiting your talk on the current ability of ExoCipher's latest breakthrough in intelligence gathering. What happened?"

Quade took a long sip of his water. "It didn't seem appropriate given the circumstances."

The duo exchanged a glance, feigning confusion. It was all an act, of course. Everything about them was a performance. They would have been savoring every minute of the moment.

"I suppose I can understand how you feel." Hernandez stopped a server and picked out some hors d'oeuvres from the tray. "If my company had dropped the ball like yours had, I might have called it off too."

"Tell us, Quade. How did you bungle this so badly?" Klauss asked. "How did ExoCipher miss the biggest attack on US soil in over sixty years?"

Quade frowned. There was a particularly vile aspect about people celebrating your failures in the wake of something so horrific. Unfortunately, they were right. ExoCipher had appeared to make a hash of it. It was his company's job to ensure what happened three days earlier never came to pass.

He finished his drink and handed it to a server passing their position in the grand hall. "Gentlemen, in the coming months, I'll likely be facing senate inquiries answering those very questions. Feel free to come along. Or at least read the transcripts. Until then, I'd suggest worrying about your own companies."

Their joviality wavered.

"Surely, you've thought about that, haven't you?" Quade continued. "If ExoCipher falls, it paints the entire private SIGINT sector in a poor light. If I lose my contract with the CIA, do you really believe they'll look for outside support next time? If I were Jeffrey Phibbs, I'd be moving those operations in-house. Don't get me wrong, I'm not relishing the fallout. But don't for a second think that if I go down, that you won't be coming along for the ride."

Fredrickson, Quade's bodyguard, approached, leaning in to whisper in his ear, "Your car's ready, sir."

The charade was finally over.

"If you'll excuse me, I have places to be," Quade said. "Enjoy your evening."

Quade walked away, leaving Hernandez and Klauss to wallow, their smug expressions fading as the realization sank in. He followed Fredrickson out of the conference building, offering others a curt nod or a few words in passing.

It was cold and dark outside, a constant patter of rain sprinkling his black suit. His limousine waited on the curb, spit and polished whenever he went to such events. He had to look the part. Fredrickson opened the door, and Quade hopped inside, sitting on one of the cool leather seats.

The privacy partition between him and the driver slid downward. "Would you like to head home, sir, or are we returning to the office?"

Fredrickson got in next to the driver.

"Unfortunately, back to work," Quade said.

"Very good, sir."

The partition slid upward, cutting him off from the outside world. Quade flipped open the laptop which was sitting beside him while the car weaved out onto the road. They made their way through the city streets, the traffic thinning the closer they got to the ExoCipher building on the other side of the town.

Outside, the rain intensified. At one with his thoughts, he sighed, feeling the weight of decisions both made and unmade. Just as the tension inside him reached boiling point, the driver jolted the steering wheel, taking evasive action.

"What the hell was that!" Quade strained to see what was happening with the partition up. He glanced out the side windows, catching another vehicle pulling up beside them. A second one materialized at the rear. They were being boxed in.

Quade's pulse raced.

The partition came down, and Fredrickson's eyes met his in the rearview mirror. "I'm not sure what this is about, sir, but we'll take care of it."

The driver had no choice but to bring them to a halt, another car appearing ahead, cutting off their path. The limo stopped on the edge of the sidewalk, and the two front doors swung open. Fredrickson and the driver got out to intercept the shadowy figures emerging from the other vehicles. Before his employees could react, tasers fired, the electric bolts striking them and sending them to the ground and out for the count.

Quade squinted through the night, trying to make out the faces of their assailants, their zipped-up jackets making it impossible in the darkness. He reached for his door to lock it.

He was not quick enough. Both flew open, gusts of cold air drifting inside the back of the limo along with two figures. To his left, a big man, tall with a sidearm in his hand. Quade recognized the individual but could not put a name to him.

Then there was the other one. Older and stockier, his movements calm and deliberate. He unzipped his jacket and sat across from Quade, closing the door behind him.

His old boss. Mentor. And trusted friend.

"Hello, Quade," Bishop said. "Let's go for a drive."

55

"All set?"

Bishop turned to Rampling as she hopped behind the wheel. With a nod, she pressed a button at her fingertips, and the privacy partition slid up between them, leaving Bishop, Hirsch, and Quade alone in the rear compartment of the limousine.

The car eased into motion, gliding past the trio of vehicles they had used to box Quade in only moments ago. Bishop focused his attention to the man in front of him. He had only seen his former deputy director once since 1993. The night only a week earlier revealed a man, similar, but different. Not only was he older but also more confident. Quade had always been a consummate professional. Now, though, there was a quiet sureness about him that he had not necessarily exuded when they had served together at Bureau 61.

They stared at each other in silence. Bishop had rehearsed the moment since he had caught the flight back to the United States from Turkey. Yet, face to face, he faltered. Quade offered nothing. No expression. No tell. Just a blank face. He had learned well. Of course he had. Bishop had taught him.

"You know what I'm going to ask, don't you?" Bishop said.

Quade's lips parted for a second before he closed them shut once again. He eyed the gun resting in Hirsch's hands. Bishop tracked the look to his mercenary and gave him a nod. Hirsch slipped the weapon back into his shoulder holster.

"If I were here to kill you, Quade, you'd have never seen it coming," Bishop told him. "You, of all people, should know that. It's time to chat."

"What would you like to talk about, boss?" Quade finally said, still using Bishop's old title from all those years ago.

"Please don't insult my intelligence. If there's one thing I hate, it's that."

Quade held his hands outstretched in a sign of peace. "What do you want me to say?"

"I want the courtesy of hearing it from you, before the authorities do. After everything we went through together, you owe me that much."

Quade frowned. Was it guilt? If it was, it was gone in an instant, the man masking it quickly. He said nothing. Bishop had expected more. Perhaps naively so. He sighed and unzipped his jacket farther, taking out a file folder. He tossed it on Quade's lap, who let it sit there without even looking at it.

"Check it out," Bishop instructed him, his tone carrying the same authority he would once have used in the old Bureau 61 offices.

Quade hesitated. His curiosity won out. He flipped it open, thumbing through the documents, his glare growing with intensity at every page.

"It's all there," Bishop continued. "It took some doing, but it's there."

He allowed Quade the time to read it, trying to discern a hint of emotion. Something. Anything.

"Let's start with ExoCipher, Quade. You built it from the ground up. In less than a few years, you turned it into the CIA's crown jewel. You became their go-to man for global signal intelligence. There was a part of me that wondered how you did it so fast. Then I found this." Bishop pointed at the files. "You had help. While you constructed it through legitimate means, you also took the darker route. Hackers. Off the street, operating all over the globe, loyal to no one but the almighty dollar. The Anca Syndicate was one of these many cells."

"I—"

"Keep reading." Bishop raised a hand, not giving Quade the luxury to lie. "My confidants have traced all the funds tied to the Anca Syndicate. It took considerable doing, digging through legitimate business deals, offshore accounts, and shell companies. But the money all led to a single place. ExoCipher. Quite a web you've spun.

"To your credit, it worked. The Turkish hackers are good operators. Probably better than any the CIA would hire. They can also work without a net, getting into places most can't reach. And that's just it, isn't it, Quade? They did go to those places. The Anca Syndicate were aware of the September Eleven attacks before they happened. And so were you."

Quade shook his head and flipped the folder shut. "You've got no proof I knew of those strikes. Sure, the authorities will have concerns about my methods, but they won't believe I was aware. I'd argue, and rightly so, that the Anca Syndicate kept that intel from ExoCipher. As far as I'm concerned, that information never crossed my desk."

Bishop nodded. "I wanted that to be the case. I hoped the hackers had some twisted loyalty to Al-Qaeda, that they held back what they'd found. But that's not the truth, is it? Unfortunately, I dug deeper. You should know, I don't do half-assed jobs. When we followed the trail of money from the Anca Syndicate to ExoCipher, I decided to examine your own personal finances."

Quade's demeanor shifted, his posture straightening in his seat and his shoulders tightening as if he were bracing for impact.

"It was a convoluted mess. I had to dig deep. Eventually, I discovered the truth. A week before September Eleven, I discovered you'd been playing the stock market more than usual. You shuffled a lot of money around. You've backed military defense contractors, because you know at some point war will come. You shorted airlines, anticipating a crash once Wall Street reopens. And then there's ExoCipher itself. You burned it to the ground by keeping that intel from the CIA. That was shorted, too, all to get your pound of flesh before it collapsed. You were set to become a very rich man. It would have been genius. If I hadn't found out."

Quade evaded his gaze, unable to meet Bishop's eyes. He finally showed some emotion. Defeat.

"Then there was the personal game you played," Bishop went on. "When I came to you for help last week, you put on a hell of a performance. You knew about Harvey Wulf already. You knew he'd stolen the intel from Anca Syndicate's servers, so you sent a man to silence him. And before you ask, yes, I know Erik Olsson is on your books, too.

"Then there was me." Bishop did his best to lace the words without contempt. He failed spectacularly. "Even with Wulf floating in the canals of Venice, you were still worried he might have made a copy. That's why you were eager for me to go to Italy. You figured if anyone was going to find it, it'd be me. Sure enough, I did. Only for your man to destroy it, per your orders. Olsson, however, stuffed up.

"He couldn't kill me. That became a problem for you. Because you knew I wouldn't stop. I followed Wulf's trail to Istanbul. When I unwittingly reached out to you, I gave away my position. You knew I was onto the Anca Syndicate. So you laid a trap for me in that warehouse. Unfortunately for you, like the cockroach I am, I crawled out alive.

"You screwed up, Quade. And now I've got everything. Every piece of dirt you tried to bury. There are so many questions I want to ask you. Only one matters." Bishop leaned closer to him, his eyes boring into the other man. "Why? Why do all of this? In the time we've been apart, what the hell happened to you? What transformed you into the person you've become?"

Quade took a slow breath, returning Bishop's stare. "It was because of you."

Bishop's jaw tightened. "What the hell are you talking about?"

"Eight years ago you stood before the brass at the CIA, warning them that shutting down Bureau 61 would mean suffering in the future. That by putting all their chips on

SIGINT instead of HUMINT, it would blow up in their faces. You were right. Even if I hadn't withheld the intel of the Al-Qaeda attacks, something would have slipped through. Intelligence is done with boots on the ground. There's no substitute for it.

"By allowing these attacks to happen, I gave the United States a head start. A necessary wake-up call. Now they know what we're up against. This isn't nation against nation anymore. It's not as simple as the Cold War. This is a twisted ideology versus our way of life. A man in a cave halfway across the world can bring us to our knees. That's the battlefield of the future. No flags. No borders.

"The current administration won't have a choice. After this, they'll be forced to return to the old approach to protect America from its new enemies. I saw which way the wind was blowing—"

"And you figured you'd make a quick buck while you were at it?"

"I wasn't going to destroy ExoCipher without taking my own cut."

"You're a real patriot, Quade," Bishop said sarcastically.

The limousine rolled to a halt. Bishop peered out the window, noticing they had veered into the gated entrance of the local FBI field office. Waiting beyond the door was a team of armed FBI agents ready to take Quade into custody.

He shifted his focus back to Quade.

"It's a shame you sent Olsson after me in Venice," he said. "If you'd handled your own dirty work, maybe you would've never been found out."

Bishop's former deputy director's face softened, a flicker of guilt finally crossing his features. "I couldn't have done that, boss."

"And why's that?" Bishop asked.

"Because I wouldn't have been able to bring myself to pull the trigger."

The door swung open, and Quade was swiftly hauled out. Within seconds, he was gone, along with the trust Bishop had held in the man.

SEPTEMBER 27, 2001

56

LANGLEY, VIRGINIA

Bishop's mind drifted to the last time he had sat in the CIA director's office. The day he had finished up as head of Bureau 61. The relationship between him and Jeffrey Phibbs had always been strained. And though there was a certain amount of professionalism shared, Bishop struggled to hide his disdain of the man.

He found himself remembering 1993 and wondering if he could have done anything different. Perhaps Phibbs deserved more respect. After all, it was not his choice to defund Bureau 61. That came from higher up. He was just doing his job.

Bishop let out a dry chuckle. Had he gone that soft? Maybe it was his marriage with Pat, which had grounded him. He pushed the thought aside. He was no longer in Anchorage. In the hustle and bustle of the big city you needed an edge about you. Your survival depended on winning the game. If you were not a player, you were being played.

He scanned the office, taking in the subtle changes. A fresh coat of paint there, a few new pictures there, and a sleek modern computer occupying the desk. It was no wonder Phibbs had served a considerable time in his post. He embodied the agency's polished exterior from top to bottom.

Bishop waited in silence until finally the door opened. Phibbs walked in with two mugs of coffee. He placed one in front of Bishop and rounded his workspace, nestling himself in his own chair. He took a sip and stared across at Bishop, his discerning eyes unsettling to say the least.

"If you're trying to make me feel uncomfortable, you're doing an excellent job of it," Bishop said.

Phibbs laughed ever so slightly. "It wasn't my intention, John. Quite the opposite. We didn't part on the best of terms eight years ago, and the last thing I wanted for you is to walk in here feeling as if you were stepping back into hostile territory."

Bishop reached for his mug and drank the harsh black brew. "I see they're still serving the same crap instant coffee they always did."

"The more refined stuff isn't in the budget."

"Of course it isn't." Bishop drank some more and set the mug down, returning the director's stare. "What am I doing here, Phibbs?"

Phibbs leaned closer to him. "You're here because I wanted to thank you in person. You've done a great service to the United States."

"I've done nothing. Thousands of people died in those attacks—"

"And thousands more would have perished if you hadn't

remained on the hunt for the intel Harvey Wulf had died for. We can all agree that in an ideal world, we would've had warning before those first planes hit. But we didn't. We can't change that." Phibbs paused. "If it wasn't for you, John, it could've been so much worse. When you received that call from Wulf, you could've chalked it up to paranoia on Wulf's part and gone back fishing. You didn't. You followed it through and made all the difference."

Bishop crossed his arms. "Only because I didn't trust you to follow up on my information."

Phibbs frowned. "Be that as it may, you jetted around the world, stuck out your neck, nearly got yourself killed, to do what some in this building thought was impossible."

"For a person of my age?"

"For a person who'd been out of the game for so long," Phibbs corrected. "Because of your work, we now understand more about Al-Qaeda than ever before. Their leadership structure, operational methods, sleeper cells, and how to hopefully stop them before they try to attack us again. On top of that, you've exposed Aaron Quade and ExoCipher, which I know couldn't have been easy for you."

Bishop stayed silent, the thought of his former protégé sitting in a cell somewhat disconcerting. What was more disturbing was what he had done to get there.

"In light of everything, its been seen fit to award you the Presidential Medal of Freedom, the highest civilian honor—"

"Please..." Bishop rolled his eyes, a heavy weariness within them. "I'm not interested in getting some medal pinned to my chest. I didn't do this for the President, or for you, or me—"

"I understand, John." Phibbs steepled his fingers on the desk. "Our reasons for being in this business are the same.

We have a love of this country. We want to see its citizens safe and protected—"

"Look, I'd like to continue chatting, Phibbs, but I've got a flight to catch back to Alaska later this morning." Bishop slipped into old habits once again, his prickly side returning. "If we can just speed things along here, that'd be most appreciated."

Phibbs nodded slowly. "Very well. Forget the medal. Forget the plaudits. I need you, John. America needs you."

Bishop froze for a moment. "What are you talking about?"

"I've been on the horn with the current administration. The Secretary of Defense, the VP, even the President himself. There's going to be a shakeup of how things are done in our field of operations. On the domestic front, don't be surprised to see a whole new agency to assist the FBI with terrorism on home soil. As for us, they're looking for another player in the game." Phibbs took a breath. "John, they want to bring back Bureau 61. They, and I, want you to head up the new branch."

Bishop remained still, gathering his thoughts as he processed Phibbs's words.

"Well, John, what do you say?"

Bishop pulled his coffee to his lips, taking another gulp. If it were in his scope to gloat, he might have indulged. Once perhaps. He was too old for that kind of crap now. "And you'd want to work together again? Us?"

"I'm a big enough to put aside the past for the greater good. I'm sure you are, too."

"If I were to consider this position, it would come with some stipulations on my part."

"Name them."

Bishop grunted, drafting an internal shopping list. How much could he get away with? "I want operational independence. Red tape gets people killed. We'll work off the books like Bureau 61 did. When we're not cleaning up the CIA's mess, we run our own leads and our own ops."

"Done."

"I want access to every CIA record ever collated. If I'm going to do this, I need the keys to the castle."

"You'll have them."

"I also get to pick those who work for me. None of your desk jockeys. And none of your operatives, unless I think they'd be of use to me. I'll have to vet everyone personally."

"Fair enough. Anything else?"

"Immunity. To build a network of assets in the field, they'll be required to do things you may not be comfortable with. Their actions cannot become public. No hearings. No scapegoats. If a new Bureau 61 is to succeed, we have to work in the shadows."

"It'll be just like the old days."

Bishop placed his mug on the desk. "Very well, I'll think about it."

Phibbs's eyes widened. "You'll think about it? But we just—"

"I'm not going to make a decision like this on the spot. You go back to the Secretary of Defense, the VP, and the President and tell them you'll have my answer shortly." Bishop stood. "Until then, I'm going home."

Phibbs rose, too, still taken aback by Bishop's bluntness. The man extended a hand regardless, and Bishop reached into his pocket, taking out a folded-up piece of paper. He popped it into Phibbs's hand.

"What's this?" the director asked.

"All that intel I gathered for you wouldn't have been possible without the people on that list. My mercenaries. The Turkish hackers. They're all there. I promised to pay them. I trust you can take care of that for me?"

Not waiting for a reply, Bishop left the office, the door clicking shut behind him. He did not look back.

Now he had a decision to make.

SEPTEMBER 30, 2001

57

NEW YORK, NEW YORK

Tyler studied the menu, the French words printed on it baffling him as much as they had last time. Some were recognizable, similar to their English counterparts. Regardless, he was not confident about deciding on a meal for himself and did not want to roll the dice.

"Need some help?"

He gazed up from the muddle of text to his sister, smiling across at him. It was not her usual grin, the mischievous glint in her eye all but dulled. She was being much more guarded.

"Yeah." Tyler handed her the menu. "If you could pick something that isn't snails and frog legs this time, that'd be great."

The server walked over to them and took their orders. As expected, Kate chose an elaborate dish, her palate clearly adapting to the high-class cuisine. For him, she ordered a steak. Plain. Simple. He had no complaints.

The server disappeared toward the kitchen, leaving them

alone once again. A hush settled over them, echoing the one that had filled the car when Kate had picked him up from JFK Airport. Normally, they would be talking over each other, eager to catch up and pry into each other's lives.

Tyler took a sip of his beer from the frosty glass in front of him. Kate swirled her wine, her gaze avoiding his. He let the silence stretch a moment longer before breaking it.

"How did Rick seem when he left for home?"

The question seemed to catch her off guard. She had some of her wine then set it down. "Same old Rick. You know how he is. Never gives much away. I told him he should come here more often. Even offered to show him around the city. As you'd imagine, he was...noncommittal."

"That sounds like him."

"Yeah." She gave her glass another swirl. "It was good to see him, though. Maybe I should make an effort to visit him more. It'd be nice to go home for a while. There are plenty of people down there I miss."

Tyler nodded. "So, you're staying then?"

Kate raised an eyebrow.

"In New York, I mean?"

"This is where my life is." She turned to the window, toward downtown where the familiar shapes which once dominated were now eerily absent in the open sky. "I might be in a new office building, but that doesn't mean I'm going to be chased away."

Tyler could not help but wonder if they would ever build on the site again. A memorial, perhaps. Two more buildings in its place. Or something even taller.

"Good for you." He genuinely meant it and raised his glass. "How's your friend?"

"Hmm?"

"The one who was in hospital. Janette."

"Oh. She's fine. Was out of there in a few days. She's back on her feet and even returned to the new office. I'm glad she is because it's all hands on deck getting everything sorted. You should see my office. It's the size of a broom closet."

The pair shared a brief laugh. It faded quickly, leaving more silence. Tyler pondered how many more other hard conversations were unfolding in the quiet corners of the city. He glanced around the restaurant. It was half full, just like his last visit there. On this occasion, the noise was subdued. New York, and America as a whole, would grieve for a very long time. And people would mourn in their own way.

"What about you?" Kate asked. "You're going back to work soon, I assume?"

"Next week," Tyler said. "They let me take the vacation time I had. My superior told me not to come back until I'd spent some time on the beach."

"After what you went through in Atlanta, you deserve it. How does it feel to be a hero?"

Tyler frowned. Hero. The term was not one he embraced. In the past, Kate would have pushed the subject, making him squirm, getting her kicks while she did. Not today.

"And did you?" she asked.

"Did I what?"

"Get plenty of time at the beach?"

"Oh." He nodded. "Yeah, it wasn't the same, though. Even down there, it felt as if the world had been put on pause. I just lay on the sand and read a good book. Several actually."

"It's not like you would've done anything differently anyway."

He chuckled. "I suppose not."

"I bet you're looking forward to work. You probably have a pile a mile high waiting for you on your desk."

"It shouldn't be too bad." Tyler took another gulp of his beer. "Monica's been keeping on top of everything while I've been gone."

Kate smiled, her expression warmer this time. "Don't let her go, Jack. When something good comes along...well, you know?"

It was Tyler's turn to raise an eyebrow. "Are we talking about work or pleasure?"

She shrugged. "I'm just saying, sometimes things happen like this and remind you we only have one shot at it all. We have to take the opportunities presented before..."

A lump formed in Tyler's throat as he wrapped his fingers around his glass, his gaze drifting back to the view. He thought of Brunelli and what could be. His sister was right. One could not afford to rest on their laurels. She put a hand on his, the tenderness of her touch seeping through him. For a moment, they watched the sun sink behind the horizon.

"We'll get through this, won't we, Jack?"

He clasped back tightly. "Yeah, we'll get through it."

In time...

NOVEMBER 2, 2001

58

ANCHORAGE, ALASKA

A stiff breeze carved through the air, stirring the dense snow underfoot. Bishop pulled his coat tighter. November had no mercy so far north, with fall having been chased away by the unforgiving advance of the cold weeks ago.

Bishop took a long drag from his cigarette, plowing through the thick blanket of white, each step a battle in his heavy boots. Over the crest, he spotted the paper birch. Like the other trees surrounding him, it stood bare, the last of the leaves buried under the veil of winter.

He stopped and coughed, his lungs straining against the bite of the tobacco and the deep fog around him. Flicking the ash from his cigarette, he pushed on, drawing closer to the paper birch, until finally he arrived. There, next to the tree, sat Pat's headstone, most of it swallowed by the snow. Bishop crouched and rubbed the cold cloak away, revealing the engraving beneath. He frowned, the memories of their short time together flashing before him.

He stood and tossed his spent cigarette to the ground, the remaining spark extinguishing instantly. Stepping to the end of the grave, he paused, his eyes fixed downward. With one hand holding a rose, he pointed to the sky with the other.

"You'd like this," he said. "Can't remember the snow coming in this thick so early in the season. I had the fire going all night. Even ended up falling asleep on the sofa in front of it. A terrible habit. Pretty sure I've got a kink in my neck now.

"Serves me right, I suppose. But going to bed hasn't been the same for a while." Bishop reached backward and dug his fingers into his shoulder blades. "I chopped up some more wood for the winter. Filled the whole shed."

He approached the headstone. "You remember, when I came back, I told you I'd been offered a job?" He let out a bitter chuckle. "Langley, of all places. They've asked me to head up Bureau 61 again. Or whatever the hell they're going to call it now. Though they won't admit it, they know they made a mistake shutting us down. I hated them for putting me out of work. I carried that anger for more time than I should've. You knew that more than most.

"Then I met you. Suddenly, none of it mattered anymore. I'm glad I experienced that, even if it was just for the four years we had together. Now..." Bishop cleared his throat. "Now they want me back. Seems I'm useful again. Perhaps I've still got something to offer."

He paused once more, as if to let Pat digest what he was about to say. Of course, the notion was absurd. And while he knew she was not really there with him, he felt he owed it to the part of her that lived inside him to explain everything to her. "I decided to say yes."

He took a step backward. "If you were still here with me, I would've told them to go to hell. Now that you're gone...

Maybe I can still do some good. Besides, they say at my age, I'll need to take regular medicals. You'd have liked that, at least?

"I've asked Derek next door to keep this area tidy. I know how much you enjoy the view, so he'll make sure no branches from the birch get in the way when the leaves come back in spring."

Overhead, the sharp thrum of a helicopter cut through the hush. Bishop glanced up, recognizing the distinct shape of the chopper moving toward his property. He walked down the edge of the grave and crouched once more. He placed the red rose at the base of the headstone, nestling it in the snow.

"I've done a lot of things." The words slipped out as barely a whisper. "The fours years I spent with you were the best days of my life. I'll never forget them. I'll never forget you. And I know wherever I go now, you'll be with me, right by my side."

He kissed his fingers and pressed them against the headstone, closing his eyes. When he reopened them, he got back on his feet, casting one last look at the resting place of his beloved before turning back to his house.

By the time he arrived, the helicopter was hovering over the front of the property, preparing to land. Painted in black with no markings, it descended slowly and touched down, its rotors winding down to a steady churn. Bishop went inside. The few belongings he had yet to ship to DC sat in two suitcases by the door. Everything else was in storage, the little furniture in the house that remained covered in sheets.

He ambled up the stairs, passing by his bedroom and entering the makeshift command center he had built when Pat had died. The old computers hummed, their monitors locked on dated screensavers. He moved over the threshold and unplugged the radios, silencing the soft hiss of static from the ceiling speakers.

As he walked out, he flipped a row of switches mounted on the inside of the doorframe. The room powered down, the lights dimming and the silence settling on the once bustling solo operation. He pivoted and headed back downstairs, where someone from the chopper had already come in and hauled his bags away.

Bishop flipped one more switch, bathing the interior of the house in complete darkness. He bowed his head and closed the door, walking the worn path to the waiting chopper. The man ahead of him climbed into the cockpit with the pilot having stored the luggage, while Bishop continued to the rear cabin. Grimsby, Bishop's new assistant, sat inside, a stack of folders on his lap.

Bishop took a deep breath, the anxiety rising within, simmering just below the surface. But he pushed it down, having come so far to turn back now. Without another thought, he hopped on board.

Grimsby handed Bishop a headset and shut the cabin door behind him. Bishop popped them on, the roar of the engines muffled immediately.

"*These are the documents you requested before we left Anchorage,*" the man said, his voice crackling through the speakers inside the headsets.

They took off, and Bishop gazed out the window. His home of eight years shrank from view, followed by the paper birch and the river which flowed mightily around the property. Soon, all that remained was the mountain range beyond. A sudden doubt crept in. He wondered if he was making a mistake.

No.

Life had to go on.

He looked down at the documents. The first folder was marked with bold embossed letters. The name of the organization he had agreed to head up: PENUMBRA DIVISION.

He stared at the name of his new home for a long moment, a low grunt escaping him. "Let's get to work..."

THE END

Stay tuned for the next Penumbra Division Thriller at samcogley.com

FROM THE AUTHOR

Thanks for reading **The Last Operator**! Writing a spin-off of my Adam Knight Thriller series has been on my to do list ever since I wrote my very first novel. It didn't disappoint. I really enjoyed writing John Bishop's character, and building the foundations of where it all began for Penumbra Division.

You can expect more Penumbra Division Thrillers set during the War on Terror era in the near future. While you wait, if you haven't yet, I'd love for you to check out my Adam Knight Thrillers—set in the present-day. You can start with the first book—**Shadow Operative.** If you loved **The Last Operator**, I'm confident you'll enjoy stepping into the shadowy world of Adam Knight.

You'll find a list of all the books I've written in the front of this book. I'd also encourage you to check out samcogley.com where you can get more information on my work. There's also a link to sign up to my newsletter. If you join, you'll receive information on new releases, special sales and updates on future happenings. You also get a free eBook and Audiobook too!

Thank you again! Sam Cogley.

Printed in Great Britain
by Amazon